COME A STRANGER

Books by Cynthia Voigt

THE BAD GIRLS SERIES

Bad Girls

Bad, Badder, Baddest

It's Not Easy Being Bad

Bad Girls in Love

Bad Girls, Bad Girls, Whatcha Gonna Do?

THE TILLERMAN SERIES

Homecoming

Dicey's Song

A Solitary Blue

The Runner

Come a Stranger

Sons from Afar

Seventeen Against the Dealer

THE KINGDOM SERIES

Jackaroo

On Fortune's Wheel

The Wings of a Falcon

Elske

OTHER BOOKS

Building Blocks

The Callender Papers

David and Jonathan

Izzy, Willy-Nilly

Orfe

Tell Me if the Lovers Are Losers

Tree by Leaf

The Vandemark Mummy

When She Hollers

COME A STRANGER

CYNTHIA VOIGT

ATHENEUM BOOKS FOR YOUNG READERS
New York London Toronto Sydney New Delhi

ATHENEUM BOOKS FOR YOUNG READERS
An imprint of Simon & Schuster Children's Publishing Division
1230 Avenue of the Americas, New York, New York 10020

Also available in an Atheneum Books for Young Readers hardcover edition
Book design by Debra Sfetsios-Conover
The text for this book is set in Baskerville.
Manufactured in the United States of America
First Atheneum Books for Young Readers paperback edition July 2012
2 4 6 8 10 9 7 5 3
The Library of Congress has cataloged the hardcover edition as follows:
Voigt, Cynthia.
Come a stranger.
Summary: Mina's deep love for a grown-up minister drives her to seek a way to give him an unforgettable remembrance, restoration of his faith.
ISBN 978-0-689-31289-2
[1. Clergy—Fiction.] I. Title.
PZ7.V874Co 1986
[Fic] 86-3610
ISBN 978-1-4424-5063-9 (hc)
ISBN 978-1-4424-2882-9 (pbk)

This one's for you, Helen:
because of the way you would always keep
on trying to stand *en point,* in your bare feet; &
for lots of other reasons too.

COME A STRANGER

CHAPTER 1

Mina jumped out over the back steps and landed in a fifth position demi-plié. Arms out, back straight, she bent her knees into grand-plié, and then up, sliding into fourth position. She leaped out, once, twice, three times, high across the yard, to the music that played inside of her head. She raised her arms slowly, lifted her right leg into a passé, and then as slowly straightened it into an arabesque, keeping one arm curved over her head, one curved in front of her. When you felt like this, there was nothing to do but dance.

At the sound of clapping, she turned around. She didn't mind if someone was watching, nothing like that ever bothered her. "Morning," she called across to Miz Hunter, who was dressed for services and sitting in the rocker on her front porch. Miz Hunter was a tiny woman, short and small boned. Her toes barely touched the wooden boards.

"Where you going to, Missy?" Miz Hunter summoned Mina over. The old lady knew who everyone was, but had trouble with names these days. Every girl she called "Missy," every boy "Sonny," because she just couldn't fetch up their names. Mina guessed maybe all their faces got jumbled together in Miz Hunter's memory with all the boys and girls she'd taught for all those years in school. "In such a hurry. And all gussied up for church."

Mina stood below the porch, looking up. Miz Hunter had her

red hat set on her head, bright as cherries. She had her gloves on and held her purse in her lap.

"I'm going to that camp in Connecticut. The dance camp. I got a scholarship."

"Where in Connecticut is that?"

"Someplace at a college. The town is called New London."

"I know where that is."

"You do?"

"You don't teach school for thirty years and not know where New London, Connecticut, is. I've never been there but I know where it is. You don't know where it is, but you're going there. It's surely funny about life sometimes, isn't it, Missy? Are you going out to tell the news?"

"Yes, ma'am."

"Careful you don't make people jealous," Miz Hunter advised.

"Kat wouldn't be jealous," Mina explained. "She knows how much I want to go."

"There's nobody born yet, except maybe the One, who didn't get jealous now and then. As you well know, Missy. Even that One too, I expect. He wouldn't be human otherwise, now would He? So you take good care of your friends."

Mina thought about that. She thought about the camp from Kat's side. Mina would be gone all of July and most of August, and even the last week in June too. Eight weeks. From Kat's side, it wasn't such good news, she guessed. "I will, ma'am," she told Miz Hunter. "Thank you for the advice."

"Although if it were up to me, I'm not sure I'd let a girl your age go off among strangers for eight weeks."

"They're not strangers," Mina argued. "They'll all be dancers."

"People you don't know are strangers," Miz Hunter corrected her, just as if Mina sat at a desk in her classroom. Mina bit back a laugh at how schoolteacherish Miz Hunter was. "Xenophobia, there's a word for you. It means fear of strangers. From *xenos*, stranger. That's Greek," Miz Hunter instructed. There was nothing wrong with her brain. Nobody could say that.

"I didn't know that. Thank you." There was never to be any slightest hint of impoliteness to Miz Hunter, Mina's parents made that clear to all of them. *She's old,* Momma said, *and deserves special politeness for that. She's lived a long, useful life before she came here. For her time, she's done wonders.* So Mina made herself stand patient for however big a bite this conversation might take out of her time with Kat. "Are you afraid of strangers?" Mina asked.

Miz Hunter smiled then, the way old people often did, as if she was remembering something far away, as if she'd like to take Mina into her memory and share it together, almost as if Mina already was a part of whatever she was looking back at. "I can't barely remember what it felt like to meet a stranger, these days," Miz Hunter said. "There aren't any strangers I've noticed around here, are there?"

"No, ma'am. My poppa, he doesn't let people stay strangers."

"You'd better run along, or you'll find yourself too late to tell all your good news."

"Yes, ma'am. Good morning to you. I thank you for the advice."

Mina walked off sedately enough, remembering now that her Mary Janes weren't dancing shoes, and it wasn't good for them, or for her, to try to make them dance. Moist sunlight floated around her. It was a fine morning. She heard Miz Hunter's rocker start up creaking behind her as she turned down the street. Birds were singing away. A baby wailed, somewhere, and a TV played, but mostly the Sunday morning quiet lay over the whole long street. Everybody was inside, getting ready for church. The porches were empty, the chairs and swings and steps had nobody sitting on them.

Front porches were for daytime sitting, Mina thought, her feet starting to skip and hurry her along. Back porches, which were screened, were for the evenings, for the families to sit together. Especially in the dark nights of deep summer, you'd hear the voices of people talking, the invisible words falling slow through the air. Like rain plopping down, relaxed and sleepy.

Mina guessed there was a lot she'd miss about being gone for the summer. She thought she'd better make Louis a cage for keeping fireflies before she left; a glass jar with wire screen fitted around its top, a preserving jar, and she'd have to wax the inside of the metal ring that would hold the wire top in place. Summer evenings, all the little children caught fireflies, and put them in cages and jars and counted up who had the most. After the children went to bed, the parents set all the fireflies loose to fly away under the dark trees, their funny little lights flicking off, flicking on.

Louis was just big enough now to be able to learn how to catch a firefly without mushing it, how to cup both hands and close them together. The firefly needed room in there to flutter around. Then you had to have someone take the top off your jar for you, so you could put your hands over the open neck and gently open them, like prayer hands unfolding, to get the firefly where you wanted him to go. Louis wasn't nearly old enough to catch a firefly one-handed; he'd mush it for sure, and then he'd feel so bad he'd cry.

Kat was upstairs, dressing for church. Mina waited by the foot of the stairs while Kat's father called up. "Katanga? Company for you."

"Come on up, Mina."

Mina looked at Mr. Beaulieu. "Go ahead, child," he said. "Tell her we'd like to get out of the house sometime before Doomsday."

Mina laughed and Mr. Beaulieu laughed with her, and Mina

laughed the harder because Mr. Beaulieu had that kind of chuckling, fat laughter that made you glad to hear it. They were laughing because the Beaulieus were always a little late, wherever they went. They just moved slower than the rest of the world. Mina thought that was because until they moved north they'd lived in New Orleans, where it was so hot you couldn't move fast without killing yourself off. "If you move slow you live longer," was Mr. Beaulieu's way of looking at it, and Kat's momma always added, "Enjoy it more too." You never knew what time dinner would get onto the Beaulieu's table, but you knew it would be delicious. At Mina's house, dinner came on at six exactly, and it was usually good enough. Mina's stomach liked being fed right on time, but it loved being fed Mrs. Beaulieu's jambalaya, all spicy and ricy and chunked up with meat and poultry and sausage.

"I'm getting hungry," she told Mr. Beaulieu.

"You're always hungry when you come here. Get Kat downstairs in ten minutes and there'll be time for biscuits, which we just happen to have fresh baked."

"Ten minutes?"

"With butter, hot biscuits with butter."

"Ten minutes isn't awfully long," Mina said.

"And honey too."

"I can do it," Mina said, charging up the stairs.

Kat had a room to herself, because she was the only girl. Her two brothers had to share, but Kat had her own small room, with a bedspread she'd picked out herself and curtains that matched, and a matched set of twin beds, dresser and desk. Kat's curtains and beds had ruffles on them too. She kept things neat.

Mina moved right in and started making the bed. Kat had her church dress hung out on the handle to her closet, and she was wearing a slip while she fixed her hair. "How old were you when you could catch a firefly in one hand?" Mina asked her.

"I don't know, I don't remember. Do you remember *that*?"

"I think I was six, or maybe seven." Mina folded back the top sheet. She always put more care into making Kat's bed than her own. Kat cared about things like that, and she didn't.

That was one of the things Mina liked about Kat. They looked alike too, which was another thing, except that Kat was short and slim while Mina was tall and skinny. Another thing was dancing.

"Do you think this barrette looks good? It doesn't match my dress, but it'll match up with the choir robe."

"It looks great," Mina said. "Okay, maybe not great, but good enough. Let's get downstairs."

"In a minute. Relax, Mina Smiths. You've never been late yet because of me."

"That's because I never do wait up for you." Mina smoothed the spread over the fluffed pillow. Kat slipped her yellow and red striped dress over her head, buttoned the buttons carefully up the front, then went back to the mirror again, fussing smooth the skirt, fussing the sleeves just right on her arms. Mina stood beside her and looked at them both.

There was something about Kat. Dainty and perfect. Kat's face had a small look to it, except for her big eyes. Mina's face looked bigger, more bony. "You're really pretty," Mina said.

Kat knew that. Ever since she'd arrived in third grade, there had been no question that Katanga Beaulieu was the prettiest girl in their class. Kat didn't put all that much importance on it, and Mina was willing to bet that even if she'd been as ugly as a potato Kat would still have dressed and groomed herself with the same care. It wasn't vanity that made her do that, it was self-respect.

"I'm going to that camp, I got the scholarship." Mina couldn't hold it in another second. She watched Kat's face in the mirror.

"Miss LaValle called up my momma yesterday, as soon as they called her."

Warned by Miz Hunter, Mina saw just a little sad expression of disappointment and jealousy flicked up in Kat's eyes and then go out. "I guess I'm not going then," Kat said, studying her own face in the mirror.

"I'd like it a whole lot better if you were," Mina said.

"But you know you're the best."

"But that doesn't mean you're not good enough," Mina answered. She didn't like anybody telling Kat she wasn't good enough.

"I guess you'll be really better when you get finished there. I guess you'll be miles ahead of the rest of us. I'm proud for you, Mina," Kat said, meeting Mina's eyes in the mirror, and meaning what she said. "I think it's great, and so will my parents when we tell them."

"You tell them later about it. For a while now, I'd like it to be just our secret."

"You can't keep any secrets," Kat teased.

"For a while I can. Then"—Mina laughed—"they just bust out. So don't wait too long."

She thought that Mr. and Mrs. Beaulieu would probably be disappointed for Kat. She thought that they'd rather get to be disappointed together, in the family, without having to cover it over with their good manners for Mina's sake. Mr. Beaulieu had a good job with the state health department, but they couldn't afford to send Kat to dance camp on their own.

"There'll be nothing to do, with you gone all summer," Kat realized. "Just dumb old Rachelle and Sabrina."

"They're not so bad."

"But they're not like you."

Mina couldn't argue with that. "I'm gonna tell my momma to

put all my babysitting jobs over to you. You've got to save up that money. So next summer, we can both go. Remember? Miss LaValle said they usually figure to give the scholarship three summers running."

"I can't earn that much money."

"If you save it, you can. Or maybe near enough."

"Oh, Mina." Kat smiled at Mina's reflected face, happy enough again. "There's nothing slows you down, is there?"

"Not if I can help it." Mina smiled back. She saw Kat's face catch some of her enthusiasm and confidence. "Best friends?" Mina asked.

"Best friends," Kat answered. They linked arms and went on downstairs.

Mina opened her mouth and sang. The melody flowed out like . . . She didn't know what it sounded like to everybody else, but it sounded like silver to her, her voice flying up above the rest of the choir; it sounded like a silver bird rising, gliding along, falling down and then soaring up.

They were all, all twenty-three of them, swaying gently with the hymn. "Where shall I be when the first trumpet sounds," she sang, they all sang together, women and girls, all in heavy black robes with starched white collars, sopranos and altos. "When it sounds so loud till it wake up the dead," Mina sang, singing out.

She could see Kat out of the corner of her eye, four robes down the line from her. For a second Mina thought about switching her swaying, pushing back against the shoulder to her right, and the way the whole line would start banging around against each other. That would give Kat the giggles. But she looked out at the congregation and saw her momma sitting in the front row, with both eyes fixed on Mina's face. Sometimes, Mina could swear her mother could read her mind. Momma's right eyebrow went up and Mina wiped the mischief off her face. And sang, hearing how her voice blended in, up above everybody else: "Where shall I be when it sounds."

When they had sat down again, and the people had rustled themselves into attention, Poppa stood up. He didn't wear a robe, just a dark suit with a shirt so white it could have been new snow. He went up to the lectern that had been set up for the readings and the sermon.

Poppa's little church didn't have a fancy altar, just a heavy wooden table with a fresh cloth on it on which the ladies had embroidered words and pictures. A silver cross stood up on top of that. They didn't have proper choir stalls, nor pews, except for half a dozen somebody had picked up at a flea market sale in Cambridge. Mina had been in a lot of churches in her day, between church-going and choir-singing, so she knew what Poppa's church didn't have. The windows were plain glass, the outside was plain wood, painted white, and the little short steeple that rose up above the steep roof had no bell to ring. What happened was, whenever they were having a drive, saving up money for something particular, like more pews so the whole room could be filled with them and not be part pews and mostly folding chairs, something always came up. There would always be some family that needed the help, or some one person in some kind of need. The deacons would empty the church pockets to help out. Like Miz Hunter, when the church took a mortgage on the little house she lived in and rented it to her for what she could afford. Nobody minded that, and nobody seemed to miss the fancy touches. Mina didn't. She liked the way the generous May sunlight poured in through the plain glass windows.

Poppa said he was pretty sure God didn't mind, because he was pretty sure God's mansion was about seventy-seven times as grand as the biggest cathedral in the biggest city in the world.

Rome was Mina's guess, but Momma had said she'd favor something in the Gothic style, with spires and arches, with steeples rising up high as man's hopes. Nobody argued with her, because Momma did a lot of reading and generally knew what she was talking about. Nursing was her vocation, she said, and her family was her life, and Poppa was her dearly beloved; but history was her passion, she always ended up saying that. Poppa always answered he'd rather be her passion, but Momma answered that she didn't think history could make much showing as a dearly beloved, so she thought she had things pretty straight. And Poppa laughed.

Mina studied her father as he opened the pages of his sermon. He was a big man, with a strong face and dark eyes that had a way of answering to what they were seeing. He had a big, quiet voice that carried through the whole church. Oh, Mina thought, with a swelling of her heart, oh, she loved her poppa. Oh, she was proud of him.

"'Now the word of the Lord came unto Jonah,'" Poppa read. He always started a sermon with a text. "'Saying, Arise, go to Nineveh, that great city, and cry against it.'" He looked up then, and all around at the people.

"I always wondered how Jonah had the heart to say no to the Lord. Did you ever wonder about that? I always did. I thought I'd have tipped my hat and said yessir so fast He'd have wondered if I truly heard Him. I would have been too frightened to do anything else. But when I study the situation, I think I can understand where Jonah's courage came from. I think it must have been the courage that comes from fear.

"What was there for Jonah to be afraid of? What could wind a man's heart around more than the voice of God speaking into his ear? Think of Jonah, think of him caught there between his two fears. What was that other fear, I ask myself.

"My guess is he was afraid to go into Nineveh. Like any man living, Jonah was afraid to go out and live among strangers. Do you blame him?"

Poppa waited, just half a minute, watching the heads shaking no, to be sure they'd got his idea down clearly.

"Strangers are a fearful people, now as then," Poppa said.

Mina folded her hands in her lap and listened.

CHAPTER 2

All the windows were open and Mrs. Landseer was keeping a close eye on the storm clouds blowing along on a gusty wind. The wind blew the air in the classroom cool. Sooner or later, Mina knew, would come the cold edge that meant that the storm was imminent. She hoped it would hold off until after lunch recess. No, she didn't; she hoped it would hold off until the middle of lunch recess. She wanted to be outside when the storm came, to see it pull at the branches of the trees, feel the wind whip around her body, and hear the long roll of thunder. She wanted to see lightning bolts, at least one, rip down through the dark sky and feel the shiver of fear go along her bones. She wanted the hard slanting rain to soak her, before she ran back into the building. Mina loved storms. Crisfield didn't get much by way of winter storms, but you could count on thunderstorms, all summer long. Kat couldn't understand it, not even when Mina dragged her over to stand at a window and watch. "It's so big," Mina would say, "it's just so—big," as a storm fought its way across the sky.

This was the season of lasts: last science experiment, last spelling list, last math chapter, last assembly. It was the last all-school assembly they were rehearsing for now. The fifth grade was giving plays. This was their last rehearsal before the performance tomorrow morning. And then, after another week, it would be the last weekend, then the last Monday, last Tuesday. Excitement was building up. Mina had already begun on her firsts for the summer. The first dinner eaten on the porch, while the long day stretched out like the bars of golden light falling across the yard. She might miss the first fireflies this year, because she would be at ballet camp, for the first time in her life.

She brought her attention back to the rehearsal. They had three short plays to perform. The biggest cast, twelve of them, had the first play, and Mina had helped out by arranging things and writing it down, so everybody knew where they were supposed to stand and how they were supposed to look. It was a pretty dumb story, Mina thought, about villagers learning how to share a magic pot that never ran out of stew. It started to get disorganized whenever the soldiers of the king (who wanted to take the pot away from the villagers) came onto the stage. She watched the soldiers enter, watched Bruce especially. He was prodding Jason and Jake with his wooden sword, getting them out of the straight lines soldiers stood in. Mina stood up at her desk. "Bruce Billings," she called out. "If you know what's good for you you'll cut that out right now." He stuck his tongue out at her and rolled his eyes toward the ceiling to show how bossy she was, but he cut it out.

The next play was all boys, four of them, doing a take-off on Mr. Rogers. Mina watched John Cooper carefully, because he had asked her how to act when he was playing Mr. Rogers, and she wanted to be sure he did things right, like the way he messed up tying his shoes. John had written the play too, and it wasn't bad at all, Mina thought. She smiled at him when they were finished, to let him know she thought he'd done okay. The rest of the boys, Mr. Speedy Delivery and King Friday and Handyman Negri, would ham it up too much, but John didn't care so much about them, so—except for a few suggestions to them—Mina kept her mouth shut. John was just a perfectionist for himself.

In Mina's play, Snow White, she played the wicked queen. She came dancing onstage, because Kat—who had chosen it and was directing it and had made up the script—and all the rest too, agreed it looked good. Mrs. Landseer stopped things when Mina did that. "Why are you dancing?"

"Because," Mina said. It was strange to dance without any music. "It's to make the queen look different, because she's got magic."

"Kat, was this your idea?" Mrs. Landseer asked. Kat was over by the classroom door, ready to be Snow White.

"Well," Kat said, looking from Mina to Mrs. Landseer.

"I thought so. This was your own idea, wasn't it, Mina?"

"Everybody said it was good."

"I'll bet they did," Mrs. Landseer said. "I'll just bet they did."

Mina knew what Mrs. Landseer meant to be saying, and she knew that Mrs. Landseer didn't really mind. "You are t-rou-ble," that was what Mrs. Landseer said to Mina, all year long. Sometimes she said it to stop whatever mischief Mina was up to. Sometimes she said it to tease her, and let Mina know she was watching her. Sometimes she said it as if she thought Mina was funny. This was one of the funny times.

"It won't do," Mrs. Landseer said now. "Wilhemina Smiths, you go have a little talk with your director and do what she tells you to do."

"Yes, ma'am," Mina said. She knew what Kat wanted her to do, because Kat had sort of suggested it quietly a couple of times. She wanted Mina to come on with big, dangerous, sneaky steps. Mina walked over to Kat that way, crossing the stage section of the classroom, and Kat giggled. "That's right," Kat said. "Thank you, Mina."

"And no more of this *Queen for a Day* act from you," Mrs. Landseer added.

Mina just grinned at her. She'd try.

The air in the classroom turned cold, chilly as October, and Mrs. Landseer ran for the windows. Mina ran too, and hesitated just a few seconds—listening to the sky growl in the distance, watching the way the leaves clutched at the branches of the trees, smelling cold rain in the wind—before she reached up and slammed down the window.

The way things were, the Smiths family had to work together, the whole family, figuring out where the money was going to come from, how it ought to be used. Poppa was a full-time minister; part of his salary came from the church, which spread out over a lot of states, and part from his own congregation; but it wasn't much money. Momma had a job at the hospital, because she'd become a nurse before she married, so that helped and it gave them all medical insurance too. The house they lived in belonged to the church. Living there was part of Poppa's pay. Taking good care of the house, the church and Miz Hunter's house was part of Poppa's job. Everything worked out. They worked everything out together.

So Mina's summer at ballet camp got worked out by the whole family. Mina's oldest sister, Eleanor, married to a man who worked for the electric company up in Cleveland, Ohio, with two little children already, sewed up some skirts and blouses and dresses from patterns Momma sent her. Charles Stuart—"CS"—was at college, a sophomore, so he couldn't help out much, but he sent down some material he'd copied at the library there about the campus where the camp was being held and the city where the college was. Mina spent saved-up allowance money for enough tights, and Zandor bought her one new pair of dance shoes. After the football season ended, he always got a job bagging groceries, so he had the extra money. "But I'm not buying you any toe shoes," he told her, standing as tall and broad as Poppa. "Those things are ex-pensive."

"If you expect me to hire you as my manager when I'm famous, you ought to be making sure I feel grateful to you now, while I'm just learning."

"Oh-ho, Miss Big Future," Zandor said.

Belle complained and started to get thirteen-year-old sulks, until Momma brought her up short with a, "No more of that, Isabelle." And Louis—well, between planning ahead how awful it was going to be with Belle in charge of him and planning on missing Poppa as usual and wondering if Mina would bring him a present back from up north—Louis kept himself busy.

Summers, the church hired Poppa extra to go around to big cities, while the minister from one of the cities came to Crisfield, to rest up. This was the third year of the project. Reverend Jefferson, the minister who had come to Crisfield for the last two summers, had gotten sick, so he was retiring back to Chicago where his people were. He stayed with the Dutleys, whose children were all grown and out of the house. Mr. Jefferson had a room there when he came south to rest up. But the new minister had a wife and three children. The church was renting him a house outside of town, on the edge of the Beerce property. The house was small, but it would make a big change from the city. It had room for the children to run around outside and a little beach just up the way, on a creek. Momma and some of the women got it cleaned up and cleared out of the wildlife that moved in during the years it was empty. They rounded up a refrigerator and some decent mattresses. The new minister had a church in New York, which was the biggest and baddest place to work. So he'd appreciate the peace and tranquility of the country, Momma said.

Poppa said he liked his two-week stint in New York least of

any of the cities he visited. He liked Richmond best, and he didn't mind Birmingham either. He kept wishing, every year, that they'd send him to New Orleans, but Momma said she thought New York might be bad, but New Orleans was Sodom and Gomorrah all rolled up into one, and she'd just as soon he steered clear of that place.

Momma missed Poppa when he was away all summer long. They all did. He called up on Sunday afternoons. He wrote letters and postcards. He even got one or two weekends home, when he was close enough by. But it wasn't the same as having him there. Poppa minded it, but he went on and did it. "It's not forever," he told them. "It's part of the work. And these men—they've earned a couple of tranquil months. We're all doing the same work, aren't we?"

"Things are different up north," Momma would back Poppa up. "Things are different down south. You children—you don't know how easy your father makes it for you."

"I wouldn't mind finding out," Belle said.

"You will, and soon enough," Momma answered. "For the time being, I advise you to count your blessings."

Belle looked around and studied everything she could see. She held up her hand as if to count on her fingers, but said there wasn't one thing she thought of to count.

Momma just laughed.

"I wish *I* was the one going away to camp for the summer," Belle said.

"So do I, honey." Momma laughed again. "So do I."

"That's not funny," Belle said, her voice going high and offended.

It was too funny, and Mina laughed out loud over it. Catch her being thirteen like that, she thought, as Belle stormed out of the room.

CHAPTER 3

From the first, Mina loved her room at camp, room 226, halfway down the long corridor. It had two beds, two windows, two dressers, two desks, and one closet which she shared with her roommate, Isadora. The beds were covered with brightly striped fabric, and the curtains matched the bedspreads. The windows looked out through the leafy branches of trees to the green quadrangle at the center of the college. Although the room was only on the second floor, there was always a breeze to keep it comfortable, because the college had been built along the ridge of the hills that bordered the broad river.

They stayed on the campus for the whole eight weeks, except for one trip into the city of New Haven, to see a performance of *Swan Lake* at Yale University. Some of the girls, especially the older ones, complained that they felt cooped up, imprisoned, but Mina never did, not for a minute.

There were seventy people living in the dormitory, and all of them were dancers. There were four dance classes, divided by age, with sixteen girls in each class. There were three dance instructors and three assistants who were taking the master classes as well as keeping an eye on the younger students. They all lived together and ate together and worked together. Music and dance, dance and music—that was what they did, all day long. They had a dance class every morning and a music class every afternoon, taught by a professor from the college. In the evenings, there was almost always something planned, either observing one of the master classes or listening to a concert given in the small college theater or watching a movie of a ballet or symphony. Sunday mornings they went to the nondenominational chapel, whose bells rang out over the quadrangle and dormitories to call people to worship. Mina sat among the dancers in an oak pew and learned a whole new set of hymns from the bound hymnals that were kept in a rack at the back of each pew with the bound prayer books. The sun shone through the stained glass windows, coloring the air with reds and greens and blues. Mina had never known how much she didn't know about dancers and about music; she looked ahead at everything she didn't know, and was glad.

There was always a song rising in her heart, one they sang at the chapel on Sundays, while the collection was being taken. "Praise God," the song rose up inside her. "Praise God from whom all blessings flow." Mina felt like praising God and thanking Him about all day long.

The majority of the girls had studied longer and more seriously than Mina had and knew more. Isadora, her roommate, was sure she was destined to become a famous ballerina. "My mom says she had a feeling, even before I was born. All the time she was pregnant, she went to at least one ballet performance a week and kept music always playing in the apartment. She named me after Isadora Duncan. I've got dance in my blood."

Mina knew what it felt like to have dance in your blood. "Who's Isadora Duncan?" she asked.

"You don't know?" Isadora looked at her, as if everybody should know, as if Mina came from a different planet.

"Nope, never heard of her. Are you going to tell me?" Mina didn't mind not knowing, she just minded not having her curiosity satisfied.

"Isadora Duncan was a great dancer, probably the greatest modern dancer. She's like Martha Graham, Twyla Tharp . . ." Mina shook her head, she hadn't heard of any of these people. She tucked the names away in her memory, to learn more about them. "Isadora Duncan was the first—she broke away from classical ballet and went back to the ancient Greeks. She wanted dance to be free from rules and things, anything artificial. She thought life shouldn't have so many rules. She danced in draperies, in bare feet, like the Greeks. Her dances were free and strong. She died young, when the scarf she was wearing got caught in the wheel of a car. See, she always wore long, long scarves around her neck." Isadora mimed wrapping a scarf around her neck, her long arms graceful. Mina could see what Isadora Duncan must have looked like. Mina was sitting on the floor by her bed, watching Isadora. "But her boyfriend had a convertible. The scarf got caught in the tire and—it just snapped her neck," Isadora concluded. "It was a tragedy. She had lots of men all madly in love with her, all the time."

"What would your mother have done if you'd been a boy?"

"Name me Isadore. There are male dancers."

Mina laughed. "I know that."

Charlie, short for Charlotte, who lived across the hall with Tansy, said that Isadora's mother was typical, a typical stage mother. Charlie often said things like that, in a superior way, as if she knew more. She acted closer to sixteen than eleven, most of the time. "Typical, pushy stage mother."

"You don't understand," Isadora said. "I'm going to be a prima ballerina. It's nothing to do with my mother, except she thinks I can, so she helps out. And all."

"—and I should know," Charlie continued, not paying any attention. "I've got one too. It's pretty pitiful in a way—it's because she wanted to be a singer. But she got married, instead.

And had kids, instead. And keeps house, instead. And nags, nags us all."

"Even your father?" Mina wondered.

"Especially Dad. Then she complains because Dad spends so much time out of town on business and nags him more." Charlie shook her head, pitying the stupidity of her mother. Charlie had no intention of going on with ballet. She wanted to be in the movies. "I'm photogenic, and—there's never the same kind of life in ballet, even if you're a success, not like movies, when you're a movie actress. Ballet teaches you how to move. An actress has to know how to . . . move right."

Charlie's roommate, Tansy, was a little plain girl, quiet and hard-working. Mina couldn't imagine why the camp had put Tansy and Charlie into the same room. Tansy had even been homesick for the first week, even though she really wanted to come to dance camp.

"How can you be homesick?" Mina had asked, trying to comfort her. "Wouldn't you rather be here?"

Charlie and Isadora had exchanged a look at that. Mina caught it, out of the corner of her eye. It was almost the kind of look kids give one another across the classroom, when they know something the teacher can't begin to understand.

"Well, I would," Mina said to the two of them. She didn't know what they thought they knew that she didn't. "Even though I miss my family too."

"Your family's different," Charlie pointed out.

"I miss my dog." Tansy snuffled.

Mina chuckled at that, and the chuckle spread out warm into a laugh. The laugh lighted up the whole dormitory room, even the farthest corners of it, and pretty soon everybody joined in, even Tansy, sitting up on the bed and blowing her nose into a tissue. She looked at Mina as if Mina was strange and wonderful.

The four of them were going to work together on the ten-minute performance that every dancer at the camp had to give for the final exercises. Their instructor, Miss Fiona Maddinton, had told them about it on the first day, after they each had an individual conference with her. In the conference, she had told each of the sixteen girls in her class what she had thought when she watched them during the audition or, in Mina's case, when she looked at the tape Miss LaValle had mailed up to New York. Miss LaValle had rented a video camera up in Cambridge and Mina had performed in front of it, the barre exercises and a dance they had worked out to part of the *Nutcracker Suite.* "You have strength," Miss Maddinton said during her conference with Mina, "and a certain rude grace. Even on that tape your presence made itself felt. A dancer has to have presence. But," she went on, when Mina opened her mouth to ask what the teacher meant, "you don't have discipline. It's discipline I will teach you. Natalie?" she called, indicating that the talk was over, summoning up the next girl. In the long working days, the hours of practice, Mina was learning what Miss Maddinton meant. Miss Maddinton seemed pleased with her. She was surely pleased with herself: She had never worked so hard and learned so much.

The performance, Miss Maddinton had told them, could be done in groups, or individually, but had to be prepared without any adult help of any kind. Even the instructors were going to take part in the final exercises, performing for ten minutes. A lot of the girls from the class had asked Mina if she wanted to work with them, but Isadora and Charlotte and Tansy had asked her first, and she would have preferred to dance with them anyway. They were going to do an original ballet, based on Narnia. The other three had decided that, because Mina had never heard of Narnia.

"But those books have been on every reading list since I was in third grade," Isadora said. "Aren't they even on your summer reading list?"

"I don't have a summer reading list."

"Then outside reading." But Mina didn't have that either. "You mean, you don't have to do book reports?"

"We do reports, sometimes, or projects," Mina said, looking around at the other three. "For science, or social studies."

"What wouldn't I give not to have to do book reports." Charlie sighed.

They all three lived in New York City and went to private schools, but different schools. Isadora's rich father sent plenty of money for her and her mother to live on, whether Isadora had a stepfather or not. Tansy's father was a special kind of dentist, called an orthodontist, and Charlie's father worked in advertising. Their mothers didn't have jobs and they had been interested to hear that Mina's mother did. About everything in their lives was different from Mina's, and she loved hearing them talk about their lives.

"I wouldn't mind book reports. I like reading," Mina said.

Charlie dismissed that. "You just don't know any better."

"Anyway," Isadora interrupted, "who has an idea for what we can do?"

Tansy did. Tansy really wanted not to dance, but to choreograph. She had an idea all worked out. "If there are two of the children, a boy and a girl—I could be the boy because I'm so small and all—and Charlie would be the girl—and Isadora would dance Aslan, all in gold, and Mina would be a Tarkaan but she'd turn into Tash, in the middle—"

"How would she do that?" Isadora asked.

"By turning around, or maybe with a mask. I know I can think of a way," Tansy said.

"Like in *Swan Lake*?" Mina asked. She had loved that moment when the magician swept his cape aside to reveal Odile, as if she had appeared by magic.

"Yes, or something like that. It would start out with the children on stage, being—happy or something—and then the Tarkaan would come in . . ." Tansy stood up from the floor of the practice room where they were working out their project and acted out the parts. "He'd try to be nice first and bribe them. Then he'd try to force them—"

"Force them to what?" Mina asked.

"To go with him, to be one of his people," Isadora explained quickly. Then she said, "I'm sorry, Mina, I didn't mean to snap at you."

Mina hadn't been offended. She didn't think Isadora had snapped at her. She waited to hear the rest of Tansy's idea.

"Then Aslan comes in and the Tarkaan seems to give up, but he turns into Tash and they fight over the children. Aslan wins and Tash—is defeated."

Mina could almost see the dance Tansy was talking about. "That sounds really good," she said. "Doesn't it?" she asked the other two.

"What about me doing the Tarkaan, instead?" Charlie asked. "Miss Maddinton says I'm the most dramatic dancer."

Tansy shook her head. "It wouldn't be as good."

"I know what you're thinking," Charlie argued.

"Don't be stupid," Isadora answered. "You're dramatic but you don't—Mina has that presence. Miss Maddinton told her that and she's right."

"Only because I'm taller than everybody else," Mina said, trying to pretend she wasn't flattered. It wasn't just being tall, she knew, it was her personality too.

"But can you be bad?" Tansy asked her. "Really, really bad—Tarkaan is bad, but Tash is—evil."

Mina stood up and turned her back to them. She thought: dark, evil, dangerous. She let that run all through her body, until she spun around to face them, tall and stiff; then slowly—to music playing *lento* in her head—she went through the five positions, feet and hands, thinking all the time of dark and of evil, and how the dark, evil thing would want to spread out and wrap itself around the three girls in the room. When she finished, she smiled at them.

"Oh, wow," Isadora said, clapping. "That was neat. See what I mean, Charlie?"

"Yeah. I guess so." But Charlie didn't sound convinced.

Tansy just looked at Mina, as if Mina was perfect. Mina knew she wasn't perfect, but she felt good. It was discipline that had enabled her to know exactly how to move through the positions, knowing where she wanted every muscle and every part of her body; she was learning discipline. "I think it'll be fun," she said.

"What music will we use?" Charlie asked.

"Something modern," Isadora suggested.

Mina had just begun to learn about music, and she kept her mouth shut. There wasn't anything she could add to this part of the planning.

"There's some Bartok," Tansy said. "Piano suites, kind of simple but not really."

"You're a walking music library," Charlie complained.

"My mom gives me anything I want."

They all knew that. They had all admired the stereo that was Tansy's own to bring to camp with her, and the stack of records. They all listened to Tansy's records. Mina listened more than anyone else except Tansy, because almost all of them were new to her; as if she had arrived in an unknown country with a wonderful geography, she was always ready to listen and hear something she'd never even heard of before dance camp.

"Mom says since I'm so mousy and all that, I'd better cultivate my brain—"

"Why do they all want us to get married?" Charlie cried out. "It's not as if they were having such a good time."

"It's crazy," Isadora agreed.

"My mother's having a good time," Tansy said. "I think. She's always going out to do something interesting, getting dressed up, you know, a show or an exhibit, meeting interesting people, artists and things, having fancy dinners."

"Who keeps your house?" Isadora asked.

"The housekeeper," Tansy told them.

That struck them as funny.

"Mrs. Welker," Tansy said. "Who keeps yours, Mina? When your mother's working?"

"We all do," Mina said. "You know, we have chores."

"Even your father?"

"Sure."

"Boy, if my mother tried to make my father do laundry," Charlie said, "or vacuum—that would be a fight that would take two weeks to blow over. We'd all starve to death in our rooms before it was safe to come down. But Dad's in advertising, and there's a lot of pressure in that. I guess your father doesn't have that kind of pressure, does he."

Mina didn't know. "We quarrel," she said. Everybody quarreled, it was human nature, and she hoped Charlie didn't feel embarrassed because her parents had fights.

Isadora's mother had been married and divorced, twice each. "Don't I know about quarrels," she said. "I'd rather think about this performance."

"I wondered," Tansy suggested in a particularly quiet voice. Mina sat up to pay close attention. She'd learned that when Tansy used that voice, it was because what she was going to say really mattered to her. Tansy looked at Mina. "If Mozart could work, for Aslan's music."

"Mozart and Bartok together?" Charlie laughed.

Mina had heard some Mozart. His name often came up in the music class. She wondered if Mozart was the kind of music you could dance to, though. She didn't say anything and nobody asked her opinion. They talked on about which of Mozart's pieces they should listen to.

"I think we ought to at least try. Whatever else, Tansy really does know what she's talking about when she talks music," Isadora finally said. "If it works, we'll be the most original I bet."

CHAPTER 4

Mina lifted her right leg onto the barre, toes pointed, and stretched her arms toward it. Watching herself in the mirror, she bent her neck so that it would follow perfectly the curve her back and arms made. Then she looked back beyond herself in the mirror, seeing the whole class, all performing the same exercise, reflected back and forth in the mirrors that lined the two long walls of the room. "Praise God," the song sang inside her, over the notes of the piano.

This was a real dance studio, as different from Miss LaValle's garage as—she didn't know anything perfect enough to compare the differences. Even though from the first minute she had stepped into it, she had felt at home, she never lost the feeling of wonder at how right the studio was. It had two narrow walls of tall windows and two long walls of mirrors that went from ceiling to floor. The upright piano filled the room with its waltz tempo for the barre exercises, as Miss Maddinton went up and down the line, correcting. "That's good, Mina," she said.

The floor was polished wood and the air was filled with light. The music went into Mina's body, and she brought her leg down in time with it, then lifted her left leg. All along the walls, mirrored back and front, fifteen girls did the same. In the mirror, thirty-two arms stretched out. Mina let a smile spread over her face.

It was coming close to the end of camp, with only a few days left before their performance. They named their dance "Narnia" and they were assigned to this same big studio for their rehearsals because they were a group so they needed more space. These days, the four of them came back every afternoon to rehearse. Mina could see why the instructors were making them work entirely without guidance, and she preferred it that way; but she wished she could hear what Miss Maddinton thought, before the performance. Mina had been careful to listen to what Tansy said when she tried to explain how things should be danced, but she thought Miss Maddinton would have some good advice. It wasn't that Mina was worried about their dance. She knew it was wonderful. She just thought she wanted it to be absolutely perfect. Miss Maddinton might catch something they'd missed.

Charlie called Miss Maddinton the "White Witch," from the Narnia books, but Mina didn't see why. It wasn't as if Miss Maddinton wore only white, or had white hair, or anything like that. Her hair was dark, inky black—dyed, Charlie said—and long. She wore grays or silvery blues or silvery pinks, her leotard, tights, and wraparound skirt all the same color. She was a professional dancer who only taught during the summer, only at this camp. Most of the year she was with a ballet company in New York.

Over the summer, Mina had written to her mother about everybody at camp, and what they were all doing. Miss Maddinton had occupied a lot of letter space, because she was a real dancer, a professional. Miss LaValle, Mina's teacher at home, had studied dance, but she was only a teacher who gave lessons in her converted garage-studio, with a record player for music. Miss LaValle was built like Miss Maddinton, both of them tall, narrow women with muscular legs, but she was older, and she wore her leotard as if it was a uniform, and it was always a plain black uniform too. Miss

LaValle had taught Mina well, Mina could tell that. She liked Miss LaValle and was grateful to her. But Miss Maddinton, Miss Fiona Maddinton—she was a real ballerina. Mina wondered what Miss Maddinton would do for her own ten-minute performance, on the night. Because it got so there wasn't anything happening to write to her mother about, Mina sometimes just wrote down her guesswork about things like that: what Miss Maddinton would do, or whether Charlie's father would lose his job because he lost a big account. Her mother wrote back the news from home, that Zandor got a fifty-cent-an-hour raise and had a new girlfriend, that Belle was bored (and boring, Mina's mother added), messages from Mina's father and from Louis, and her own opinions about the summer minister's sermons and his family. It sounded like Mina's mother liked the minister fine, but wasn't sure about his wife. "We don't see much of her," Momma wrote.

Mina had started off writing to Kat, just silly things, and Kat had written back, but after a couple of weeks that had tapered off. Kat couldn't possibly understand how wonderful it was. Mina couldn't have explained, for instance, how much she liked learning about music, its history, the names of composers, and listening to their different music, the different forms music could be written in. Mr. Tattodine, who liked Mina because she asked so many questions, had white hair that flopped over his forehead, and a way—when the class was listening to a record—of getting entirely engrossed in the music, until his face looked half asleep and his hand would come up to mark the beat, as if he was conducting the piece.

It was Mr. Tattodine who had given Tansy the idea for where to find the right Mozart music for Aslan. Tansy had been trying movements from symphonies and string quartets, but nothing worked. Nothing made a dance. During the classes on opera, when he was talking about Mozart's life and the reasons that people thought he was a genius, Mr. Tattodine had mentioned *The Magic Flute.* "It was considered at the time that he had written a low piece of work, a popular effort, written for money. Well, he did need money, he always needed money. But it is now taken as one of his richest works, musically speaking," Mr. Tattodine said. Then he smiled at them and said, "I'm sorry, I'm lecturing at you again, I keep forgetting. Let's have a question. Who can define the differences between opera and ballet. The musical differences, that is, because many operas—like *The Magic Flute*—do include dance." Tansy nudged Mina then.

Mina knew four of the seven differences that were given and realized once again how glad she was to be at camp. Mr. Tattodine said the way she learned she was like a sponge or a vacuum cleaner; "But not in the bad sense," he said. Mina wasn't worried about bad or good senses; she knew she could remember almost everything she was told, and she learned that she could hear not only musical phrases and forms, not only harmony and counterpoint, but also the several individual instruments that played together. She loved the whole range of strings, the variety of percussions, the winds and the reeds. Mr. Tattodine had them try playing every instrument, just to get sound out of it. Mina's favorites were the reeds, because to play them you needed to hold the reed properly in your mouth and blow through it properly, which took discipline; but it was also a matter of your breath going through the wooden tube. The reeds seemed the most complicated and natural.

The brasses were her next favorite. When she had the French horn in her hands, in class, she got a long clear note out of it, without any trouble, a round winding sound that made you sit up at attention and called out to you. "I've just got a lot of hot air," Mina said laughing and passed the horn to Isadora. "That's why I'm not having any trouble with it."

Once Tansy had listened to *The Magic Flute* and found passages of music that she wanted in it, passages that would be like counterpoint to Tarkaan's Bartok, they moved ahead with their dance. It took work, hours of practicing to get the steps right, to get each individual performance right, to get everything put together right so that the dance worked the way Tansy wanted it to. But hours of work were no trouble. Charlie and Isadora complained, sometimes, but Mina never even felt like it.

"What are you, some goody-goody?" Charlie demanded during their second-to-last rehearsal.

"It's because her daddy's a minister," Isadora, stretched out on the floor beside Charlie, said. Tansy had been called out to the phone, which was odd because parents usually called during the hour the girls had free before lights out. Mina was trying to get Charlie to go over the part where Tarkaan was trying to win over the human girl. Charlie didn't see the point of doing it without having Tansy there to watch, because they'd just have to do it all over again for Tansy.

"I think she's just stronger than we are," Charlie said. "You don't get as tired, Mina; you can't argue that."

Mina didn't know what it was, except she liked what she was doing so much that she never got tired doing it. She decided to listen to the Bartok again.

Mr. Tattodine had explained to her the way the rhythm worked and the reasons for the notes being what they were and the different scale Bartok was using. She didn't really understand, but she could hear the dance in the music now. Mr. Tattodine was an immigrant, from Hungary, which was Bartok's homeland. He said maybe that was why the music made sense to him. Mina listened to the fragmented chords of the Bartok, standing still but feeling as if her body was moving to the dance.

Tansy came back through the big door at the end of the room. She looked serious. "Everything okay?" Isadora asked.

"My grandfather died."

"Oh. That's too bad," Isadora said.

"Were you close?" Charlie asked.

Tansy shook her head. "I've barely seen him since he went into the nursing home."

"Was he sick?" Mina asked.

"Maybe we ought to stop the rehearsal," Charlie suggested.

"The performance is the day after tomorrow," Tansy said. "We don't have enough time as it is. I'm sort of sad, but it's not as if . . . He wasn't sick, he just got too old to take care of himself, so he went into a home."

Charlie and Isadora started telling stories about old relatives of their parents who had gone into nursing homes, or retired to places where there were a lot of old people gathered together. Mina didn't say anything, because her one living set of grandparents lived with her mother's brother in Georgia, and the grandparents who had died when she was still a baby had lived just around the corner. She thought of Miz Hunter, but didn't mention her either. After a while, Tansy said it was time to get back to work, "If that's okay?"

They were the last of the youngest class to give their performance. By the time they moved onstage, Mina had been so nervous for so long she was too tired to be tense. Mr. Tattodine played the tape they had put together. Mina listened to the first bars of music and watched the curtain draw apart. She wore her black leotard and a mask over her eyes, a black Halloween mask that she had edged with red and gold glitter. Isadora, with her long hair loose, like Aslan's golden mane, wore a golden leotard and tights; Charlie wore white, with a skirt wrapped around it, and Tansy wore green. The other three had to buy new leotards, but Mina just had to buy the mask, which was lucky. Tansy had thought everything out. Mina's part required angular steps and positions, while Isadora, as Aslan, moved in arcs and circles. Isadora never came into Mina's part of the stage, until the end; Mina sometimes moved a little into Isadora's part, like the tip of a triangle, but she danced out quickly. The two children in Narnia went back and forth.

When Mina changed into Tash himself, all she did was take the mask off. They had painted her eyebrows dark and her mouth red and larger than it was. The music's sharp lines of melody, broken off, matched her steps. As Tansy had explained it to them, Tash made triangles and Aslan circles. All the dancing showed that, just as the music clashed and couldn't ever be made to play together. So Isadora moved in circles, leaping, turning, golden, while Mina moved dark and strong and cruel to the points of triangles. At the end, Aslan's circles wound all around Tash, and he was driven from the stage. Then the two children and Aslan danced together, to Mozart.

When they took their bows at the end, everybody in the audience stood up to clap. They held hands and bowed and bowed, still breathing heavily, smiling at one another and at the audience. At the reception afterward, punch and cookies served in the dormitory living room, just about everybody in the camp came up to tell Mina what a good job she'd done.

"Thanks." She smiled. She couldn't stop smiling. She wished—that they hadn't performed yet and that it was something she could do again, right away.

Miss Maddinton came up, with another instructor, while Mina was getting another cup of punch. "It was very good, Mina," Miss Maddinton said. "You've learned a lot this summer, haven't you?"

"Yes." Mina knew she had.

"I envy you that class, Fiona," the other instructor said. "And you, young lady, you were absolutely frightening. I was on the edge of my chair."

"It's Tansy, really," Mina said. "It was her dance, her idea, and all."

"You don't have to be so modest," Miss Maddinton corrected her.

Mina smiled. She felt goofy smiling so much, but she couldn't stop. "Thank you. But it really was Tansy."

"I know that; do you think I don't know that?" Miss Maddinton said.

Mr. Tattodine came up to the four of them. "You've had the success of the evening, and I'm very proud of you. It was good theater," he said to Tansy.

Tansy lowered her head, embarrassed and pleased. Mina smiled.

"And well danced, all of you. You have shown me that ballet is still a living art. Oh, I've enjoyed your performance."

They all had trouble going to sleep that night. They all sat around in Mina's room, in the dark, talking in low voices. It was the last night of camp, and Mina suddenly felt as if she couldn't bear to wait the whole school year before she came back.

"It's not that we were the best," Tansy was saying, trying to put their feelings into words.

"Except that we were awfully good for our age," Isadora said.

"I hate that for-your-age stuff, don't you?" Charlie protested.

"We were the only really original ones," Mina said. "Everybody else, except the instructor for the oldest class, danced the usual dances and even hers—she danced to jazz but it was still traditional. Ours wasn't like anybody else's." She smiled.

"It was worth all that work, Tansy, I'll admit it," Charlie said.

"Yeah, thanks," Isadora agreed. "And to Mina too—did you

hear the way somebody gasped when you took off your mask, Mina? I don't know what they expected to see. It was like a horror show."

Mina smiled. "Thanks a lot," she joked.

"You know what I mean."

"I'm already wondering what Tansy's going to ask us to do next year, aren't you?" Mina asked them. She had gotten so much better in just the weeks here. She could work every day, practically, if she got organized, and by next summer— "Oh, I'm looking forward to next summer," she said.

"Mina! We've still got two weeks of vacation. What's wrong with you?" Charlie demanded. "Don't wish away my only vacation time."

Mina thought that camp was her vacation, but she didn't say so. They heard the college bell chime two in the morning before they finally were sleepy enough to go to bed.

Miss Maddinton was the one who greeted Mina's father when he drove up. She made her report as he loaded Mina's suitcase into the backseat of the dusty car. "She's learned a lot about discipline this summer."

All around them, girls were greeting their families, saying good-bye to their friends, getting into cars, driving away. Mina waved and waved at Tansy, going off in a red sports car with her father, who looked as small and mousy as Tansy.

"I've enjoyed having her in class. It seems to have been a good experience for everybody."

"I know she's had a good time here," Mina's father said. "We thank you."

"See you next summer, Mina," Miss Maddinton answered. "Keep practicing."

"Oh, I will," Mina promised.

She got into the car. Her father got into the car. She turned her head to look at him. "You better belt in," he said. Then he reached out a big arm to hug her, and she hugged him back. There hadn't been any hugging or hand-holding or putting arms around all summer long. Mina thought, for a minute, that she thought there should have been, but then she dismissed the idea: It wouldn't have been right for dance camp; it wouldn't have suited.

"We've got a long drive ahead," her father said. He drove down the road beside the river, then along the ramp and out into the speeding traffic. He didn't talk. Her father didn't like these crowded thruways, Mina remembered. He was concentrating hard. She didn't like them much either, once it stopped being exciting to be hurtling along, rushing, once the sad feelings started coming up again inside her, at leaving and having to be gone from camp for so long. The truck motors roared in her ears, the hot air smelled of gasoline and oil, and the scenery at the roadside was mostly the backs of houses, backs of shopping centers, backs of factories. Mina sat quiet, remembering, feeling sad.

"Mina?" her father asked.

Mina turned her head to look at him. She had forgotten how rich the sound of his voice was.

"Were you the only little black girl there at camp?"

"I guess so," Mina said.

"Why was that?"

"I was the only one good enough, I guess," Mina said.

CHAPTER 5

Mina and her mother were sitting at the kitchen table, sorting through a pile of pictures, to decide which ones would go into the album Zandor had given their parents for Christmas. An icy January rain drummed on the tin roof over the back porch, and darkness lay outside the windows.

Mina was downstairs because it was Belle's turn for the record player. Even in the kitchen, you could hear the heavy rhythm of rock music, and the sound of Belle's feet, dancing around their room. Louis was asleep while Zandor did homework. Zandor would be sitting there at his desk, in a pool of light, turning pages of textbooks or maybe scratching his pencil over his notebook. He had exams coming up. Dad was out at a meeting that night. He'd gone right after dinner, bundled up in his overcoat.

"It was a pretty paltry effort, that Christmas tree," Mina's mother said, studying a photograph.

Mina was working her way through the pile of pictures from the summer, sorting out the ones where the focus was bad, or the people had moved at the last minute. She didn't study them, she just flipped through. Last summer she had been at camp. It felt like about a hundred years ago, and it felt like another hundred years before she could go back again.

"Mina? Did you hear what I said?"

"Yes, Mom."

"Don't you have anything to say?"

"Not anything I haven't said before. I told you, I think we should have made some popcorn and cranberry strings. That would have helped a lot."

"I wish Ellie'd been able to get home."

"You wouldn't have wanted her to leave her husband alone over the holidays," Mina reminded her. She got up to throw the rejects into the wastebasket under the sink. While she was up, she thought she'd have a glass of milk. "Heat me a cup of coffee, would you, honey?" her mother asked.

"Won't it keep you awake?"

"Nothing'll keep me awake tonight."

"You work too hard," Mina said, lighting the burner under the coffeepot. They never used a pilot light; it cost less to use matches. Zandor had once worked out just how much it saved and it wasn't terribly much, Mina remembered.

"Working too hard is when you're doing it for somebody else's purposes," her mother said.

"Like school," Mina agreed.

"Maybe," her mother said. "Maybe it is."

Uh-oh, Mina thought. There was something her mother wanted to talk with her about. That was why she'd asked Mina to help with the photographs, Mina was willing to bet on it. Her mother wanted to get them sitting down, just the two of them. Mina guessed she'd known it was coming. In their family, you couldn't go from straight A's to straight B's without somebody saying something. She poured out the cup of coffee, adding sugar and cream.

"That'll be too sweet," her mother observed.

"You need the energy," Mina said.

Her mother tasted it. "You're right, this tastes perfect. Thanks." She put the cup down. "I was actually thinking about slavery."

Mina just kept herself from groaning aloud as she sat down again and picked up the stack of good photographs. They acted as if slavery wasn't dead and gone, a hundred years ago and more. They acted as if—as if people around now were the same ones who had owned slaves.

"Your father's worried about you," her mother said.

They didn't look at one another.

"I'm sorry," Mina said. She thought, These must be pictures of the Fourth of July picnic. She remembered where she'd been, Fourth of July.

"I notice you aren't asking why."

Mina wasn't asking why because she had a pretty good idea of why, and she didn't want to talk about it. "Is this the summer minister?" she asked, pointing to some people she'd never seen before, a man and wife, a girl, and two little children.

Her mother said yes, it was.

"She's awfully pretty, isn't she?" Mina asked, her eyes drawn to the woman, who looked especially dainty standing beside her husband, her tiny waist emphasized by the brightly colored belt wrapped at the waist of her wide skirts. That woman knew how to dress. Mina liked the plain pink dress and contrasting colors of the wide striped belt.

"Oh yes, Alice is that. She's like your friend Kat—or, your used-to-be friend."

"But your letters sounded like you didn't like her much. Alice."

"I didn't mind her personally. She just isn't much use to her husband, she's one of those women who always seems to need taking care of and never seems able to take care of anyone else."

Alice wore dainty high-heeled sandals, even though it was an outdoor picnic on a field. "How did she manage, with those shoes," Mina wondered.

"Honey, I'm trying to talk with you."

"I know."

"And you're avoiding me."

"Well . . ." Mina laughed. ". . . I'm trying to." Her mother laughed too, so Mina knew that she wasn't in line for a scolding.

"Your poppa doesn't agree with me. I guess, I'm just never so confident in my opinions as he is."

"Dad has God on his side."

"Don't be fresh, Mina. But I can't believe it's so bad for you to learn something about music, and listen to . . . all that."

All that, Mina thought, smiling because her mother was lumping Beethoven and Tchaikovsky and Brahms into a pile, and calling the pile *all that.*

"Your father doesn't really understand."

"I know, Mom," Mina said. "I don't mind."

"Not because he's not smart," her mother said quickly. "You got your brains from both of us, as I hope you know. But there are different ways of being smart and he's not the man for studying something, reading about it. He values education, that's not what I mean, only . . ."

Mina thought she knew what her mother meant. "I'm not upset," she promised.

"I think I am," her mother said. Mina's head jerked up and she just stared at her mother. "All these things put together, and I read too many history books to think that you can get away without putting things together, if you want to understand."

"All what things?" Mina asked.

"These symphonies and things that you listen to. The way you've been blow-drying your hair, as bad as Belle about how you look. Practicing so much at Miss LaValle's—which, if you were going to be a professional ballerina, might make sense."

"How do you know I won't?"

Her mother was not to be diverted. "Then Mrs. Parker asked me to come in for a meeting."

"About my grades," Mina decided.

"No, although we've been wondering."

Her mother waited.

"Wondering about your grades," she added, and then waited again. She was giving Mina a place to step in and explain, but Mina didn't want to.

"No, Mrs. Parker wanted to talk about your attitude. She says you're a debilitating influence. Those were her exact words. Do you know what that means?"

"Yes, ma'am."

"She says she doesn't mind a lively child—she's got three children of her own, she knows about children."

"I didn't know that," Mina said. "How old are they?"

"Don't you try to derail me, young lady," her mother answered, and Mina laughed. "She says you act the wit. I did tell her that you've always had a good sense of humor."

Mina grinned at her mother. "Thanks, Mom."

"But she said that acting the class clown is different. And she's right."

But, Mina thought, but it was different, but—

"And she says that you're directing your remarks only to a select audience. The white girls, as if . . ." Mina's mother didn't finish the sentence and Mina didn't feel like asking her what she almost said. "Mrs. Parker told us she was pleased and surprised when you asked in September if you could do book reports."

"She was surprised, that's for sure."

"But that you don't read the books she recommends. She says they're good books."

Mina shrugged.

"And she asked me how you felt about all the growing you've been doing. If it worried you."

Mina had gone back to sorting pictures, which would only take about one-quarter of her attention.

"I told her I was a nurse and we were pretty frank about puberty. She said it wasn't only that, she wondered if maybe you were ashamed about looking so mature. And I hadn't ever thought of that, which didn't please me too much, but she's right. She said someone like you, she'd expect bold colors, bright things."

"They're loud," Mina answered. "I can dress the way I want to, can't I? Just because I'm developing, and all that, doesn't mean I have to act like I'm trying to be Belle, does it? I can read what I want to too." She thought her mother might really understand this, so she really tried to explain. "*You* read what you want to. Nobody says you shouldn't read something just because it's not about black people, do they? And how would you like it, if they did?"

Mina's mother just looked at her and looked at her. Mina thought, I should've kept my mouth shut.

"Does Mrs. Parker tell you to read about black people?"

Mina shrugged.

"What do you do?"

"I write it down, title and author, and then I go to the library and look for something I want to read. The thing is, Mom, except for slavery, nothing ever happened to black people. I like England," Mina said, knowing it sounded disconnected. "They had the Middle Ages. And knights. And all. I don't think you can understand," she said, hoping that when she said that her mother would prove that she *did* understand.

"Me, not understand? With all six of my children named what they are?" Her mother was angry, instead.

"Naming people after kings and queens isn't the same as understanding," Mina said.

"I'll tell you who doesn't understand," her mother said.

"Nobody does, that's who," Mina said. She felt unhappiness start to block up her throat. "So let's just get this job done, all right?"

"Yes, maybe," her mother said. Both of them went to work, and neither of them tried to speak, because, Mina thought, both of them knew there wasn't anything that could be said. She wondered, not for the first time, why God made some people black and some white. And why, if He did that, he made Mina one of the black ones. She knew there was no use to wondering about that, but she still wondered.

Mina worked her way through pictures, selecting those that had the family in them: Louis digging in the sand, Belle and three of her friends dressed up to go to a dance, CS at a picnic table. There was one of everybody who had been at home that summer, with her mother at the head of the line and then, from youngest to oldest, Louis, Belle, Zandor. "You didn't have much to do this summer, did you?" Mina asked, before she remembered that they had given up speaking for a while.

"It was easier, with only half of you around. I'll give you that. CS got home for some weekends."

Mina came to a family picture of the summer minister, a portrait pose. The little children were on their parents' laps. It looked like a church occasion of some kind. The girl stood between her parents. Mina's eyes were drawn again to the woman, Alice. Her white button earrings matched her necklace, the sundress she wore made green folds over her knees, her legs were slim, crossed at the ankles: She was a pleasure to look at. Her face, and the expression on it . . . "She looks like she's crazy about him. Was she?"

"In her own way, I think so," Mina's mother answered, looking across at the picture.

"Does he love her as much?" Mina hoped he did. It wouldn't be right if Alice wasn't loved back.

"I expect so. She's the kind of woman men idolize and spoil. You'll be able to date the pictures from the fall, so you take these while I do the summer ones. We didn't get any pictures from your camp, did we. I'd have liked one or two. I don't even know what it looks like."

"Oh," Mina said, "it's beautiful. It's up on a hill, and the buildings are stone and the grass stays green. It doesn't dry out like here; it's like, like a carpet. Lots of tall trees, really old trees."

"I can't picture it."

"I can. I can remember it perfectly. Everything about it."

"*Are* you thinking of a career in dance?"

"Why?"

"I'm interested, as you know very well. It's not an easy life."

"All the competition?"

"That. And a lot of other things too. Look at Irene LaValle, look at her life. Your father's a little concerned, and so am I."

"I don't want to be a nurse, Mom."

"Neither did I. But I like my work fine. Let's get these into the album, so I can get to bed. I'm pretty nearly wiped out."

Mina's mother peeled back the plastic sheet that covered the first page.

"Did you want to be something like a doctor?" Mina asked. She couldn't imagine her mother a doctor; it didn't seem right somehow.

"I thought about that, maybe once or twice altogether, but never seriously. My parents couldn't have afforded the schooling, and I wasn't smart enough to get a scholarship. I had a choice between nursing or teaching or social work; you can find positions anywhere in those fields. Then, when I met Poppa, well, I just wanted to have my courses finished so that we could get married."

She arranged four pictures on the page. Mina looked at them and nodded. Mina put the plastic cover back over the page and smoothed it down with her hand.

"Poppa never did live out of Crisfield, except when he went to school," her mother said. "If I hadn't been there, I never would have met him. He's always wanted to live here."

"I know," Mina said.

"I think maybe that's why he's so—He never got his feet knocked out from under him. Being a service brat," Mina's mother went on, "I kept getting my feet knocked out from under me. Every two or three years we'd move, every time we moved we had to get to know a whole new bunch of people. I always wondered if that's why Poppa seems so much surer of himself than other people."

"I thought it was religion," Mina said.

Her mother ignored her. "Almost everybody says you've changed. Miz Hunter too; but she says anybody worth his salt gets unsettled while they're growing up." Mrs. Smiths smiled to herself. "I'm surely glad we have her around to talk sense."

Mina realized that her father was the one mostly saying she'd changed.

"Helene Beaulieu said Kat thinks the summer turned you into a snob."

Did she then? Mina thought. Did she just think that? "All they want to do is form clubs. All the clubs do is leave people out, because you know how Rachelle likes leaving people out."

"And making sure the people know they're left out. I know how that is."

"And—I'm just not interested in their stupid clubs."

"Did they ask you to join?"

"Not really."

"Why not?"

"I guess, they don't like me anymore."

They weren't looking at each other, just arranging pictures on pages and setting them under the plastic covers, working pretty fast.

"Mina—you know they like you."

"I guess. But—"

"But they don't know anything about you?"

Mina guessed that was about it. Mina guessed there was an awful lot her mother did understand. "At first, we started a reading club. To do book reports too. But—"

Mrs. Smiths waited, then asked, "But?"

"It was my club, really, it was my idea, and I started it and picked the people, with Kat."

"So I guess you had an idea about how it would work."

"Yeah."

"And their ideas were different."

"They said I was being bossy and showing off. But, Mom, didn't you ever think? There are all these myths about gods and goddesses, because the ancient Greeks believed in them, and the Romans, and all we ever had was Brer Rabbit. And the Ananse stories. And things like that. Even the Bible, we didn't write that. . . ." Mina's voice drifted off.

"I imagine only the Jews could write the Bible—the Old Testament."

"What do you mean?"

"They're a minority too, Mina."

But that wasn't what Mina meant, at all. Her mother yawned, turned over a page of the album and selected the next four pictures. They were Halloween pictures, Louis as a ghost, Belle as a

Spanish gypsy and Mina herself wearing a tutu Miss LaValle had loaned her and a little crown she had made herself out of wire and foil. She had made her regular dancing shoes look like toe shoes by winding silky ribbons up her legs. She told anybody who asked that she was Odette, but only Kat knew who that was. Looking at the picture, Mina realized that it didn't matter what name she had taken, she could have been about anybody from any of the stories, Giselle or Juliet or anybody. Not the Firebird, though. Next year, I'll try the Firebird, Mina thought to herself. If I'm still going out on Halloween.

"Poppa says he guesses you're just beginning to realize the realities; waking up, he says. He thinks you're too young."

"You've been talking about me. You've been talking to everyone about me," Mina complained.

"What do you expect? I love you, and I don't think you're particularly happy."

"I'm fine, I'm just fine," Mina protested. Except for wanting to be at camp, she was.

"You've been going around making things hard on yourself. You know you have, so don't try to deny it. A lot of people care about you, honey."

Since that had nothing to do with anything, Mina wasn't going to bother denying it.

They worked quickly. Thanksgiving, with Eleanor and John and the babies, CS too, at home, then Christmas, four pictures to a page. It was like filling in the pages of the year, Mina thought.

"What do *you* think? Do you think I'm so different?" Mina asked, as she smoothed the plastic sheet over the last pictures. She didn't know if she wanted her mother to understand or not.

"I think it's puberty, if you want to know. All those hormones shooting around." Mrs. Smiths chuckled. "But it's hard on you, and I respect that." Her mother kissed Mina on the head, putting her dirty cup in the sink to be washed with the breakfast dishes. "I'm going upstairs. I go on duty at six in the morning tomorrow."

"Good-night, Mom," Mina said. She watched her mother leave the room, a strong woman, with her broad back and her heavy legs. Her mother's strength—even when she was tired, like now—showed in every move her body made.

Mina folded the album closed, but didn't get up. She thought she was right not to tell anybody what was going on. How could you say to your own parents that you didn't feel at home with them?

Just about everything felt wrong to Mina—like underwear that didn't fit properly—just about every day—like a wrong-sized bra, something tight and uncomfortable underneath whatever you had on. The only thing that didn't feel wrong was choir singing, even though her voice was getting lower, even though she was changing there too. She was closer to an alto these days, which seemed to match all the filling out her frame had been doing. It wasn't fat though, it was muscle. You couldn't work the way Mina did every morning in her room and most afternoons at Miss LaValle's studio and be fat; dancing had never been such hard work before.

Mina sang softly, "Jacob's Ladder." "We are climbing Jacob's ladder." Inside her head, she added two harmony parts, a third above and a third below. She was beginning to think that there was something too show-offy about singing soprano anyway, singing solos, as if you were always trying to be the star of everything.

But all the rest of her life—she minded about all the rest of it. She wished the year were over and she was back at summer, back at camp, back with dancers. Back where she really belonged.

She looked down at her hands, but she didn't recognize them

as her own, those hands resting on the photograph album. Mina closed her eyes. The house around her was silent, except for the pattering noises of people going to bed, or the muted sounds of people already sleeping. The wind blew around the house, and the sound of rain on the tin roof got sharper, so that she thought the rain had turned to sleet. Sleet would blow down sharp through the dark air.

In her mind, she saw a high hill, with stone buildings on it among tall, leafy trees, and the great golden lion pacing there. He would know her, who she really was; with him, she would be who she really was. In her mind, she heard the overture to *Swan Lake*, all the orchestral instruments playing together, in harmony. She could almost smell the studio, a mixture of wax and sweat and the perfume Miss Maddinton wore.

Mina opened her eyes. The hands lay flat on the bright fabric with which the album was covered. She looked at them, at the square fingernails and the black skin. She turned them over to see the pinky skin of her palms. She felt as if these hands didn't belong to her and she didn't want them to. But could you feel that way about your own hands?

CHAPTER 6

Mina tackled Kat on the subject the next time they were alone together. That occurred when they walked to Miss LaValle's for dance class. They had class twice a week, Tuesdays and Thursdays, from five to six. They always walked together, because their parents said they had to. It wasn't dangerous, not Crisfield, but it wasn't smart for girls to go walking around alone in the dark of evening. They both carried their slippers in plastic sacks, against the damp; they both had already changed into leotards, because the one changing room in the garage, with a plastic curtain hanging down over it, wasn't a very nice place to change clothes in.

"What do you mean, telling your mother I'm a snob?" Mina demanded.

For a long time, Kat didn't say anything. Mina didn't look at her. She watched the sidewalk pass under her feet instead. They didn't walk close anymore, they were too old to walk around hand in hand the way they used to.

Finally Kat said, "That's the way you act."

Mina didn't know, really, why she'd asked. She didn't care, really, what Kat thought. She just wasn't going to let Kat get away with saying things like that, without Mina letting her know that she knew about it.

"It *is*," Kat said. "All you'll talk about is that boring music, all you do is—and boasting about camp, or going off to babysit somewhere—"

"You know I need the money, for tights, and slippers. It isn't as if my parents can afford those things, the way yours—"

"That too," Kat interrupted. She stopped and turned to face Mina. Her face was twisted up with anger and didn't look at all pretty, Mina noticed. "I don't know you anymore. You're always criticizing me these days."

"Like when?"

"Like right now, as if there was something wrong with my father earning good money. Oh, you don't say anything, you don't do it with words, you do it with your eyes, as if there's something wrong with the way I dress and talk and act, as if— And all you do is write letters to those camp people. I bet they don't even write you back. Answer me that."

Mina didn't answer.

"And trying to make me different too, make me read books and listen to your music. And they're boring and dumb—the Narnia books. It's just pretend, fairy-tale stuff, with magic, and if I don't like them, you look at me as if I'm stupid. I'm not stupid. I don't know you anymore and it's not my doing."

Kat was breathing heavily. The white breaths floated away in the darkening air. The trees around them were bare branches, except for a big magnolia behind a fence. Mina didn't know why Kat was so worked up. Looking at the girl, Mina thought probably Kat was jealous. It was as if jealousy had gotten into her and twisted up her face.

"You said we were best friends, but you don't act like a friend at all." Kat started to cry.

Mina guessed maybe they weren't friends. People changed. But if they weren't, she didn't see why Kat was so worked up. She started moving again. "We don't want to be late," she said. "I only told you to read Narnia because I wanted you to understand about Tansy's dance," Mina reminded Kat. "You said you wanted to hear about it."

"I did, but not over and over again. As if there was nothing else in the world. And nobody else."

"Besides, everybody says they're really good books, and they are too."

"Who everybody? I know who. Your new friends, your white friends. That's who. I notice what part they gave to *you.* But you don't notice, because that would be criticizing them, and they're perfect."

"You don't understand," Mina said.

"Oh yeah? I bet—if you could—you'd go up there and live with them and be just like them—"

So what if she would, Mina said to herself. Kat didn't even know what she didn't know. Who was she to act so uppity at Mina?

"—You act—at school too, I've seen it—as if you're ashamed of us."

For that matter, sometimes Mina was; she knew that. It was too bad, but it was true.

Kat snuffled along beside her for a while, then said, "Everybody says that anyway."

"Says what?"

"You're a snob."

Just because you were interested in other things they called you a snob, just because . . . that was just the kind of thing the kids here did.

"Yeah, well, nobody says it to my face, do they," Mina answered.

"That's because everybody likes you," Kat told her.

Mina started to laugh. It was so completely illogical—

"You may think it's funny but I don't. I think it's sad," Kat cried.

—but true too, Mina thought, not laughing anymore. She was popular, but she didn't have friends, not here. The funny thing was that they seemed to care about it more than she did.

"I don't know why you complain anyway," Kat said as they came to the cement driveway that led to the studio. "Since you've got so many better things to do than be friends. Since you don't care."

"I wasn't complaining," Mina pointed out.

"Well, then," Kat said, her face looking purple as a plum under the street light.

"I don't see that I've got anything to complain about," Mina added, to let Kat know that she was perfectly contented with the way things were. "But I don't like you telling things like that, when your mother repeats them to my mother," she warned Kat. "It made Mom worry. I don't want her worrying."

Kat wanted to quarrel back, but she didn't dare. Mina could see that. It wasn't that Kat was afraid to, not exactly. It was more that she knew Mina was right. Mina was usually right, because she was smarter and had broader experience, she read more and knew more and asked the right questions. Mina knew Kat wouldn't quarrel back, and she knew she could make Kat do what she wanted.

"You're going to get yourself in trouble one day," Kat prophesied.

"It sounds like you hope you're there to see it," Mina answered. T-rou-ble, that was what she was around here, and she didn't mind a bit. To start with, it was miles better than being just nobody, like everybody else was.

"How can you say that?" Kat asked her. "How could I feel that way when we're friends and have been for ages? You talk like I don't like you, Mina."

"It sounds like maybe you don't," Mina reminded her.

"But that doesn't mean I want something awful to happen to you. You've really changed, Mina."

Mina had had enough of the conversation. She'd said what she wanted to say, and her mother wouldn't be hearing any more, she guessed. They were wasting time they could use dancing, hanging around out here.

Miss LaValle's studio still had the green plastic crowsfoot firs hung around the walls, with little Christmas lights blinking on and off, red and blue and green and orange and white, blinking on, blinking off. The studio had originally been the two-car garage for the little one-bedroom, one-story house. Miss LaValle had remodeled it herself, painting the walls, purchasing and hanging the long, cheap mirrors, which were now mottled with some kind of rusty stains. Overhead, fluorescent lights in long bars gave off uneven light. Mina worked by herself at the far end of the barre.

The floor was the hardest part of the job, Miss LaValle had told her once. She'd had to learn how to lay wooden flooring herself, measuring, cutting, and laying the long, narrow strips. Then she'd sanded it smooth with a rented sander and waxed and polished it herself. The floor was always cold in winter, because it had been put down over the cement slab that was the garage floor. Most of the wax had worn off and Miss LaValle hadn't gotten around to rewaxing it. As Mina did her warming-up exercises, she tried not to hear the scratchiness of the record Miss LaValle was playing, for the class that was taking place at the other end of the room. The record was a waltz, "The Blue Danube," so worn with use that the violins sounded as if they were being played with metal bows and the winds seemed to be gasping for breath. Now that Mina knew how the instruments could sound, and should sound, she almost couldn't stand to listen to Miss LaValle's records.

While the class was working at the barre, Mina moved to the center of the room, back at the far end, near where the changing room had been made catty-corner, where the clothes and bags were piled up against a wall. She worked adagio and allegro, then did batteries, increasing her elevation. Her muscles had to work hard because her body seemed to protest; and it wasn't long before she was working up a sweat.

Miss LaValle changed the record, to *Nutcracker* selections, but Mina barely noticed. The record gave her rhythm for the two enchainements she had worked out, but it wasn't music. As she went over the arrangements of steps, doing both completely each time, she tried to watch herself in the mirror. It didn't feel quite right, but she couldn't figure out what she was doing wrong. She was too often too close to off balance, she knew that. The steps in an enchainement were supposed to flow, one into the other, but hers didn't feel like they were doing that. Mina concentrated hard, slowed down to regain fluidity of movement, then pushed up to the proper tempo. She heard Miss LaValle working with the class—the teacher was too patient, Mina thought. It was better to make the girls do more, work to higher standards, if you were going to teach them how to dance. Dance class shouldn't be a social occasion.

There wasn't anything more Miss LaValle could teach Mina; Mina had realized that right away. She continued coming for class time and giving Miss LaValle a five dollar bill at the end of each week. Mina had used to think that being a dance teacher like Miss LaValle would be a perfect life. You could dance all day long, if you wanted. Now, looking at her former teacher, she wondered. Miss LaValle's dance slippers were scuffed and worn, she wore the same black leotard and tights Mina had always seen her wearing, and her hair wasn't long. A dancer needed long hair. Mina was growing hers, which was a pain but was necessary. Miss LaValle kept hers short and curly, which looked good on her, but wasn't what a dancer should do.

Miss LaValle was built like a dancer, long legs and muscular calves, a narrow torso, long arms and neck. Narrow shoulders. She had a flat stomach and small breasts. She looked weak and delicate, but she was actually strong.

There had been a time when Mina could imagine nothing more rewarding than living the kind of life Miss LaValle lived; now she could imagine more, so much more. . . . The bad side of that was that, now, she didn't feel like she belonged even here, in the dance studio, anymore.

She was always feeling out of place these days, Mina realized. She thought of it during her silent walk back with Kat and again in her own kitchen, where Louis read at the table he'd have to set in a couple of minutes, once their mother got home. Mina had put the burner on under a stew and preheated the oven for biscuits. She had the biscuits mixed and shaped when her mother came in the door. "Go over to the church and tell your father his dinner will be on in—?"

"Twelve to fifteen minutes," Mina said, slipping the two cookie pans into the oven.

"Take a jacket," her mother called.

"It's not far," Mina called back. "I won't be cold." She didn't take her jacket.

She went slowly down the front steps, rather enjoying the icy cold of the damp winter air on her bare arms and bare legs. From Miz Hunter's porch came the question. "Where you going to, Missy?"

Mina halted in the concealing darkness. Miz Hunter probably stepped out onto her porch to say hello to Mina's mother, coming back from work. Miz Hunter's tiny body was silhouetted against the yellow light at the open front door.

"Where you going to, Missy?" Miz Hunter asked again.

I don't know, Mina thought, and everybody's getting in my way. Stop *asking*, she thought. "I'm going across to bring Dad home for supper," she said.

"Well, you have a good evening."

"You too," Mina responded.

September, October, November, December—they were all gone and done with. January was almost over. It wasn't that long now anymore.

CHAPTER 7

Mina's heart was beating so fast, and so hard, she thought for sure it must show, thumping away under her blouse. Her father was driving slowly through the city of New London and then, slowly, up the river road. They had been riding for hours, without talking much, and Mina had made herself be patient. But now they were so close, and the car was going so slowly, waiting to turn and enter between the stone pillars and creeping up the road to the quadrangle.

When the car finally stopped, Mina burst out and took her suitcase from the backseat. Her father greeted Miss Maddinton. They talked about nothing in particular. Mina looked at her sneakers and felt her heart, beating.

It all soaked into her skin, and that was enough for now. If she looked around, at the stone buildings and trees, at all the familiar remembered places, she would start running around to touch everything, and her father would know—he'd know for sure what he'd only guessed, that she was gladder to be back at camp than anywhere else, that she could barely wait for him to leave so she could be by herself and be her own self again. She didn't want to hurt her father's feelings by letting him know that, so she stood there with her eyes closed, being there.

At last, he started to leave. "Have a good time, Mina." He hugged her close and she hugged him back, her head almost up to his shoulder now. "Behave yourself."

"I will. Have a good summer, Dad."

She made herself stand and wave while the car drove away, a dusty black sedan with the Maryland license plate a little white square. Then she turned slowly around, and smiled.

"You're in room three-o-seven," Miss Maddinton said to her, consulting a list she had on her clipboard. She was wearing a silvery gray suit; her hair was in dark braids that she'd wound around her head like a corona. She looked busy, she looked distant and calm, she looked beautiful.

Mina was back where there was music around everywhere, every day. She was back where if you said Prokofiev, nobody said, "Who?"

"You've grown," Miss Maddinton said, sounding doubtful, looking doubtful.

What did she expect Mina to do? Not grow? Mina laughed out loud. "I guess. My mom says I've been shooting up and shooting out."

"You can find your own way, can't you? I've got to greet the new girls."

"Three-o-seven?" Mina asked, not that she didn't remember, but just to savor this first minute a little longer. "Is Tansy here yet?"

"She's up there," Miss Maddinton said.

At that, Mina couldn't wait another minute. She grabbed her suitcase and hurrying as fast as she could with the heavy case banging against her leg went into the dormitory, went home.

Room 307 was on the third floor. The second floor was for the littlest girls, the top floor for the fourteen year olds. Mina climbed two flights of stairs and pushed through the heavy door onto the corridor. She heard voices, she heard music. Looking at the numbers painted on the doors, she went on down the hall. Her feet wanted to jump and run, her heart wanted to stop it all from going by so fast already. Room 307 was down toward the far end of the corridor. The door was open, but no music came out. Mina guessed Tansy was probably in somebody else's room, visiting.

But the room had only one bed in it. The room was too small for two beds anyway. The room was a single room.

Mina put her suitcase down on the floor and sat on the bed. For a long minute her mind was empty—blank and silent, a cold white emptiness. Then she understood.

They were seeing the outside of her.

Because nobody, not even Tansy, had wanted to be her roommate. So the adults had put her into a single room too.

Mina got up and set her suitcase on the bed. She unpacked her clothes into the dresser, then made up the bed and thought. She just hadn't understood, she guessed; but as soon as she thought that she knew she was wrong. They *had* all been friends, they had all gotten along just fine. It was what her father had said, though, what he had noticed right away when he picked her up: She was the only little black girl there.

Mina laughed out loud and dropped the pillow on the bed. Little? Well, she wasn't any too little anymore. There were bras and a box of Kotex she'd unpacked with the rest of her things. She guessed, if they thought she was little, in any way, they were underestimating her. She guessed she was going to have to make friends with them all over again. She stretched her arms out, her broad shoulders up, and flexed her fingers. She didn't mind that. She always liked making friends.

The first thing that she wanted to do, now, had changed. Now the first thing she wanted to do was go outside and wander around a little. She wanted to have her bare feet on the grass that covered these hills. She wanted to put her palms up against the bark of the trees, to feel how strong and solid the trees were. She wanted to hear the way the wind blew through leafy branches, and she wanted to put her eyes once again on the gray stone buildings that looked like they had grown up out of the earth to make the college. Once she had touched all of those things, once she'd gotten back in touch with those things that didn't look at her and see just the outside, Mina would come back inside and start dealing with the human things.

When Mina found Tansy, it was in a room with Isadora. They were sitting on their beds, not talking, not playing Tansy's music, not doing anything. Tansy looked like her same mousy self. Isadora had grown up. You could see what she would look like when she finished growing, Mina thought; Isadora looked like a dancer.

Mina smiled and sat down and pretended she didn't notice the quick, worried glance Isadora sent to Tansy. Last year, when she had been asleep to what was really going on, Mina had mostly caught only the ends of those looks and had been puzzled. Now that she was awake, she could see what they were. They separated her from everybody else, from everybody white. She thought she could show them that wasn't necessary.

"Hey hi. It's good to see you." Because it was. "Isn't it fun to be back? Have you seen Charlie?"

Isadora knew the answer to that. "She's going to a drama camp, instead. Near Philadelphia. She said she's gotten all ballet has to offer her."

"Oh-ho," Mina guessed without stopping to think, "and I bet we call her Charlotte from here on."

Isadora looked up at her and laughed. "How'd you know? Honestly, Mina, you wouldn't have believed it. She came, Charlotte, to spend the night, sometime in April. We'd planned it for ages, and then all she could talk about was this camp, and the opportunities it offered. She was like—she was like she was twenty-two and talking about her career. The first thing she said to me was exactly that: I had to call her Charlotte. How'd you know?"

"It was a guess." Mina smiled another hello at Tansy, noticing for the first time what a shy smile Tansy had. Her mouth barely moved.

"And she was wearing stockings and three-inch heels to come spend the night."

"You've got braces," Mina said to Tansy, whose mouth was filled with silver metal. "Do they hurt?"

"A little."

"I liked your Christmas card." It had a picture of Tansy's whole family on it, dressed up, standing in front of a big fireplace. Rich folks, Zandor had commented. "Your mother's pretty."

Tansy nodded.

"Have you made up any new dances?" Mina asked her. That got Tansy going, and Isadora drifted out of the room saying she'd be back to go down to dinner with them, so they should be sure to wait.

It didn't take Mina long to figure it out. They didn't mind being friends with her, but they didn't want to be roommates. They thought she wouldn't notice, as if she could be smart about other things but not about this. It was pretty funny, when she thought about it. Most of the time it was funny, she admitted to herself, alone in her room at night; sometimes, especially alone in her room, it felt like teeth biting into her heart. Like sharp pointed teeth biting into where her feelings were and cutting off bites to chew on. "But what did you think?" she asked herself at such times. "Didn't you know you were black?"

She wasn't going to let it trouble her.

What did trouble her was that for some reason the classes weren't going right. Mina had worked hard to maintain her dance, harder than she'd ever worked at anything. But she seemed to have fallen behind even so. What used to be easy was hard now, as if she couldn't do things everybody else could. Or as if her body couldn't do what she wanted it to. When they had their dance classes, Mina would be distracted by the mirrors, because they reflected her blackness back and back, among the white skin of the other girls. That was the hardest place, the dance class, to remember not to see just the outside of herself, not to notice how different it was from everybody else. The other girls sat out in the sun to get tan, Mina thought; but she was darker than any of them, and it was funny that they didn't see how funny that was. Mina felt trapped in her skin, locked in it, like a jail. She was always aware of being the only one.

Miss Maddinton didn't seem to think anything was wrong, even when Mina found herself sweating after doing what should be simple floor exercises. Miss Maddinton never had any complaints about Mina. So Mina figured whatever felt so wrong was all in her own head. The theory class was still terrific, listening to different composers, learning about harmonics, watching Mr. Tattodine bounce around getting all excited about the music.

The first week of camp lasted about a hundred years. Mina never could relax, unless she was alone outside. Alone inside, she had to keep pushing back thoughts she didn't want to face. With other people, she felt confused, trying to figure out what really was going on. They liked her, the other girls; they didn't mind sitting with her at the table or anything like that, and they included her in the things they did, and they laughed when she was silly and listened to what she had to say. They talked to her. But Mina couldn't tell if it was her, Mina, inside her skin, they liked, or if they were being nice to the one black girl at camp. If you were walking down a street and you saw somebody all crippled up and walking peculiarly, you'd go out of your way to show that it didn't make any difference, to act natural and friendly, to smile and all that. You'd do it because you didn't want the person to think you were thinking what you were thinking.

When they talked, nobody asked her questions. She asked them questions and they answered, as if they were the interesting ones and it was only natural that she should want to know more about them and that they shouldn't be interested in knowing anything about her. So Mina was always listening to what was being talked about, trying to figure out what it really meant. There were also some things that never got mentioned, as if they weren't visible. Like anything to do with black skin.

What did it all mean? When the questions crowded into her mind too closely, Mina would go outside, alone. She would sit back against a tree and close her eyes. She could feel the tree behind her, connected to its roots under the earth and growing straight up into the sky, strong. She could feel the ground under her legs, the grass-growing soil that covered the rocks that shaped the hills. Neither the trees nor the earth had any eyes to see what color she was.

In Narnia, Mina would want to be a dryad, a tree creature, with her roots dug into the earth and her body strong and lasting, untroubled by questions that blew through her like a wind blowing through branches. Trees were peaceful. They knew what was really true.

As soon as Mina thought that, however, and just when a smile was starting up in her heart and her whole body was relaxing against the grass and the tree, she would remember that dryads came from Greek mythology. They belonged to the white world. Then she would have to jump up with the feeling that jumped up inside her. Because they had so much, they had everything, and they kept reminding her that it wasn't any of it hers.

Mina was so tired at the end of that first week of camp she didn't think she'd ever have made it through without the company of the trees. The trees were stronger and older, wiser and truer too.

The second week was just about as bad. Mina was at ease only when she was alone, or during Mr. Tattodine's class listening to music. She thought about how many of the instruments were made out of wood—violins and piano, cello, and the reeds, the oboe, the clarinet, the resonating bassoon. She picked out their individual voices as she listened. The Fourth of July came at the end of the second week. The girls at the camp had been invited to a big bicentennial display of fireworks over at the naval base across the river, so after supper that night they went to get dressed for the occasion. Mina, alone in her room, used the blow drier to make her shoulder length hair into a smooth pageboy. She got a little too much of the straightening gel into it, so it looked as if it had been lacquered into place, not soft the way it was supposed to. She didn't have time to wash it out and redo it. She put on the dress Eleanor had made from a pattern Mina sent. It was a pale blue dress, with a sleeveless blouse top over an A-line skirt. Mina checked herself in the mirror, letting the noises from the other rooms slide in and out of her ears. Then she went to the window.

The sun was low in the sky, a heavy summer sun, sinking. There was no wind for a change, and the air lay heavy and gold. The trees stood patiently, enduring.

Mina closed her eyes. She wanted to be back with her own family, with her own people, at the annual Fourth of July church picnic. They didn't have fireworks, except for a few sparklers for the little children, but they had fried chicken and potato salad and singing. There were three or four churches that got together for the occasion, a big, noisy crowd of people. The stars were fireworks enough. Mina didn't think fireworks were so special. Right now, she could almost see the long tables set out, covered with food, and hear the people talking. She wished she was there where she wasn't pretending every waking hour not to be different, pretending she was something she wasn't, acting as if she wanted to be white.

Mina's eyes flew open. They were making her act as if she was white, or as if she wished she was.

"Who's making you do that, Missy?" she asked herself. She asked it out loud, but answered it silently: I am, or I'm letting them, which is about the same thing. And she was ashamed of herself. Angry too.

No more, she promised herself. She was going to be herself, Mina Smiths, t-rou-ble. She felt the devilment rising up in her.

Mina went right to the big seat that ran across the rear of the school bus. That way, there was room for anybody who wanted to sit with her, but nobody who didn't want to would have to. Tansy and Isadora and Natalie came back to join her. They watched people get into the bus. The oldest girls were dressed up pretty fine, Mina noticed, with as much eyeshadow as they thought they could get away with. "Because of the sailors over there," Isadora explained.

Isadora had mascara on, Mina saw, and lipstick. "You're doing it too—don't try and kid me."

"Don't be—" Isadora started to say, then she saw something on Mina's face that made her giggle instead. "They're awfully cute in those uniforms. You're just jealous."

"Don't you wish," Mina said, and the girls around them said, "That's telling her." But Mina looked around her, at the heads of hair that shone silky clean in so many colors, and at the slender necks that looked delicate even though they were, she knew, strong. She looked strong, she knew that, big and strong. And she was too.

"We'll have to get you introduced to one of them," she said to Isadora. "Maybe, you should fall into the river."

"I can swim."

"You can pretend, can't you? Splash around and yell for help. Then he comes to rescue you."

Many faces were turned around to watch this conversation.

"I couldn't do that," Isadora said.

"Okay, then I'll push you."

Miss Maddinton told them to be quiet, to behave with some dignity, please, and the bus started up.

As the sun went down, they watched the flag being lowered, while a bugle blew taps. Everybody stood quiet to watch, listening to the sad, lonely notes of the bugle. Four marines stood at attention, while two others lowered the flag and folded it. Mina looked around at the crowd: officers and their families, lots of children standing quiet, sailors in bright white uniforms, and civilian groups. Except for a couple of the marines, she was the only black person there. She felt as if everybody must be noticing her, standing there among the girls from the camp.

She wasn't going to let that get her down. When they sang "The Star-Spangled Banner" to music from the loudspeaker, Mina just went ahead and sang out. All around her, quiet white voices sang in a reined-in way, fading away on the high notes. Not Mina; Mina sang strong and true, letting her voice dominate. Let people notice her, if they wanted to.

"You have a nice voice," Tansy whispered as they sat down, getting ready to watch the fireworks.

"You bet," Mina said. She heard people chuckling at her reply, because what they would have said was something modest, like, "Oh, do you think so?" or "Not really, I just like singing the anthem."

While they waited, the last light faded out of the sky, and a little breeze came up along the river. They were sitting fairly far back from the river's edge, all of the dance camp girls together, supervised by the teachers. Mina wanted to sit closer to the water, because that would be a better view. She whispered to Isadora, asking if she wanted to move up.

"We have to stay here."

"Nobody'll know, nobody'll see us, because it's dark."

Isadora's shadowed face looked around. She got up, while Mina told Tansy, who didn't want to come with them. Mina and Isadora moved along the edge of their group, like shadows, Mina thought.

But not enough like shadows to escape Miss Maddinton. "Isadora?" she called. "Where do you think you're off to?"

She said it as if it was Isadora's idea, as if Mina was just following Isadora. It was as if she wasn't going to call out at Mina because then she would be picking on Mina because she was black. As if Mina was a mouse like Tansy and couldn't get herself into her own trouble. As if she got special treatment. All of this rushed through Mina's mind in a second and fed the devilment.

"We's gwine down to de lebee," Mina called out. "To pick us some wateymelon." She barely got the words out before she doubled over laughing. Everyone around started laughing too, and she and Isadora returned to their places. "Honestly, Mina," they said. "How could you?" they giggled.

A light exploded in the sky, a huge white light that plumed out like a chrysanthemum, and then two more exploded behind it. It knocked the breath out of Mina. When the three crackers went off, like cannon across the skies, she wanted to jump up and cry out something. *Whoo-ee*, that was what was in her mouth. The audience clapped, instead.

Mina just shook her head. If this was what a super big fireworks display was like, she guessed she could see why they thought it was such a big thing. She couldn't figure out why they just applauded, like it was a theater. She went along with them, patting her palms together, but that wasn't the way to do justice to what was going on in the sky overhead.

The sky filled, over and again, with explosions of white and red and orange, with whirligigs that spun upward and then showered down like falling stars. Mina watched with big eyes. The fireworks shone out against the sky. When they faded, the black sky waited there, pricked with stars, silent, until the next explosion of light and sound.

Finally, Mina couldn't hold it in, because she didn't want to. "Whoo-eee," she called out, like a trumpet, to the falling fires. All around, voices shushed her.

CHAPTER 8

On Monday of the third week, Mr. Tattodine came to their dance class with a video camera to record them. Miss Maddinton told them to ignore it, and after a few minutes they could. Mina found it easy to forget the white head with its eye fixed into the viewer of the black box. Mina was working hard, as usual. She wondered—while she concentrated on getting her legs right and her arms right, to keep her body in the balance Miss Maddinton showed them—if she was in some kind of transition stage in her dancing. She didn't remember that it used to be this much trouble. It used to be as natural as breathing. The class, warmed up now by the barre exercises, moved to the center of the room. Mina continued to wonder.

If it was like—like being a seed in your seed case; there would come a time when you had to break out of the case and force your roots through. Or like being pregnant, and then the labor of having your baby; it was easy to get pregnant, and her mother always talked about how good her body felt when she was carrying her children, close inside her. But before the baby could have its own life, it and the mother had to work it out. The class did the port de bras movements, while the piano played a theme from *Swan Lake.* And Mina wondered, feeling how her muscles seemed to pull at her shoulder bones, feeling big and clumsy among the swaying torsos.

Belle and she had once watched a crab go through the final stages of shedding its old shell. They had found it hidden among the grass at the edge of a creek. Crabs shed their old shells when they got too big for them, Mina had always known that. At the season of every full moon, people went looking among the shallow waters for the soft-shelled crabs, which could be fried up whole and eaten. Mina didn't much care for soft shells, except for the crunchy thin legs. But after they had watched the crab pulling itself out of its outgrown undersized shell—after she had seen the contractions of muscles under the flesh as it patiently pulled each leg free, working backward out of the old shell . . . it looked like someone with no fingers trying to take off his socks. It hurt Mina and made her impatient, watching it. She wanted the process to be over, even though she knew that the crab would be helpless for the next day or so while it grew its new shell. She knew that other crabs, who weren't shedding, would come through the shallow waters, looking for dinner, as would the herons and egrets. The process of shedding was so painful to watch—as the crab gathered its dwindling strength to pull its legs free and force itself backward through a narrow crack in the hard old shell, achieving another quarter-inch of freedom—Mina ran away, that long ago summer day. This day, however, she wasn't going to run away. She thought something like shedding was happening to her.

Miss Maddinton called out for the class to do batterie en demi-pointe and Mina pulled her muscles together to try it. It was not too successful, but she kept trying and kept smiling, kept pulling up into the air and beating with her foot. It almost always missed one beat, and she grinned, thinking of how it must look.

Miss Maddinton had a private conference with everyone in her class. She met with them in the dormitory living room. First they watched the tape, then they talked about technique and poise and what needed improvement. Mina was one of the first, although not the very first. Sitting in the big armchair, watching the square screen, Mina saw more clearly than anytime before exactly how much she stood out. She tried to watch the whole class, or the whole performing group, but she kept seeing the one black person there. Miss Maddinton didn't say anything while they watched, except to hurry on past parts where Mina didn't appear. She didn't stop the tape to discuss any special problem.

Mina watched the big black girl on the screen. The girl looked clumsy. Not clumsy by ordinary standards, but clumsy in comparison to everyone else there dancing.

Then Miss Maddinton put in another tape: It was Mina's audition tape, a little black girl who wasn't too skillful, but danced easily, naturally, and with a pleasure that made you smile to see her.

After both tapes were finished, Miss Maddinton sat back in her chair, her legs stretched out in front of her. Miss Maddinton always wore dancing slippers for shoes. "What do you think?" she asked Mina. "You see what I mean, don't you?"

"Do you think I'm more disciplined?" Mina asked. "I think I am." She was a little frightened, and she was afraid she knew why.

Miss Maddinton stood up. She went over to one of the long windows that looked out on the trees and grass. She turned around to face Mina.

"I don't know what to do about you," she said. "I don't know what's the right thing to do."

"What's the matter?" Mina asked.

"You saw it. I know you did. I guess I can't expect you to make it easy for me, after you've fought so hard to come this far. You've grown uncoordinated, Mina," she said. "You're too far behind the rest of the class, and falling farther behind every day. I think you know that."

No, Mina hadn't known that. She couldn't kid herself about not seeing it, when she watched the tape. But she hadn't thought that it was happening because she wasn't good enough. "It's not that bad," she said.

"I'm not saying it's your fault. There's nothing you can do about it. This just happens, with singers as well as dancers, at puberty. Nobody can really predict how a body will develop over the years of change. Your people develop earlier, which is why it's happened to you this year."

"It's because I'm black, isn't it," Mina asked. Maybe the girls could avoid talking about it, but they were children and Miss Maddinton was a grown-up.

"That's ridiculous." Miss Maddinton sounded like she had known Mina was going to ask that.

"No," Mina said. "No, I don't think it is. You just said it was, in fact."

"What I just said, Mina, is that you're awkward and ungainly. That's what I meant and that's what I said. Although, you don't see many black ballerinas—"

"And what about the Harlem Dance Theater?" Mina demanded. If she'd talked like that at home, her mother would have stopped her mouth. But she wasn't at home.

"Not in the classical ballet," Miss Maddinton went on, as if she was thinking out loud. "I don't know . . . Next time I'm going to insist on at least two of you, you'd have felt better with someone like you here, wouldn't you? Or four, if we must have any, if we must have the federal funding. The trouble is, you're so mature. Not only physically, so it's hard to know—Georges Tattodine says you do well in theory, he says you've an excellent memory and a perfect ear and—but it's not fair to you, nor to our executive committee. It costs money, for room and board if nothing else."

"I could try harder," Mina said. She sat very still in her chair.

"You know as well as I do how hard you're trying right now. You have, as you rightly said, learned discipline."

"Then why don't you give me a chance?" Mina demanded. Miss Maddinton's eyes grew cold.

"Why do you think I've delayed making this decision? I thought this would happen, and I saw it right away, but I thought, maybe—Oh, I wanted to avoid trouble too."

"I'm not any trouble," Mina insisted. "I try. I practice. I'm more serious than a lot of them. You know that's true."

"But it's not getting any better, and it's certainly not getting any easier. It can't be a happy time for you," Miss Maddinton insisted.

"I'm not unhappy," Mina said.

"Because," Miss Maddinton went on, thinking correctly that Mina was trying to avoid the main point, "you're starting to clown around, to turn errors and clumsiness and slowness to learn into a joke. Mina?"

"Yes, ma'am," Mina said, collapsing inside herself, like a tree finally felled. Miss Maddinton was right. But she didn't want to say so out loud. That was all Mina wanted, now, just not to have to say out loud, herself, that she was no longer good enough.

"What do you think, Mina?" Miss Maddinton kept after her. For these conferences, she wore white slacks and a silvery pink, pale shirt. She stood in front of the window, not moving, and Mina knew that until she'd said what Miss Maddinton wanted to hear, the conversation wouldn't be over.

"I'm the worst in the class," Mina admitted.

Miss Maddinton waited. Mina felt helpless. She was helpless against Miss Maddinton's cold discipline, and she was about not to be able to control her tears any longer, so she was helpless against herself too.

"What do you want me to do?" Mina asked, almost pleading

with Miss Maddinton, just to say something, make some decision and then make Mina obey, just to have this finished with.

"Mr. Tattodine notwithstanding, you're going to have to go home."

"Go home? Why do I have to do that?"

Miss Maddinton sighed and shook her head at Mina's stupidity.

"I could drop the ballet class. I don't have to take that if you think I'm so bad. But I could still take theory and do the evening things. I don't want to go home."

"Pull yourself together, Mina. *Faites attention.* Oh, you get along well with the girls, I'll admit that; I've been surprised at how successful that's been. You handle yourself with real maturity. But it won't do to have a girl here who isn't taking dance. You know that as well as I. We have neither staff nor courses to take that responsibility. It's always hard to admit that you've failed—"

At that, Mina was so angry that she did burst into tears. She was so angry she just wept. She was weeping so hard she couldn't speak. Just growing wasn't failure, you couldn't say someone had failed just because her body grew bosoms and hips and the muscles worked differently.

"But, Mina, what do you want me to say? What can I do? What do you want to do?"

"I want to go home," Mina wailed, miserable, angry, and ashamed.

"Good," Miss Maddinton said, ushering Mina out of the room now that Mina had said what she wanted to hear.

It was all settled by the next day. Most of the girls avoided Mina, as if she had some horrible contagious disease. "That's tough," Isadora said. "I'm glad I've still got a dancer's body. I'll keep it, my parents are both slight."

Tansy had been kinder. "I'll miss you, you make things more

fun," Tansy said, her big brown mouse eyes showing that she meant it. For all the difference that made.

Mina didn't know what to say to anybody, so she didn't say anything. When Mr. Tattodine put her on the morning train to go south, he told her to keep on studying music. "You've got real ability," he said, his face looking worried.

Mina just nodded. She shook the hand he held out for her to shake.

She sat by herself on the train, with her suitcase on the rack above her. There were several other people on the train and Mina just kept looking out the window so that she wouldn't see them looking at her. Everything was quiet except for the train noises. The train went on south, stopping at places, New Haven and Bridgeport, Stamford, and then it went underground to get into New York. Mina sat still and waited. They'd given her some money for lunch, but she wasn't hungry. They'd told her that her family knew when she was getting into Wilmington and would meet her, but she didn't wonder about that, even though she remembered that her father had the car.

At New York, there were a lot more people who got on the train, and the car started to fill up with music from radios, and with voices talking, and with little children. Mina stared out the window, seeing no difference between the dark tunnel of New York and the industrial towns of New Jersey and the rolling countryside past Philadelphia.

She didn't know what she was going to do, she couldn't think of anything she wanted to do. She knew the camp hadn't turned her out, not exactly, but she felt like they had. She knew that they had turned her out because of the dancing, but she felt like they had done it because she was black. She was afraid they'd only let her come in the first place just because she was black.

CHAPTER 9

A lot of people were getting off in Wilmington. Mina stepped off the air-conditioned train and into what felt like a solid wall of heat. She hesitated briefly, then moved away from the throngs, moving along the platform, looking up and down the platform.

It was hot on the asphalt and the air shimmered with heat and moisture. Her blouse stuck to her skin, but the air felt good as it wrapped around her body. She didn't mind nobody being right there, mostly because she didn't know what she'd say to Zandor or her mother. She guessed she might never say anything again because when she looked down her throat to find words, there weren't any there. She felt locked away into the silence she had been moving around in for the last twenty-four hours.

They sure got her out of there fast enough, once they got moving. As if they couldn't wait to get rid of her.

People moved away and the platform got empty. The sun poured down through the thick air. There was a city smell to the air, metal and engine fumes. City noises were moving, off in some distance. Mina stood. She wasn't waiting, because she didn't much look forward to being picked up. She didn't know what she was going to say to anybody, especially when she knew perfectly well that what she'd been thinking—for the last year and more—had been getting-away-from-them thoughts.

But she wanted to see her mother, she wanted Momma's arms

and love wrapped around her. Her momma would be angry at the camp, she'd be all on Mina's side no matter what. Mina wanted some of the kind of love Momma gave to her children, where love was the first and deepest thing, and the questions came later and the answers wouldn't matter much measured up against the love.

But she didn't want to see her momma, because she didn't know what to say.

When a big man, dressed up fine in a dark suit and tie, his shoes polished to high gloss, came walking up toward her, Mina got ready to run if she had to. She'd leave her suitcase. It had only dance things in it anyway, and she wouldn't need those. She didn't know if she'd have to run, but she thought if he looked like he might grab for her she'd take off, go inside to the waiting room where there were people around. Just because someone was black didn't mean you could trust them.

"Wilhemina Smiths? I'm sorry to be late, I had trouble parking. I'm supposed to escort you home," his voice went on talking. Mina stared at him, not hearing what he was saying.

He looked vaguely familiar, with heavy straight eyebrows and round, sympathetic eyes, as he introduced himself and reached out to take her suitcase for her. Then she could identify him, although she'd missed his name. He was Alice's husband, the summer minister. She wondered if she was about to meet Alice, and she hoped so at the same time as she didn't want to. Not now, not like this.

She walked along beside the man. He tried asking her a couple of questions, how her trip was, whether she minded traveling alone. Mina just nodded or shook her head. She wondered why her mother hadn't come. She hoped her mother wasn't angry with her.

The summer minister had a big, dusty station wagon. He put

Mina's suitcase in the back. The rear seat had two child car seats strapped on it. He asked her if she wanted to sit in front or in back. Mina sat in the front seat. He told her to strap in, and Mina pulled the seat belt down and latched it. He asked her to be sure she knew how to unlatch it, so she did. She wished she could get some words out, to thank him for meeting her, or ask where her mother was, but she couldn't. He was going to think she was pretty weird.

And she felt pretty weird. She felt as if she hadn't done anything wrong, except be black and grow up, which there wasn't much she could do anything about; but she still felt ashamed, as if she'd done something wrong and was being punished.

The car pulled out of the parking lot and into traffic. The summer minister stopped talking and concentrated on driving through the city streets.

Mina looked straight ahead. "Your people mature earlier," that was what Miss Maddinton had said, but she didn't know what she was talking about. After Mina, the most physically mature girl in her class was white. Almost all the girls wore bras by the end of sixth grade, not just black girls. Besides, Kat didn't yet and she was black. Mina wished she'd said those things to Miss Maddinton. She wished she'd pushed Miss Maddinton out of the window, or something—done or said something to someone to let them know they couldn't just push her around like this. Even though they could, because they did.

The car left the city on an elevated highway, moving along over the tops of row houses and stores. The highway merged with several other highways to form a new road, jammed with trucks and cars and heavy white heat. Stoplights came up, one after the other, quickly. At every one, brakes groaned and people honked their horns. All along the side of the road there were fast-food restaurants and motels and stores.

The summer minister, Alice's husband, drove on south. The signs overhead said Annapolis and Baltimore and Dover. He picked Dover, sticking to the main road. All the car windows were open, so it was cool enough when they were moving, although it was noisy from the motors working all around them.

Mina looked out her window, to catch the breeze and keep her face private. All of the feelings churning around inside her were looking for words so that she could understand them. But she couldn't find any words, and she didn't know why her mother hadn't come to meet her, because Momma could guess how she'd be feeling. She was heading home, but Mina didn't know what she'd be able to say when she got there.

She was so sorry for all the things she'd thought. She was sorry for herself too, because they'd taken dance camp away from her. Because she wasn't good enough. Because she was black. She'd worked hard to be good enough, as hard as she could. But she couldn't work hard enough. She was disappointed in the people at camp and angry at them for not wanting her anymore. The same ideas ticked over and over inside her head, as the minutes ticked by and the car moved on south.

It was still a highway, but it had farms beside it now, except for crossroads where there would be a gas station, or a little restaurant. Mina wondered how far they'd gone, and how much time had passed. She felt the summer minister studying the back of her head. She felt him trying to start a conversation. But she didn't want to talk to him. If she didn't have any words for her own family, she couldn't have anything at all to say to a perfect stranger. Mina concentrated on the fields they were passing, and the occasional house.

"So," she heard his voice begin. He had a quiet voice, deep. "How does it feel to be an ex-token black?"

Mina turned her head slowly to look at him. He had spoken

words that connected so directly to her that she didn't know what to think. His eyes were on the road.

"A former token black? Or retired. Token black, retired," he said.

What a thing to say, Mina thought, as she burst out laughing and burst out crying, all at once together. Whenever the laughter was about to take over, Mina would remember how bad things were and the tears would continue. Whenever the tears started to dominate, she would hear his voice asking her those questions and she would keep up laughing.

"My wife usually has tissues in the glove compartment," he said after a while.

Mina needed several tissues before she finished with her nose and her eyes. She crumpled them up into her pocket when she was through.

"Thank you," she said. "I don't know what I'm going to do now," she told him.

He thought about that. "Do you mean now, here and now, or now, ever in your life?" He didn't wait for her to answer, which was just as well because Mina didn't know which she meant. She only knew it was true. "Your mother didn't come because she's sitting with Miz Hunter, who's had a bad summer virus. She's on the mend but when you're that old you've got to be careful with yourself."

Of course Momma would be there, helping out. Mina wondered why Alice didn't do it, to free Momma. But she couldn't ask him that, and she remembered that Alice had those three children, two of them pretty young.

"She's pretty. Your wife, I mean. I saw some pictures from last summer, and she's really pretty."

"Isn't she?" the man said, as if just thinking about Alice made him glad. "We've been married over nine years now, and every time I see her—I think, what fine work God did when He made Alice."

Mina liked the picture he made, of God up there like a sculptor, shaping the bodies and the faces.

"You know, you never answered me. Have you had lunch?"

"No," Mina said. "They gave me money for it, but I didn't."

"Are you hungry?"

"I think I am," Mina realized. It was midafternoon.

"If we pool our resources—I was up in Wilmington interviewing for a position and they gave me some travel expenses—I've got twenty dollars. How much do you have?"

"Five."

"How about it then, will you have lunch with me, Miss Wilhemina Smiths, whatever else you figure out you're going to do now?"

He really did understand, Mina thought. She thought she'd like to have lunch, and she liked this summer minister. He was funny.

"We can afford a respectable meal. They're not expecting us back until after supper anyway. There are some good restaurants around Easton. Can you wait another forty-five minutes?"

"Sure. But I don't know your name. I wasn't listening when you said it. What *is* your name?" Mina asked. She was studying his profile now, as they drove along westward across Delaware. His hair was short, curling close to his head, and his eyes were set deep in their sockets. He had a broad mouth and good teeth, well-kept hands and long legs. He was a handsome man. His suit didn't look rumpled at all, even though the day was so hot and sticky.

"My name's Shipp. Tamer Shipp."

"Reverend Shipp," Mina repeated, trying the name on.

"I'd be more comfortable if you'd call me Tamer," he said.

"I didn't mean—" Mina started to say.

"It's that name, 'reverend.' Because I have trouble feeling like—I should be revered. You know?"

"It's not a name, it's a title," Mina pointed out, amused because he was taking words so exactly.

"A title's a kind of label. It's also a name, if you think about it."

Mina thought about it. She could see what he meant.

"Your father, now, I could call him 'reverend.' Though I've never met him, because he's always gone by the time I get here. I've met up with his work, over and over."

"What do you mean?"

"You can't step into a man's shoes, into his job like I do, into his life, and not learn a lot about him."

"I guess not," Mina said, thinking about the dancing slippers she had packed away in her suitcase. She planned to throw all that away as soon as she got home.

"I envy him, I think. My people—"

"Up in Harlem?"

"Harlem—the Harlem I see—the ghetto I serve—is down," he said. "Down from everywhere. Wherever else you might be, if you go to Harlem you're going down."

He was being exact again. But he sounded tired when he said that, and his voice lost some of its richness. "I don't want to think about that right now," he said.

"Sure, Mr. Shipp."

"The kids I know, the kids I work with, all call me Tamer."

"Even at home?"

"My home or your home?"

"Crisfield."

"Yep."

"Why?" Mina asked, before she thought to keep her mouth shut.

He didn't answer right away. Fields of corn, coming up green, flowed past the car windows. The fields were edged by rows of trees, like high green fences. The sky, bleached white by summer heat, stretched out overhead. Mina figured, after a couple of minutes, that he wasn't going to answer her question.

But, "I can't think of why," he said, sounding surprised. "I've never thought about it, and I don't know why I didn't. Because I tend to think about things," he said.

"Oh," Mina said, not knowing what else to say.

"Drives Alice crazy." He turned to smile at her. There was something sure and strong in him, and his eyes, resting briefly on Mina, looked amused and interested and sympathetic. They looked knowing too, she thought, as if he knew a lot about her.

Mina was willing to bet that Momma had sent him up on purpose to meet her. But he said he'd had a job interview, so it couldn't have been that, and he said Momma was sitting with Miz Hunter, so she would have come with him if she could have. So it was just good luck he'd been the one, unless it was what her father called God's good time.

They had lunch in a little restaurant in the town of Easton, a couple of miles off of Route 50. They were the only ones eating lunch at that hour. Mr. Shipp thought Mina should order crab cakes, because she'd been away from crab country, but Mina explained about how when you were used to crab cakes as good as her mother's were, anything else wasn't worth the money. She had chicken instead. Mr. Shipp couldn't decide. "My mother could give your wife the recipe," Mina said. "Or I could. They're easy."

He shook his head. "TV dinners are what Alice thinks of as easy. Roast chicken counts as hard. I'm hoping one of my girls will turn out to be a cook. I guess I'll compromise with stuffed shrimp." He smiled up at the waitress—who looked about thirty-five and worn out—who didn't smile back at him. "Baked potato, house dressing, and a glass of iced tea," Mr. Shipp said, before she had to ask him. She nodded to show she'd heard, but her blue eyes never left the ticket she was writing. Mina watched her walk away, noting her thick-soled shoes and the bend of her neck, and the way she put her shoulder not her hand on the swinging door into the kitchen, as if she needed her shoulder's strength for the task of getting through that door. Mina got just a glimpse into the kitchen—long stainless counter and two black men at work.

"Did you notice her ring?" Mr. Shipp asked her.

"She wasn't married."

"That faint mark, where her finger wasn't tanned. Like a ghost of a wedding band," he said. He took his water glass and drank it half down. "A woman her age, probably there are children. I think an unreasonably large tip is in order, don't you?"

"Because you feel sorry for her?" Mina guessed.

"Because I know about how she feels," Mr. Shipp corrected her.

"But, Tamer," Mina said, his name uncomfortable in her mouth, "you're not divorced, are you?"

He shook his head.

"Have you been a waiter?"

He shook his head again, smiling, teasing, waiting for her to work it out.

"And you're not a woman, and you're not white."

He just waited.

"And I'm not going to call you Tamer, either; I'm going to call you Mr. Shipp," Mina finished up.

He laughed then, and Mina joined in.

"You can't say I didn't try," he said. "So, are you beginning to look forward to getting home?"

Mina realized that she was. It was going to be all right, she realized.

They didn't hurry over their meal. They didn't dawdle. Mina had a slice of pecan pie for dessert, while Mr. Shipp drank his coffee. They left almost ten dollars for a tip.

Back in the car, strapped in, back on the highway south, Mina asked him, "Did you get the job?"

"What job"

"The one you interviewed for."

"Oh, that's right, I did have an interview. No, I don't think so."

"Did you want to get it?"

"Only partly. I keep thinking about my family living in Harlem, my kids growing up there, where there's so little room to grow, and it's dangerous. . . . Then I keep thinking about my work, and the people who destroy themselves because they think they're being destroyed. And they are too." It was anger she heard now. "I think about . . . what it is I'm meant to be doing. If that doesn't sound too conceited."

"No, it doesn't."

They traveled on without talking for some time. They went over the Choptank River, broad and blue at Cambridge. They crossed the little humped bridge at Vienna over the Nanticoke. The land flattened out around them and the air began to smell like home.

"Looks like there's been rain this summer," Mina said, breaking the long silence.

"There's been some good rainy days. I like this part of the world," Mr. Shipp said, his head moving to watch a chicken farm go by his window. "I always did like it. I lived around here for a couple of years when I was younger. For the last two years of high school," he answered her unspoken question, "when we were first married, Alice and I."

"It's really different from Connecticut," Mina told him.

"Worse?"

“No, just really different. I liked the hills and the trees up there, especially the trees. Connecticut is up, isn’t it?”

“Definitely up,” he answered. “You’re finished with the grief then.”

Mina wasn’t surprised that he was understanding her. “I guess so. I guess it wasn’t all that serious.”

“Oh, I don’t know.” She watched his face. His skin fitted smooth over his forehead and cheekbones. He had a good strong jaw. “Some grief is sharp and sudden, and some is slower and longer. Sounds to me like you had the first kind, which is the easier—once it’s behind you.”

“Both would be pretty bad. Having both together.”

He didn’t answer, just nodded his head. Mina didn’t know if that was to say he agreed with her, or just that he’d heard her. She wondered why he didn’t answer, since he seemed to have something to say about almost everything. She wondered what he was remembering and understood that he didn’t want to talk about it, so she changed the subject.

“I like this country too.”

“Do you mean this country America? Or this country Dorchester County.”

“I mean Crisfield. I’m not too sure about America.”

“Really? Because of being black? Because of slavery?”

“I don’t know,” Mina said, because she didn’t. “I just don’t feel comfortable, feel like I belong . . . I don’t know.” She’d never thought of that before, but it was true.

“I used to think, to wonder—I used to complain too, to Him—why God didn’t lead us out of America the same way He led the Jews out of Egypt. There was a lot the same in the situations,” Mr. Shipp said.

“I guess there was,” Mina said, thinking about it.

“I’d wonder why we didn’t have any Moses. Then—if there

was a Moses coming along. Dr. King, I thought, might be the man to lead us back to our own country."

"Except, of course, Moses wasn't black. The Jews weren't," Mina explained.

"Neither am I," Mr. Shipp said.

Mina almost laughed. It had to be a joke. Then she saw that it wasn't a joke.

She couldn't think of what to say. She wondered if he had a patch of craziness in him, that let him pretend to himself that he wasn't black. She thought she must have been wrong about him being strong and at peace, and that was depressing. She didn't know what she could possibly say to him now. Somehow, she knew that the one thing she felt like saying—"You are too"—was the one thing she couldn't say. She turned her face to the fields again.

"But I'm not, Mina, and neither are you. Look at me. Look at yourself. We're not black, are we?"

Mina looked at the skin of her hands. It looked black to her. She looked back out the window, embarrassed.

Between the rows of soybeans the earth showed brown, the dark brown that meant rich soil, but lightened by the clay characteristic of this low land. This soil was dark, but not really black-brown like the soil where the bay ate away at the marsh grasses.

"I'm brown, really," Mr. Shipp said to her silence. "We are. Shades of brown. We call ourselves black because—the other words have been used and used derogatively. Negro—that's black too, in another language."

"Spanish," Mina mumbled, a little embarrassed at herself now.

"But I wouldn't like to be called brownie, would you?"

Mina giggled.

"Blacks, it's what we call ourselves, so that's all right."

"What would you rather be called?" Mina wondered.

"I always liked colored," Mr. Shipp said. "Because that covers just about everything."

Mina was looking at him again, and she saw he was half teasing. She thought about that, about all the colors the blacks were. There was dark, like Mr. Shipp, dark, dark brown so that in certain lights you could see the purply black that went into it. Her skin was like a chocolate candy bar, a Hershey bar to be precise. Kat's had coppery tints in it. Some blacks were so light they were beige, almost, and some had golden tones and—She started to laugh, because he was exactly right about it.

"What's so funny?" he asked. But she was willing to bet he already knew the answer.

"I'm not surprised you didn't get the job," she told him.

Mr. Shipp's dark eyebrows went up, surprised, and his surprised laughter poured out of him into the warm air. "I'm going to have to watch out for you, Mina Smiths," he said. "You're—"

She waited.

He said what everybody had always been saying about her, all of her life, except at camp. "You are t-rou-ble."

Mina wished he'd said something else. Something different from what everybody else always said.

Then he added, "I haven't known you but three hours, and already—"

"Already what?" she asked, when he didn't finish the sentence.

"Already you've got me talking with you like a friend," he said.

She was glad to hear him say that.

"I've got a congregation, and people I work with. I've got a family and a wife. But friends are in short supply. Unless maybe you count God, but I can't make out if He's my friend or what."

He didn't say that as if he minded not knowing, or even

minded feeling as if he didn't have what he'd call friends. Mina didn't mind him thinking she was trouble, if that was how he thought about it.

She looked across at Mr. Shipp, at his heavy, dark eyebrows and at his dark hands on the wheel of the car. There was a smile building up in her, of mischief and gladness and being free. They thought they were turning her out, turning their backs on her, but really they were sending her home.

CHAPTER 10

Momma was in Miz Hunter's bedroom, not waiting in their own kitchen, but that was the only thing different from the way Mina had imagined things. Momma wrapped her arms around Mina and Mina wrapped her arms around her mother. Even though she was almost as tall as her mother, the arms made her feel little again, and safe. She breathed in the faint odors of rubbing alcohol and hand lotion that Momma carried around with her. "I know it's selfish, but I'm glad you're home. I miss your company," Momma's voice said in her ear. They drew apart, but Momma went on. "You look crumpled, you've got that travel look to you. You go right on home and take a bath, get your laundry sorted. It's fried chicken for dinner and you can imagine Belle is going to be glad you're here to help her out."

Mina slipped back into summer, like slipping into a comfortable old bathrobe. She took her mother's place sitting with Miz Hunter for the last recovery days. Mina would go over to the old lady's house late in the morning and make her some lunch. Then, while Mina swept and dusted the three rooms, Miz Hunter would get washed up and dressed, with Mina nearby to help in case she fell or felt suddenly weak. They spent the afternoons sitting on the front porch, with Louis under orders to stay close. They talked sometimes, and they played Scrabble. Mr. Shipp usually dropped by, for a shorter or longer visit. Mina's mother brought over a covered plate for Miz Hunter's supper before she went off to work. More and more Miz Hunter got well enough to look after herself.

It was a peaceful few days for Mina. She didn't see much of anybody, because nobody much knew she was home. Miz Hunter asked her, right off, if she'd gotten tired of living among strangers.

"Yes and no," Mina said. They had a little table set out between them on the front porch with the Scrabble board on it. "I learned a lot." She arranged her seven squares on the rack.

"Yes, your daddy does keep you all wound around in your cocoon here. But it doesn't seem to have done the older two any harm, so maybe it won't hurt you either, Missy."

"Actually," Mina said, "I meant learned like—learned things I never knew anything about. Books and music and stuff."

"I heard some of that music, last year, coming from your room. I haven't heard any since you've been back."

Mina hadn't played any records, she hadn't wanted to. In the same way she hadn't wanted to dance, or anything.

"I hope you like learning," Miz Hunter said. "I did myself. I still do. Education learning, that is." Her little hand, brown as a sparrow's back, made the word *lease.* Mina could use that S, if she could find a good enough word to attach to it. She shuffled her letters around, trying to find a word with an H and a Y both, that could end in S. Her mind kept skittering around, coming up with words she didn't have the right letters for, like *hyphen* or *hyena. History* had the S in the middle, and it was long too, but she didn't have a T or an I or an R.

On Sunday morning, she rejoined the choir. It was kind of fun watching the expression on peoples' faces when they saw her up there. From where she sat, she could look over the whole congregation. Mina saw the fine summer dresses and caught her first glimpse of Alice sitting up front, with Momma and Miz Hunter. Miz Hunter had her red straw hat bright on her gray head, but Alice didn't wear a hat. Instead, she braided her hair into many little braids, each one woven through with colored ribbons. The colors danced whenever Alice moved her head. She was as pretty as her pictures, as pretty as a picture, and Mina stared at her for a long time. She had big, big, dark eyes under curved eyebrows, a nose that turned up just a little at the end, and a red mouth that looked kissable. That was all Mina could think of, looking at Alice's mouth with its red lipstick, that it looked like what they called a kissable mouth, and she didn't think she ought to be thinking like that during church. A little girl, about eight or nine Mina guessed, sat beside Alice, her hair in three thicker braids, one down the back of her head and two at the sides. Mina thought they must have spent hours getting their hair ready. Beside the girl sat a thin little boy in a suit that was too big for him, with glasses. The littlest child sat on Zandor's lap, pulling at his nose while Zandor talked over the heads of the children to Alice, as if he couldn't take his eyes off her. Mina didn't blame her brother.

When the service started, Mina looked over and around the congregation, at the different colors of the faces. Mr. Shipp was right, she thought, colored was the best name for them. The service went on around her, Bible readings, hymns, collection, and Mina looked around her. There was as much variety of color as you would see in a furniture store, Mina thought. The faces were all the colors of wood, seasoned and stained, oak and pecan, maple, pine. Mr. Shipp, she thought, her eyes resting on the back of his neck, was darker, like black locust that had been around for years and years, stained by smoke, maybe.

Outside the windows it was a low, gray morning, and it would rain before the day was out, she was sure. The air had that close, squeezing weight to it, of moisture building up. She settled back to hear what Mr. Shipp's sermon would be like. Her eyes settled over the congregation, contented to be among the warm, woody colors of her own people, in her poppa's church. Mr. Shipp was about the most interesting person she'd ever met in her whole life; she thought, with a rush of gratitude, that he was one of her people.

Mr. Shipp talked about Judas, who betrayed Jesus for thirty pieces of silver. But he didn't talk about Jesus's sacrifice, how he had allowed himself to be crucified so that everybody's sins could be forgiven; Mr. Shipp ignored that part of it altogether. Instead, he talked about what Judas did after he had betrayed his Master, how he had tried to return the silver pieces, how he had gone out and killed himself. He talked about why Judas might have done that, until Mina felt so sorry for Judas; she almost felt sorrier for him than for Jesus. Then Mr. Shipp changed the subject, sort of, to talk about an old Italian named Dante. Dante wrote a long poem about Hell and Heaven. This Dante said that in Hell the people who committed suicide got a worse punishment than the pitch and the flames and the tormenting devils, they were trapped inside trees. When you broke off a twig of one of these trees, the tree bled.

That was a different kind of tree from the dryad tree Mina had imagined, even though it was the same. Mina felt her mind stretching to understand the differences and samenesses as her eyes rested on Mr. Shipp.

At the Last Judgement, alone of everybody, these suicides were going to get their bodies back, Dante said. God would throw their poor dead bodies down, and the bodies would hang there from the trees. Because, Mr. Shipp said, they despised the body. They despised their own bodies.

"Judas betrayed twice, once his Master and Our Lord and

once himself. This burden of double sin—how far could a man carry such a burden? Judas did not go far before he tried to rid himself of the unbearable weight. The first sin is easy to recognize, so we can choose not to have to carry it. But that second sin, let us guard against it. My body, your body, these are God's work; to despise them is to despise God's work. Instead, look around to see the handiwork of the Lord. The eyes that can see, the ears to hear with, the strength of bone and muscle over organs that function with extraordinary efficiency, so perfectly that even scientists stand breathless before it. And the skin, fitted so close and tight over all, to contain and protect it. This must be God's work, upon us, and for us. To despise it is to despise God. To despair of it is to despair of God. I will not burden my soul with that second sin," Mr. Shipp concluded.

Mina rose to sing the final hymn with her mind churning.

"Does he always talk like that?" she asked her mother when they were back home, setting the table for lunch. They would eat inside, because of the threat of rain. Miz Hunter was well enough to come and join them.

"Pretty much. Could you follow him? Sometimes I do and sometimes—like today—Well, my mind wandered. A lot of people don't care for his way of making sermons. But nobody dislikes his ministry, as far as I've heard. And I guess, being Poppa's wife, I'd be the first to hear. Did you enjoy it?"

"I don't know. It—got me thinking," Mina said. "Yes, I did. He's different from Poppa."

Her mother laid out knives and forks and spoons. Mina folded the paper napkins.

"Poppa keeps his feet in the plain everyday things. Tamer—he's walking out there among the ideas, like along the mountaintops." Momma stood looking at the table. The smell of stew filled the house. "Set out the glasses, will you, Mina?"

"Can we have him and his family for dinner sometime? He's never had good crab cakes."

Momma looked at her, as if Mina had said something that didn't make sense. "How'd you know a thing like that?"

"When we had lunch, I was telling him about yours."

"What would you say he was sermonizing about today?" Momma asked.

"About being black," Mina answered, setting an empty glass at each place. "Except, I can't figure out what Judas had to do with it."

"I didn't tell you," Momma said. She stood still, not setting anything out, not going back to the kitchen, "but your Miss LaValle, she tried to kill herself."

"Because of me?" Mina was shocked.

"The world does not revolve around you, young lady." Momma's voice was angry. "Believe it or not, there are people who think some things are more important than you being sent home from that camp." Then she came over and hugged Mina. "I'm sorry, child. I shouldn't have said that—I know how much it mattered to you."

But Mina couldn't think of why else Miss LaValle . . . "But why?" she asked. "What's wrong?"

"Her man left her," Momma said.

"What man?"

"The man who's been paying her bills. I was sure you knew. You didn't think she supported herself just from ballet lessons, did you? We've got to get the biscuits made."

"But, Momma—" Mina followed her mother into the kitchen. Her mother dropped mounds of soft dough onto the pan. Mina dipped her fingers into cold water and shaped the dough into smooth-topped rounds. "Did she love him that much?"

"Who ever knows, about love. Maybe she did, or maybe—at

her age—she was afraid of starting out again, afraid of being on her own."

"She's not so old."

"She's my age. If Poppa were to leave me—"

"He wouldn't do that."

"Men die, you know. There are always accidents to happen. If that did happen, then I'm so tangled up in my life, children and grandchildren, my job, all the friends we have, the church—I wouldn't go under. But she didn't have anything. Not a single child. I always felt so sorry for her."

This was an entirely different person from the Miss LaValle Mina had known for years, the woman who had taught her how to dance. It was like a horror movie on TV, a Friday late-night horror movie, where the monster peels back the mask-face to reveal his true, horrible face. "I should go see her," Mina said.

"She's gone."

"You mean she died?"

"No, although she tried. No, she moved out, moved away, clean away. She's gone to the West Coast, where she has friends, people she met when she worked as a professional dancer up north."

"She was a ballerina?" Miss Maddinton could be wrong, there could be black ballerinas.

"No. She said once she wanted to, but she couldn't."

"She wasn't good enough?"

"I wouldn't know about that. They don't let blacks in—or at least they didn't when I was a girl. Irene danced in chorus lines. She was actually on Broadway twice, or so she told us. It was years ago." Momma put the two trays of biscuits into the oven and then just stood there with her back to Mina, her shoulders sagged. When she turned around, she had to wipe her eyes.

"Momma? What's the matter?"

"Oh, I don't know. Sometimes, it just seems like so much uphill work—she must have been awfully good, to get as far as she did, being black, and a woman, and then she ends up in the emergency room having her stomach pumped and wanting to die. If Tamer hadn't been there . . ."

"But she didn't go to our church," Mina asked.

"She didn't go to any church. But you know how it is, Mina; we all know all about one another, and we take care of each other. No matter what church anybody goes to." Then Momma seemed to relax and feel better. "I thought *that* was what Tamer was sermonizing about, about Miss LaValle. He's not the young man to let things go unspoken when people want to avoid them. Everybody's been gossiping and I guess he just thought we needed a little bringing up short."

Mina didn't want to think about it anymore. "Will you ask them to supper?"

"If you'll help out. Don't even bother answering; I know you. You go ahead and ask them, honey. I'm only working nights for a few more days, then I go back to days, so it'll be fine next week. Do you want to slice the tomatoes or drain the beans?"

They got back to work. One thing about a big family, Mina thought, hefting the pot of green beans over to drain through the colander, the jobs got split up. Mina helped her mother with the cooking, because it was what she liked. Belle and Zandor wanted to hang around after church and see people, so they would do the washing up. When Zandor went off to college in the fall, Louis would take over most of the jobs he did, because he was about old enough. They *did* take care of one another, Mina thought. Her mother was right about that. Then Mina thought—alone in the kitchen, moving the baked biscuits from the trays onto the serving platter, piling the layers up—how lucky she was that this was where she was. She liked being where people knew how to keep close to one another; she liked having these people her people.

Mina heard her family gathering in the dining room and she heard the slow summer rain start plopping down outside. She looked at the plates of food standing ready on the Formica table close up to the wall. The kitchen wasn't any too large, and it wasn't any too fancied up, but the air was warm and filled with food smells, the meaty smell of beef stew and the bready smell of biscuits and, lighter in the air, the smells of vegetables. Mina felt so snug in there, among shelves of glasses and dishes and food in cans and bags and boxes, she almost didn't want to go out to the table. In a fit of contentment, sharper for thinking of Miss LaValle, Mina brought down the honey jar. Louis loved honey and butter mixed together to spread on his biscuits. She'd sit next to him and show him how to mix them, so Momma wouldn't have to worry about him making sticky messes.

CHAPTER 11

Mina got back in touch with Kat that week. Kat didn't ask her for any apologies, but she made a brief one anyway, and that was that. Through Kat, she got back in touch with Rachelle and Sabrina and all the rest. They were a little standoffish with her, but she figured that wouldn't last long. They didn't ask her about what had happened, except for Kat, privately. To Kat she said quite honestly that it turned out she had the wrong build to study ballet, and the wrong color. Kat didn't say anything, but she kept her eyes on the ground and her lips pursed up just a little, so Mina could guess what she was thinking, that it might have been better, after all, not to have been the one chosen. Mina didn't say so out loud, but she sort of agreed. Anyway, she told Kat, absolutely honestly, she was glad to be back home.

They went to the beach every day, where they horsed around with the boys and girls there. Kat was crazy about Lije Wilstrum. Lije worked on his uncle's boat during the summer, so he'd show up around midafternoon, after the mornings haul of crabs had been taken care of. Kat would eyeball him from her towel or go down to the water's edge and sit alone, making holes in the sand, hoping Lije would go in for a swim and say a word as he passed by. He was a couple of years older and Kat looked like a little girl, so she didn't get much of his attention. He knew she had a crush on him, though. Mina could tell that by the way he made sure to strut by close to where Kat was. If he came over, it was Mina or Rachelle he'd talk to, but he'd keep an eye on Kat. It was fun on the beach, with the radios going and a bunch of people around and the sea nettles just starting to come in, so you could still swim without worrying if you'd get stung. Once you'd been in the water to cool down, the heat didn't seem so bad. The beach was a long, narrow strip of dirty sand, and it was black people exclusively who used it. They stretched out along the sand, kids at one end, families in the middle, all stretched out to enjoy themselves. Relaxed, Mina wondered why she hadn't known how unrelaxed she had been the last year. Her eyes found Louis among the dark bodies and bright suits. When he looked up, she smiled at him. He came over then, and she hugged him, pulling him down beside her on the towel, keeping an arm around him.

Mina kept on visiting with Miz Hunter too. The Scrabble games were fun. She was getting good enough to come close to winning, sometimes. Miz Hunter told her about books she should read when she got older, and some she should have read already. They talked a lot about Africa, because Miz Hunter was an Africa freak. She'd always wanted to go to Africa, she said. "There's always been an African movement, ever since the War Between the States," she told Mina.

They were sitting on her porch, drinking lemonade, just watching whatever life went by on the quiet street. It was too hot and humid to move around. Even Louis lay quiet, coloring on old newspapers under a shady dogwood. "Liberia's the place."

Looking around her, Mina wondered why anyone would leave. The houses lined up neatly and a few air conditioners hummed. The leaves drooped with heat, like beet greens too long in the store; nobody was expecting anybody to do anything in this weather. Everything was hot and moist and lazy. The lemonade slid cool down her throat.

"That's a functioning political state, and it's a black state," Miz Hunter said. "I'd have liked to be part of it. There's something about the idea of building a country."

"Why didn't you?"

"Oh, it was dangerous, I guess. Pioneering always is. You have to be pretty adventurous, or in pretty much trouble at home, to go out and be a pioneer." Miz Hunter lifted her glass to her mouth and drank.

"Like the frontiersmen," Mina said. "I'd have been terrified," she added, thinking about what it would be like to be scalped or captured by Indians.

"You'd have managed, Missy. It'll get you nowhere to underestimate yourself."

"You never even went to visit Liberia?"

"It's awfully expensive. I had family here, and friends, and then—when I finally married"—Miz Hunter laughed—"I had Mr. Hunter and the children."

Mina hadn't known that Miz Hunter had children. She wondered where they were.

"But it was always my dream. It was always—I wondered what it would feel like to be part of the majority. If I'd feel different."

"We're the majority around here," Mina pointed out.

"You think so?"

Well, Mina did. She almost never saw white people, except downtown. It was like Connecticut, only reversed.

"We're about half and half, around here," Miz Hunter told her. "Where I lived in Alabama, we were the real majority. But there are majorities and majorities, there's more to it than just numbers. I spent some long nights dreaming about Africa."

"I know what you mean," Mina said, thinking about dancing. "But I can see how you wouldn't have wanted to leave all this." She looked down the street, and up the street.

The church was on one side, then her own house on the other, with its two shade trees by the front porch, then the Westers' house and the Phillipses' . . . She went on, naming them to herself. She knew every family, on both sides of the street, and all around the blocks.

Miz Hunter chuckled. "Oh, it wasn't like this. This here is next to heaven. For our people, it is. Down south, we were still too close to slavery."

"But it's been years, over a century."

"That's not so long a time. It feels long, but it isn't. My grandmother was born a slave, in Louisiana, and I was eight when she died. I remember her. Her mother, my great-grandmother, was a house slave. My great-grandaddy worked in the cane fields until he disappeared."

"Disappeared?"

"I'm pretty sure he died, but my grandmother's mother never knew. He ran off, to get North. They never said exactly why, probably they didn't know. There'd have been any number of reasons why a man would want to run off North."

"To be free."

"And to come back and buy his family free. My grandmother used to tell us, all her childhood she was waiting for this big handsome man to come for her. He was big, she said, and strong and handsome. He went off into the swamps one night and never was seen again. They went after him with the dogs, but they never got him."

"So maybe he did get away," Mina said.

"I used to think that. So I went down there, out of curiosity, one summer vacation. He'd taken up a lot of my dream-time too, that big handsome black man who wouldn't be kept down in slavery. I took a bus down below New Orleans into the area where they lived. There was a kind of National Park, if you can call it that, with paths laid out through the swamp. Nobody much ever went there. I did."

Miz Hunter drank and swallowed. "Nobody needs to see that place, Missy. I had a clean room waiting. I had a friend waiting in New Orleans who would prepare me a fine dinner. I had a job to keep me, a good, secure job. Even so, looking at that place made me want to give up and die." Her eyes looked out across some distance. Her words came slow. "The water was still, dead still, and green slime all along the top. Those cypress trees—between the dead stumps coming up black out of the water and the live trees tangled up overhead with vines to keep the sun out and keep the wind out and keep anything clean out . . . I almost couldn't make myself walk into it. He'd have had nothing with him, nothing but the clothes he wore and his bare hands and his bare courage. You could hear the trees creaking, sometimes. And bugs—and—it was the kind of place snakes love; it felt like the kind of place anything bad would be at home in. There were little hummocks of land, sometimes, and the water looking like pea soup gone bad on the stove. I was on a pathway, no more than half a mile from a town road, and I felt it reaching out for my soul. No, he died in there. As soon as I saw it I knew that. What made me wonder was what a man's life could be like to make him go in there in the first place. Any man walking into that swamp was walking into death—so whatever lay behind him must have been worse than death."

Mina felt cold. She could see it, almost, and she thought that he would have looked like Mr. Shipp. It could have been Mr. Shipp born in slavery, sold into slavery. The painted boards of the porch floor felt thin, flimsy; when they gave out there was a swamp waiting underneath.

"That's terrible," she said.

"What's most terrible," Miz Hunter answered her, although

her thin old voice didn't sound like it was so terrible, "was that if he'd just waited a few years, he'd have been freed. It wasn't ten years later that the war was finished. He couldn't know, probably didn't even know war was coming. The ignorance of slaves—nobody told them anything, nobody taught them—But if he'd only waited, he'd have had his freedom and his life."

"Oh no," Mina said.

"You have to look with a long eye, Missy. Some people never learn that, and I'd guess that my great-grandfather was that kind. We live in a blink of time, but God looks with a long eye."

"That wasn't much over a hundred years ago," Mina said.

"And it's been quite a road since then," Miz Hunter told her. "If you look down that road with a long eye—as your poppa does—its almost a miracle how much territory has been covered."

But Mina's imagination was stuck there in the green swamp, with a man who looked like Mr. Shipp, half in and half out of the water, alone, and his skin crawling over with bugs and covered with slime, the black skin that covered his strong muscles. She'd never understood before. Because that kind of man wouldn't be quiet under any master.

She put her glass down, even though her mouth was dry. She couldn't have swallowed anything. She couldn't have gotten anything down past the anger and misery, the pity and the bitterness all mixed up in her throat. She was looking with a long eye, and that man lay too close to be forgotten about.

CHAPTER 12

The day the Shipps came for supper, Mina and Louis, with Kat helping too, steamed and picked a bushel of crabs. They were at it all morning long. Belle was supposed to help, Momma had told her to, but once she got out of bed she decided it was too hot for work. She took her towel and went off to the beach. Steaming the crabs was easy, but the picking was tedious.

Louis took the legs off, opened the shells and cleared out the gills. As a reward, Mina let him eat as many of the big pincers as he wanted. She and Kat did the finer work of picking the meat out of the many-chambered body. It was midafternoon before they had the big bowl of crab meat in the refrigerator. "Okay, Louis, now let's go get some corn and tomatoes," Mina said. She had an eye on the clock. There wasn't any press for time, but there wasn't any time to waste either. She was enjoying getting ready for the evening. She was looking forward to the dinner.

"Can I come?" Kat asked.

"Sure, but don't you want to go to the beach?"

"I thought I wouldn't, today. There's such a thing as being too available, you know."

"There's such a thing as being too young," Mina teased.

"He's not so much older, only three years."

"We'd like to have you along, wouldn't we, Louis? But we're going to have to bike out to Milson's."

"It's something to do," Kat said. Mina knew she was having a hard time staying away from the beach, where Lije might be. She wasn't sure exactly why Kat had decided not to go today, but she could sympathize with how hard it was, and she thought Kat's decision was pretty smart.

"And it'll be good for your figure," Mina said.

"There's nothing wrong with my figure, except I'm too flat."

"Then it'll be good for my figure," Mina said.

They were walking Mina's bike over to Kat's house.

"There's nothing wrong with your figure either. We're just both of us out of step, that's all." Mina stared at Kat's coppery skin, inherited from Creole ancestors Kat had told her. When did Kat get so smart, she wondered.

Louis balanced on Mina's handlebars, facing front, his legs held out. He was pretty heavy, but he'd helped out so patiently all morning long that Mina didn't have the heart to leave him behind. At the vegetable stand, they bought two dozen ears of corn and several pounds of tomatoes from a high-school boy whose nose had one of those constant summer burns that blond whites sometimes got. Kat packed the two bags of corn into the carriers on each side of her rear wheel. "I hate it," she muttered, looking back at the stand where the boy now waited on some people from a car.

"Hate what?"

"Hate the way they don't even look at us. As if we weren't worth looking at. Didn't you notice?"

"What does that matter? Although he *is* cute."

"Mina Smiths. You just shut your mouth. I didn't mean anything like that and you know it."

"He's white anyway."

"And Lije could beat him hollow if it came to a fight," Kat said, satisfied.

Mina wasn't so sure about that, but if it came to a fight it would be a lively one, from the look of the blond boy. They rode off toward town, more slowly with their more awkward loads, riding side by side. Louis held the paper bag of vegetables under one arm and gripped the handlebars with his free hand. Things were pretty precarious.

"Do you really think he's cute?" Kat asked.

"No, but he's someone they'd think was cute, if you know what I mean."

"Who *do* you think is—good looking?"

"Like, handsome? Oh, Mr. Shipp is. And Bailey Westers. I like Bailey's looks."

"Mina, he's built like a broomstick. And his mouth is huge."

"I don't mind. I just said I liked his looks, that's all. I'm not going to marry him, or anything."

Because she'd helped out so much, Mina asked Kat to stay and eat with them. It was almost a party, with the five of the Smiths family, and Kat, Miz Hunter, and Mr. Shipp's family too. Mina mixed and formed the crab cakes, then fried them gently on the big griddle Poppa gave Momma for Christmas four years ago. Even so, there were so many crab cakes that she had to do them in two batches. They ate at the table on the back porch, where it was cooler. Poppa had made the table out of a door he'd bought at a hardware store, with legs he'd bought and nailed on. It wasn't exactly beautiful, but it was a big, steady table.

As soon as the Shipps arrived, Mina set out the platters of food, which Kat carried out to the table. Two platters of crab cakes, piled up high, each platter decorated with lemon wedges, went out first. Then a bowl of mixed sliced cucumbers and tomatoes, tossed in Mrs. Beaulieu's special dressing. Mina wrapped the corn around with dishtowels, to keep it hot. She had a bowl of fruit in the icebox, chilling for dessert, and she had made brownies. The kids had glasses of lemonade, the grown-ups had glasses of beer.

Big as the table was, they were all crowded around it, eating and talking, passing things up and down. Mr. Shipp really liked the crab cakes, Mina could tell as she watched him take his first bites. He sat at one end of the table and her mother sat at the other. Mr. Shipp finished his first crab cake pretty quickly. Alice ate daintily, slowly.

"Your daughter was right; these are wonderful," Mr. Shipp said to Mina's mother. "What's in them?"

"Mostly crab," Momma answered. "It was Mina who made them."

"Did she?" he asked. "Did you?"

Mina nodded, wishing her mother hadn't said anything about it.

"She and Kat made this whole dinner, if you must know. I just came home and showered and changed. That's my contribution."

"Well, now, then, we certainly thank you girls."

"It's very nice," Alice said.

"Is there anything you can't do?" Mr. Shipp asked Mina, teasing. Mina looked up at him, from where she was buttering an ear of corn for his youngest daughter. He was treating her like she was about Selma's age, about three years old, with that jolly teasing voice.

"Dance," she answered, putting a stop to that conversation.

Everybody got uncomfortable for a few seconds. Mina could almost feel eyes looking at her quickly and then away. She wondered if maybe she'd gone too far, and thought probably she had and wished she hadn't tried to be so smart. Being t-rou-ble. But Mr. Shipp kept on looking at her, and she wasn't going to look away. His eyes were what she liked best about his face, maybe, she thought. They were really looking at her, as if he were thinking about her and interested and amused and sorry for her, all at once.

Then he smiled, just a small, quiet smile, as if he knew what she was up to. She thought maybe his smile was what she liked best.

"Why that's perfectly ridiculous," Alice said. "Anybody can dance. Everybody can."

Mina looked at her. She had missed entirely the undertone of what Mina said. But even Louis had gotten it, and Kat was looking at Mina as if she felt sorry for her, whereas Alice . . . but Alice must have known.

"Even Tamer can dance, when he wants to," Alice added, to prove her point.

Mina kept herself from giggling, but she couldn't stop the grin that spread over her face. Because the bows on the shoulders of her sundress, which Kat had been admiring, were more important to Alice than whether or not Mina Smiths was happy, or what. Alice was like a butterfly, who would land briefly on one leaf of a tree, paying no attention to the branches going back to the trunk, or the trunk going down to the ground, or the roots digging deep through the earth. It would be an easier life, being a butterfly.

"You used to take me dancing," Alice reminded her husband.

"I did, didn't I?" Mr. Shipp said. "Tell you what, honey. For our tenth anniversary I'll take you out for an evening, a first-class evening, dinner and dancing." He was teasing again.

"Downtown?" Alice asked. His eyes stayed on her.

"Downtown. We'll go to"—he considered it, watching her face as she waited for him to finish—"the Persian Room at the Plaza Hotel."

"Oh, Tamer," she said.

"Take me too," the oldest girl, Dream, said. "I could get a new dress. I can dance."

"This is for grown-ups," Alice explained, while the rest of the people tried not to encourage Dream by laughing.

They lingered over dessert and coffee, while the little children went out into the yard to run around in the last of the sunlight. Selma fell asleep in her father's lap. The voices blended together, floating out from the screened porch to join in with other voices from other houses, everybody relaxing at the end of a day. Mina listened as Kat and Belle asked Alice about hairstyles in New York, as her mother told Mr. Shipp about something called the Hundred Years' War, in Europe, because he had said he had never understood what it was about, and Momma said it was about economics, as always. Mina sat back, her stomach full, tired after the work of the dinner, her mind resting. She wished her father was here.

Mr. Shipp seemed to think the same. "I would like to know your husband, Raymonda," he said, right in the middle of things.

"Amos says the same," she answered. They leaned down the table toward one another to talk, while Mina tucked away the knowledge of the way her mind and Mr. Shipp's mind ran along the same lines.

Darkness settled down through the air, and the children went inside to watch TV on the Smithses' little black-and-white set. "It's better than nothing," Alice said. "We don't have one out at the Beerce house." She went in with them to select the program and stayed with them to watch. They let Selma sleep on the sofa. Mr. Shipp walked Miz Hunter across to her own house and then walked Kat to her house. Momma helped Belle and Zandor with the dishes. Mina would have liked to walk along with Mr. Shipp through the dark evening air, but thought she'd better not say so and she wasn't asked.

After everything was cleaned up, Belle, Zandor, Momma, Mina, and Mr. Shipp sat around the table, just sitting there, not talking about anything much. Momma had citronella candles burning, and the light flickered over the dark faces. Mina didn't think she'd ever felt so good. She felt contented, from the soles of her feet to the ends of her pigtails contented.

"Say, Belle, you must have a radio or a record player, don't you?" Mr. Shipp asked. "Unless I misunderstand human nature entirely."

"I couldn't live without it," Belle answered.

"Do you have any music a man could dance to?"

"You aren't going to go lugging that thing downstairs," Momma objected.

"We'll open the windows. It won't be loud, Raymonda," Mr. Shipp said. "One of the things I enjoy most about summers here is the quiet. The simple quiet. I just wanted to ask Miss Mina to tread the boards with me."

"The boards?" Mina wondered.

"The grass, precisely," he said. "It piques my curiosity when a young lady says she can't dance."

"But," Mina began, but by then Belle was already on her way upstairs. "Not too loud," Momma called after her.

The music fell down from the open window like a fine summer rain. Belle dragged Zandor out to dance with her, while Louis and Momma watched from the porch. "I picked light rock," Belle told Mr. Shipp.

"I'm glad to hear that," he answered solemnly, and then, when she had grabbed Zandor's hands and started in dancing, he lifted his eyebrows at Mina as if to say he didn't know what Belle was talking about. Mina giggled. She felt weird, standing there in their backyard, in the shadowy air. He held out his hands for her to take, and she hesitated, feeling weird. Then the music began to wrap itself around her feet with its steady beat, and the melody started to move in her shoulders, while the singers' voices got into her ears; and they danced. Mina heard his voice humming along the way hers was. She was surprised at his coordination, as they stepped out and then stepped in together, but she didn't know why she should be. He was a good dancer, she thought, as their hands separated and their arms went out, moving from the shoulders down to the wrist. They backed around each other, moving together in the dance. At the end he just said, "I thought so," before the next song started up.

Louis brought Dream out to dance, and Alice claimed her husband from the steps. "I want to dance with you," Alice said, sounding happy. "Mina won't mind."

Mina didn't mind. She went up into the house to fetch Samuel out. "I can't," he said, his eyes solemn behind his glasses.

"It's easy, you just—move around to the music," she told him. He was miles shorter than she was and moved with funny little jerky steps, self-conscious, until they both started laughing and he relaxed. Then he took off his glasses, running up to set them on the table, and ran back. "Okay," he said, satisfied. "You're a good teacher."

Everybody danced with everybody, switching partners. But nobody could persuade Momma to join them. "I'm not built for this. I've been on my feet all day, and it's no relaxation for me to get back on them to—jump around."

"I can fox trot," Mr. Shipp called up, but she shook her head. "You're as bad as your daughter," he told her, his voice floating through the dark air.

"You said I was a good dancer," Mina protested.

"You know what I mean." She heard his laughter but she couldn't see his face. "Don't you make trouble, Miss T-rou-ble. I haven't danced for years, have I, honey?" he asked Alice.

Even after everyone had gone home, the house was filled with the good time they'd had, as if it could linger in the air like the voices and music lingered in memory. Mina wrapped the memory up and put it in her heart; there was a quiet gladness, deep like a tree and tall in her.

CHAPTER 13

A couple of days after that, Mina and Kat and Louis rode out to the Shipps' house. Alice had told them to come on out, anytime, anytime soon, because she got pretty lonely out there all day with just the children. She had some magazines she was sure Kat would enjoy, she said. There was a little beach just down the way, on a creek, but it had sand. They put on bathing suits and shorts and rode out the three miles to the Beerce farm.

Alice was still in her bathrobe, but she didn't mind having them come over. While Alice was upstairs dressing, Mina and Kat washed up the breakfast dishes for her. Then they all sat on the porch, drinking Kool-Aid, and talking. Alice didn't like the house much. It had no air conditioning, no dishwasher, no TV for the kids. The linoleum floors always looked dirty and the windows had to be propped up with pieces of wood. Mina thought it was a fine house, set among the fields the way it was, with a few straggly wild cherry trees behind it and a couple of locusts out front. The heat built up and she listened, picking at the paint of the porch with her fingers.

"Can't we go swimming?" Louis finally asked. Alice said it was all right, but she didn't want to go with them. She asked if Mina would mind watching the children, and Mina said it was no trouble. So Kat stayed behind while Mina walked off with Dream and Selma. Samuel was upstairs, doing something, so she didn't ask if he wanted to come with them, but he came running after them, in a sweat.

"You should have called," he said, angry at her. His bathing suit was twisted wrong at his skinny waist and his glasses were halfway down his nose. He couldn't fix them without dropping the towel.

"I said I was sorry once," Mina reminded him. If he was going to just be cross, she wished he'd go back to whatever he'd been doing.

"It wasn't fair," he said.

Mina ignored him. Selma had such short legs, she wondered if she should offer to carry the little girl, but she suspected that Selma wanted to do things all by herself.

"You never even said you were here, when you came," he continued.

"Cut it out, will you?" Mina told him. Louis had run on ahead along the path that ran between two cornfields. She hoped he'd have sense enough to wait for them before going into the water. She had no idea of how deep it was, or anything. "If you feel like this, why didn't you stay home?"

Samuel walked along ahead of her, studying the path. It was close in there among the tall corn. The heat multiplied itself, and there were more bugs than Mina cared for. Sweat sat prickly on her skin. She wondered how much farther they had to go. She wondered if the line of scrawny trees ahead marked the creek, because such trees often grew up beside the creeks. She wondered if Selma would have a fit if Mina suggested carrying her, so they could move a little faster.

"I wanted to go swimming more than I wanted to be angry," Samuel said, turning around and walking backward.

"Hunh?"

"You asked me why I didn't stay in the house," Samuel reminded her.

He didn't call it home, Mina noticed. She looked at his little face. He didn't look that much like his father. "How old are you?" she asked.

"Five. I'm going to first grade. There it is."

They stepped out from between walls of corn into some trampled underbrush and then onto a narrow beach. Louis was sitting with his legs in the water. The creek was narrow, and another cornfield lay across it. But a little breeze ruffled the water, here where there was room for air to move, and the trees gave some shade. They spread out their towels and splashed into the water.

It was shallow, never over Mina's knees, but deep enough to splash in. She lay around in the water and then walked out, wetted down thoroughly, to sit and watch the little children play. It was entirely private, entirely their own, rather like a swimming pool in their backyard.

Mina hadn't planned to stay too long at the beach, but she did. She watched Selma potter around at the water's edge and Samuel resolutely try to teach himself how to swim. Louis peeled himself a fishing rod and Dream sat weaving long grasses together, lost in her own thoughts. Mina sat on her towel to watch, flopping back into the water whenever she got too hot. Kat and Alice knew where they were. It was funny that she called Alice, Alice, but couldn't imagine calling Mr. Shipp, Tamer.

The late morning sun poured down over the creek and beach, sparkling along the surface of the water. In spells of silence, you could hear the little noises the water made. There weren't many spells of silence, not with three children from one family to start games and then quarrel them to an end. Selma was the best quarreler. The little girl consistently got exactly what she wanted, even from Louis. By sheer stubbornness and refusing to give up ever, that was how she did it. Mina was amused. She was willing to bet that Selma's short hair was because Alice would be easily defeated during quarrels about braiding Selma's hair.

Samuel told her about what school was going to be like, as if he didn't realize she'd been six years in school herself. She listened to him with half of her mind as he walked around in front of her, talking. She looked at the field opposite and the clear hot sky overhead, at her own big feet digging into the rough sand. The Shipp kids took this for granted, she thought; they'd have been just as happy with a plastic pool in the dirt of the backyard.

"Are you listening?" Samuel demanded, stopping right in front of her with his feet planted and his hands on his skinny hips. She started to just say she was, then she realized that he knew better.

"I wasn't, but I am now." Laughter bubbled up in her voice, and she hoped he wouldn't notice.

"So I'm going to learn how to really read." He stayed right in front of her, to be sure he kept her attention.

"What do you mean really read. Can you already read things?"

Louis splashed water over Dream, but gently, as if he was making her a private waterfall. Dream rewarded him with laughter. Louis would think Samuel was boasting, but Mina wasn't sure.

"I can read Sesame Street, but that's not like reading books."

Mina stared at him.

"Daddy said my school will have a library. There's going to be bad kids there, but I'll ignore them. There'll seem like there're more bad kids than good kids, but Daddy said that's just the way it seems."

Mina stared.

"Not the way it is." Samuel clarified himself, in case she misunderstood.

Mina couldn't stop herself. She reached out and grabbed him close, and hugged him close. He was so little, with his little shoulders and his little bathing suit with his pipe-cleaner legs sticking out of it. She didn't wait until he started to struggle free, but let him go right away. "That was because I like you."

"Good," he said. That made Mina laugh.

"I like the way you laugh," he told her. She knew what he meant, just as she thought she knew why Selma came up just then to drop wet, muddy sand on the front of Mina's bathing suit.

They stayed out at the Shipps' almost the whole day, going back to the house for lunch, where Mina made peanut butter and jelly sandwiches for everyone, and more Kool-Aid. They sat on the porch, not moving much. Dream and Kat and Alice, who had the only chair, studied magazines, talking about dress styles and hair styles and makeup styles. Selma fell asleep, so Mina carried her upstairs to the room she shared with Dream. None of the beds was made, not even the double bed. The bathroom had towels on the floor, which she picked up. She could sympathize with Alice, too bowed down by heat to bother polishing the house up. It wasn't the kind of house that any amount of polishing would make look good anyway.

Back with the others again, Mina studied the house from her seat on the porch. The wood had never been painted. It had just weathered down to gray. Overhead, the tin roof glared up against the sunlight, hot silver. The other three turned pages of magazines while Samuel and Louis, at the far end of the porch, built with clay. Mina leaned back against the wooden post.

All around her the day was quiet. No cars, no radio or TV sounds, only occasional voices. The corn grew silently. Bugs whirred or buzzed quietly. Except for the two bikes parked just on the side, under a dilapidated-looking loblolly, it could have been any time at all. It could have been a hundred years ago. In more peaceful times, Mina thought. It could be anytime. But if it were just a hundred and fifty years ago . . . they would have been slaves.

That thought sat her up straight. For the little kids, things would be about the same—the slow, hot summer hours. Except they'd belong to someone, who could sell them just the way that blond boy sold corn and tomatoes. And the man who wasn't there, he could have been sold away, or he could have tried to run away, heading up north to freedom, however he could. Or he'd be out in the fields, working. So would Alice; except someone as pretty as Alice would probably be a house slave, dressed plain and waiting on her mistress, or maybe working in a washhouse. Kat would never be there, Mina thought, looking at her friend who was entirely engrossed in the glossy magazine. She'd be down in Louisiana, near the swamps Miz Hunter talked about. And Dream—looking at Dream a hundred and fifty years ago, Mina's heart twisted with pain, because Dream was going to be too pretty, and she'd be noticed. If you were a slave, it wasn't good to get noticed.

Samuel's bony spine stuck out as he bent over his clay. He'd never have learned how to read or had glasses even if his eyes needed them. He'd have learned never to open his mouth and say what he was thinking. Selma would have her stubbornness whipped out of her if they couldn't teach it out of her. They'd try to teach it out of her, her parents, or her mother, if her father wasn't around for some reason, just like they'd try to teach Samuel's way of thinking true out of him.

And herself? Mina looked at her legs, lined up neat, two strong thighs and the knees flexed at the joint, long calves and big feet. She registered her bust under the bathing suit and knew she looked much older than she was. A hundred and fifty years ago, it wouldn't have mattered how old she was; she'd have been treated like a woman grown. Broken to slavery from day one of her life.

She'd have been entirely different. She'd never have had a chance. There were so many people, then, who never did have a chance, no choices to make, not about what to eat or where to go or what to do. She'd never even have had a chance to make her own mistakes. A black girl who was t-rou-ble didn't make anybody smile a hundred and fifty years ago. And all because of the color of her skin, all because the skin covering that bony back at the far end of the porch was dark skin.

But the blood under it was red, and the bones were white.

Looking with a long eye, Mina saw how close they sat to a hundred and fifty years ago, and fear ran along her blood. Her stomach closed up in fear and pity. Her heart rose up in anger, against the whites that had done this.

It wasn't just a hundred and fifty years ago, she thought, remembering dance camp. A black girl who was t-rou-ble at dance camp got sent home. As if she'd failed, as if she couldn't dance because she couldn't dance their way.

Mina couldn't sit still. She got up and walked back to the driveway. Her legs moved long over the ground, and she turned around to look at the faded house, with the people sitting under the sagging porch roof, and at the pile of bricks holding the floor of the house up from the ground. Her fists clenched. She guessed she'd show them. She guessed she wouldn't let them drive her into any swamp to die.

"Hey," she called. All the faces turned to her. "Let's go," she called. There was a moment's hesitation and then they scrambled up.

"You'll come back? Come back real soon," Alice asked from her chair.

Louis and Kat hurried out to join Mina. Samuel trailed along. "Where are you going?" he asked.

"Ask Mina." Louis sulked, because he wanted to stay longer.

Mina realized she didn't know the answer, except "Home." Then she added, to Samuel's solemn face, "I've got things to do," although she wasn't sure exactly what they were.

Even carrying Louis on her handlebars, she stayed ahead of Kat, racing along the black roadway all the way.

CHAPTER 14

August just lay down on Crisfield like a dog, panting, too hot to do more than hang its tongue out. All day long, all the long days, the heat built up and the air hung heavier and heavier, as the hours rolled on by and the sun rolled across the sky. About four times during August, Alice called Mina up in the morning. "I've gotta get out of here and some friends are going up to the mall," she'd say. "I'm going stir-crazy," she'd say. "Can you possibly watch the children?"

Mina would ride out there to find Alice waiting on the porch, looking fresh and cool from a shower, her perfume a cloud around her, her hair done up fancy. Alice would go off for the day and Mina would stay with the children. Sometimes Louis came along with her, and sometimes Kat too.

They'd clean the house, while the heat was still bearable, then go on up to the creek for the worst of the day. Alice was usually back by the time they returned, in the late afternoon. Sometimes she'd be silly and giggly, and they'd all get silly together. Sometimes they'd find her sleeping on her bed, with her shoes off and her dress getting crumpled. If Alice was asleep, Mina would stay around either until she woke up or Mr. Shipp got home.

One of those afternoons, the storm that had been grumbling in the distance all afternoon finally broke. It woke Alice up, but she kept the kids inside with her. Mina and Mr. Shipp went out on the porch to watch. Rain beat down on the high stalks of corn. Wind blew the dark clouds across the sky and pulled at the branches of the trees. Lightning, visible for miles out here, it seemed like, cracked down through the sky. The thunder growled. The air cooled in the slanting rain. They didn't talk, Mr. Shipp and Mina; they just stood there watching and listening, leaning against the posts. Mina didn't know what expression was on her face until, as she turned around from the tail end of the storm to go in and say good-bye, Mr. Shipp said, "This is your kind of weather, isn't it?"

"I like it," Mina told him, careful as she always was to try to be exact with Mr. Shipp. "But I wouldn't say it's my kind of weather. Or the only kind."

"I know what you mean," he said, and she thought he did.

Riding home along the slippery roadway, riding right through the shallow puddles when they crept up the side of the road, Mina wished she knew Mr. Shipp well enough to ask him about dance camp. She almost never thought about it, partly because she was having a good summer, partly because she didn't want to. But when she did think about it and try to understand, she couldn't think because it was like teeth in her heart. She couldn't think while those sharp teeth were cutting away. All she could do was replay that scene with Miss Maddinton and all the things Miss Maddinton came so close to saying she might as well have said them right out: That Mina had only been allowed to go, and given the scholarship, because she was black. That she wasn't good enough and she never had been. That she was just a way for the camp to get money from the federal government, which it used to train the real dancers.

But how could Mina have been so stupid about herself? Unless Miss Maddinton just never could see the truth, because she always only saw that Mina was a black, different. That meant it didn't mean anything what Miss Maddinton said. But Mina had been wrong about her friends there, even Tansy, about them liking her. She remembered walking into her single room and the teeth cut into her heart.

Maybe she would ask Mr. Shipp about it, about how he managed. Maybe in another couple of summers she wouldn't be embarrassed to ask him about it. She could believe what he'd say.

With the Shipps, Mina felt like a big sister, older, wiser, more responsible. Being a big sister suited her. Mr. Shipp said he wished she'd come back to New York with them. "But you'd hate it, down in Harlem," he told her. Mina knew from that that he hated it. He thought Alice liked the city, but Alice said she didn't. "If we could move downtown," Alice said, "but it's so expensive, we can't. It would be something, though, to walk out of your door and see nice things in the store windows. I do that, sometimes, when my mother-in-law comes to take care of the kids. I take the bus to Fifth Avenue and Fifty-ninth Street and just walk on down, looking in the windows. Oh, Mina, you'd die if you could see the things they have. But Tamer'll never leave Harlem, not in a hundred years. How'd they call him up in the middle of the night, if he wasn't nearby? Everybody needs him, and especially when they're in trouble. I tell him, sometimes, he should open a law office and start charging people. But I worry, because some of those people, they'll turn on you for no reason. I wish he'd let us move, before one of them cuts him up."

One day, they were gone. Mina felt curiously aimless then. She played Scrabble with Miz Hunter in the afternoon, but half her mind was on where the Shipps would be, and what their apartment was like. She got Miz Hunter talking about them and that eased the empty feeling a little, even though the old lady was pretty critical of Alice and her butterfly ways.

The day after the Shipps drove off up north, a few days before school began, her father came home. Mina's mother took one look at him and chased him off to bed: "You're skin and bones, you look like you haven't slept for a week, and listen to that cough. You're not a young man anymore, Amos Smiths, and I've half a mind to tell that board what I think of them, sending you all over the place."

"It's good to see you too, Ray," Poppa said, giving her a bear hug before he went obediently upstairs to flop down on the bed and fall asleep.

Mina's father spent about a week in bed, letting the deacon take that Sunday service. He was mostly tired, Momma said, telling them not to worry, and he had a feverish cold, and she was going to get him healthy before she let him go back to work. And that was all there was to be said about that.

Mina watched this and thought that Alice would never talk like that to Mr. Shipp. But the Shipps loved each other, like her parents did. Mina thought there were times when Alice should talk like that and take care of her husband; and she thought it would be better if her mother prettied herself up more, like Alice did, because she thought her father would like that.

Mina thought about a lot of things, but almost never about the dance camp and the people up there, the white people. She wanted to write them a letter and tell them. She wanted to get famous, really famous, and be on a talk show and laugh at them. She wanted—she wanted not to feel so restless and unhappy with things. She was eager for school to begin, so she'd have something to do.

Once school started, Mina sat in her seventh grade classroom like a storm about to explode across the sky. She could take down some branches, she thought, and she could knock out electricity. She looked around her, at the black kids who made up more than half of the class, at the white kids, and she felt all her smartness and all her energy building up, ready to be used. She knew where she was heading: so far to the top that nobody would come close even to her heels.

The second day of school, Mr. Bryce, the principal who also taught them Social Studies, came in to administer a battery of achievement and aptitude tests. He took the class with painful slowness through the filling-in of their names and school, their ages and the date. Then he started to explain about the rules, how they weren't allowed to talk or ask questions, how they had to concentrate and do their best work because these tests were going to be used for placement, now and in the high school.

Mina never minded tests. But Rachelle, sitting next to Kat, raised her hand. Mr. Bryce went on talking, about going back to check if you had time at the end of each section, about how to erase the answers so the machines that corrected the tests wouldn't get it wrong. Rachelle sat there, with her hand up. Mr. Bryce looked at her occasionally, but didn't call on her. Finally, Rachelle called out, "Aren't these tests biased in favor of the whites?"

Mr. Bryce, who was of course white, looked at Rachelle for about half a minute. "I hope," he finally said, "that you're not in the habit of speaking before you're called on."

"I was just wondering if that got considered, in the scoring," Rachelle asked. Her voice wavered a little bit, like a violin losing the note. "Because if it's not, I wonder if I should take this."

"I don't think you have any choice if you're in this school system," Mr. Bryce said.

Uh-oh, Mina thought. He wasn't any too pleased with that question, or with Rachelle. "Let's just take it, 'Chelle, and get it over with," she said.

Mr. Bryce's eyes turned to her, and he wasn't too pleased with her either. Rachelle shrugged and didn't say anything more. Mina got set to get to work. She knew what Rachelle meant. There had been magazine articles about how these tests were designed for people who had grown up in the white environment. But Mina didn't see what they could do about that. She felt helpless, because there weren't any tests designed for blacks that she'd heard of, so the only tests there were were biased toward whites, and you had to take the tests. There wasn't anything she could do about the situation, and she didn't like that feeling, not one bit. But she didn't think they could give her any test she wouldn't do well on. They hadn't yet. She felt powerful, sitting there with the two sharpened pencils in front of her, waiting to begin. Maybe the test was biased, but they weren't going to be able to trip her up with it.

Mina went up to Rachelle during recess, to apologize for butting in. "Yeah," Rachelle said.

"I only did it because he was threatening to expel you," Mina explained.

"He was not. He couldn't do that."

"I don't know if he could, but it's what he was thinking. Don't you think, Kat?"

"Do you think that's what he meant by 'in this school system?'" Kat asked.

"I think," Mina said.

"I was so angry, I barely listened," Rachelle said. "Although, come to think of it, I'm not so sure I care. We're just diddling our days away in school. Letting them think they can have it all their own way." Rachelle was short and round and liked a fight.

"You know what the Bible says: 'Render unto Caesar that which is Caesar's,'" Kat reminded her.

"That's okay for you," Rachelle said, "but my father's sick, and my mother can't find work and they keep jiving her about welfare . . . as if they owned the world."

"I know how you feel," Kat said. "I'm really sorry." Kat meant what she said. It was in the tone of her voice, she really did feel sorry for Rachelle, and in a good way, not a pitying way. "My mother says there are some times so bad, you don't know how you'll get through them."

"Your mother? Really? But she looks like—" Rachelle didn't finish that sentence.

"Well, they don't own me," Mina said. "I'm just glad we only have one class a day with Mr. Bryce."

"Tell me about it," they both said. Then they all laughed and linked arms, to stroll together on around the playground.

Mina had other things to think about than school, or her own stormy feelings, for a while after that. Miz Hunter took sick, and the sickness settled in her chest. She was dying. She knew it, but she still didn't want to go into the hospital. Mina's mother nursed her, and a lot of the older people came to sit with her when Momma had to go off to work. Mina was needed at home. She kept a supply of food going over to the little house and kept their own house running. Louis helped out, as much as he could. The second Saturday of school he spent the whole evening working with her to make up coffee cakes for the next morning. But Miz Hunter died that night, just slipped away in her sleep, Momma reported. It was a good death, after a good life, Momma said. Mina, despite feeling a sadness like slow, steady rain, knew what her mother meant. It was as if Miz Hunter came to the end of her road and stepped off onto the next.

The funeral was Tuesday. Both Mina and Kat missed school to sing in the choir for the service. The choir sang, "You shall reap just what you sow." Poppa's eulogy was about Miz Hunter's whole life and the good things she sowed. He read it out to Mina

Monday evening, to hear how it sounded. She was looking forward to hearing him read it out in church.

Looking out over the solemn faces in the crowded church, Mina saw the door open. Mr. Shipp slipped into the room.

She saw Mr. Shipp and her heart flopped painfully over in her breast.

Mina stared at her father, not hearing a word he said. She just hadn't known, she hadn't even suspected. She had never figured it out, how much she had missed Mr. Shipp, even though she had noticed how he kept walking across her nighttime dreams. Her cheeks felt hot when she understood.

She didn't mind. Just the opposite. She was just surprised that she hadn't known that the hollow place she'd been feeling inside her wasn't an empty place at all—it was the place where her feelings for Tamer Shipp were waiting to be given their right name.

Now she knew what that was, she knew how she'd missed seeing him and his family, missed hearing his ideas, his mind laid out for her to understand in Sunday sermons. She always and every day wanted to watch him walk into a room, and maybe smile. She wanted to look into his eyes and see all the complicated and comprehending feelings he gave to the world.

Watching him, as he knelt for a brief prayer then sat back in his chair to listen, Mina wondered how the sky felt when a lightning bolt blazed through it. She thought that was about the way she was feeling, right then. She looked away from him, understanding: During the trip down from Wilmington that July afternoon, the long car ride, the long lunch, Mina had fallen in love with him. She'd fallen so fast, she didn't even know until now how deep she'd fallen.

She didn't know if Mr. Shipp looked at her, because she didn't dare look at him again. Besides, she thought, bringing her mind back to her father's eulogy, this wasn't the time or the place. She brought her mind back to Miz Hunter, even though that was no less confusing than anything else in her life. She was sorry Miz Hunter was dead. She would miss the old lady's presence in the little house next door, she would miss their conversations. But Miz Hunter's trials were over now, and she was resting now.

When the choir stood up to sing Miz Hunter out of the church, it was "Deep River" they sang. They sang it *a cappella*—just the voices, singing. Mina's voice sounded to her all filled up with sorrow and gladness for Miz Hunter, over Jordan now, just like the song said, and with joy to see Mr. Shipp, and with belonging, here in her father's church.

"Where you going to, Missy," she remembered Miz Hunter asking, all the time. Everybody was going someplace, she thought, singing out deep, watching the people follow the coffin out while the choir sang them on their way. Miz Hunter was just way on ahead now, over Jordan, sitting down to the gospel feast in the song.

Mina didn't know about this place where Miz Hunter had gone to, nobody did for sure. But she did know for sure that she'd go where she wanted to go—in this world that had Tamer Shipp in it. Not just go where somebody else said she had to because she probably wouldn't be able to do any better for herself, because she was black.

CHAPTER 15

Mina didn't know what Mr. Shipp thought of her, except that he approved. She knew he was a married man, and he loved his wife, and he had a family, and she was years too young for him. But that didn't mean she couldn't love him. But sometimes she wished she'd never met him, or he hadn't been the one to come pick her up that day in Wilmington. Sometimes she envied Kat the way she moved from crush to crush, with no boy ever really mattering to her for himself. Kat was having a good time growing up.

Sometimes, Mina just daydreamed about Tamer Shipp. Some of her daydreams were goopier than others. Often, he was there in her night dreams, and now she knew why. She wondered if she was ever in his dreams, although she doubted it. She wondered what he'd think of her and how she was doing in school. She thought he'd approve. Half the reason she was working like she was was for Tamer Shipp.

She paid attention in classes, not surprised that she knew any answer the teachers asked for. She did her homework, and then some. She did a lot of reading on the side and a lot of that was the books her sixth grade teacher had recommended to her, books about blacks and books by blacks. Math, Science, Literature, Language Arts, the perfect papers just kept rolling back to her. It didn't surprise Mina that it was so easy for her.

She also made sure that everybody in the class knew who she was, Mina Smiths, knew that Mina Smiths wasn't going to come in second to anybody, knew that Mina Smiths was someone to be reckoned with, t-rou-ble. They thought she had to be who they wanted her to be, but they didn't know anything about her.

Mr. Shipp knew something about her, she thought.

She wondered what he would make of Mr. Bryce and the Social Studies class. The course was the history of Maryland, with Fridays given over to current events, when everybody had to report on a newspaper article. She knew what she made of Mr. Bryce, who ran a military-strict classroom where everything had to be done exactly his way, even the place where the date went on your papers and the way the date was written, first the number, then the month, then the year. There was only one particular set of words that made an answer right. Social Studies met at the end of the day. Mr. Bryce came in expecting them to behave badly, seventh graders at the end of the school day, and he sat on anything he thought might be trouble before it could even begin.

Mr. Bryce was an overweight middle-aged man whose hair was thinning and who had the big belly of a man whose once athletic body hadn't been exercised for a long time. At first, he'd call on Mina, but after a couple of days he dismissed her questions, without seeming to hear them even though he was looking right at her. He ignored questions about blacks during the colonial period, whether there were free blacks as well as slaves in Maryland, about what legal rights a free black had. He didn't even call on Mina after the first few days. He didn't like her, he really didn't like her. The look on his face when he took attendance told her that he thought she was trouble, and she'd better look out.

She did look out, everybody did around Mr. Bryce, who was the school principal too; but that didn't mean she was going to shut up. Mina thought about Mr. Shipp, and whether he'd let anybody treat him this way. She wondered if, if Mr. Shipp was in their class as a student, she'd let anyone treat him the way Mr. Bryce treated the black kids, barely taking the time to tell them they were pretty stupid. So Mina made a point of standing up for blacks in general, and the kids in her class too.

"What would your father say about your manners," Mr. Bryce asked Mina one day, in front of everybody, when she had asked a question about three times, waiting for him to respond to her. "What would he say about how rude you are. He's a minister, isn't he?" Mr. Bryce added, looking around the class to make sure everybody got that point.

Mina didn't know how to answer him. She did know that she hadn't been rude, in any way, not even in her tone of voice and barely in what she'd been thinking about the man. She didn't want to answer his question, however, because it would look like a quarrel, whatever she answered. Mr. Bryce was setting up a quarrel.

"Well?" he insisted, staring at her in the front row, where he had moved her the third day of class.

He was pushing at her with the full force of his personality. Everyone got quiet, uncomfortable and a little eager for any kind of excitement, even if it was only somebody getting sent out. Mina didn't want to get sent out of the room for a discipline report. She also didn't want to apologize, because she didn't think she had been rude. She wasn't going to let him make her lie either, by forcing an "I'm sorry" out of her. But the way he'd asked the question, she couldn't think of what she could say without it looking like a quarrel, unless she lied.

Then she thought if there was going to be a quarrel, she wouldn't lose it. She was a match for this man, she thought, feeling the storminess building up in her. But she thought of what

Mr. Shipp would think was right, and even though she was afraid of a real quarrel she thought that for Tamer Shipp she ought to answer. So she tried an answer, looking right back into his unfriendly eyes, not smiling, not looking smart, keeping her voice level. "Yes, my father is a minister, over at the Oak Street Church. He takes a pretty firm line on rudeness, you're right."

She wondered how he'd answer that, and she watched him wonder too. Mr. Bryce wanted to make an example of her, to make sure everybody knew he was in control. He wanted to put her down.

But if he kept on with it, everyone would know that it was him making the quarrel, by picking on her. Things were tense in the room, but not—Mina noticed—in her. Then one of the white kids raised a hand at the same time as two of the black kids did. Mr. Bryce called on the white boy, and Mina didn't let her expression give anything away.

After that, Mina didn't make any issues, but she didn't lie low either. On Fridays, when they reported on current events, she talked about newspaper articles that had interested her, like race riots in Cape Town in South Africa, where sixteen blacks had been killed, but for the first time the rioting had taken place within the white areas. That interested Mina, as did what was going on in Rhodesia. Mr. Bryce wanted them to concentrate on the election, so most everybody talked about the issues and the debates, week after week, because they knew that would get a good grade. Some of the boys reported on science, especially the Viking expedition, and on natural disasters, like Hurricane Liza. Bailey Wester had the reports Mina looked forward to. He always picked some obscure incident—like when Allied Chemical was fined thirteen million dollars for polluting the James River, or the time Serbo-Croatian Nationalists hijacked a TWA jet, with a fake bomb. But Mina was the only one Mr. Bryce kept saying it to: "The assignment was to cover the significant news."

When Mina saw on her first report card that her Social Studies grade was a C, she wasn't surprised. Mr. Bryce should have given her an A, she knew; all of her homework papers were perfect, all of her test papers were perfect. He wanted to fail her, she thought, but he didn't dare to. He didn't even dare give her a D. So he gave her a C and wrote a comment in the blank where teacher comments went: "Wilhemina is disruptive."

The whole thing just made Mina laugh. She guessed she'd gotten through to him, all right. It made her laugh also to see that whole row of A's, everything straight A's, even PE, and then this C. Everybody else had written something like "Excellent" or "Exceptional," and Mr. Bryce complained that she was disruptive. Well, maybe she was, if disruptive meant asking questions he couldn't answer or bringing up subjects he'd planned to avoid.

Mina thought everybody would be as amused by the report card as she was. She knew Mr. Shipp would be, and she wished she could tell him about it, to see him smile; but her parents took it seriously. There were just five of them at the table these days, with Zandor off partying his days away at college, if his letters told the truth. Belle and Louis had done what their parents expected them to do on their report cards, Louis mostly B's, Belle mostly C's. So Mina got the attention. As she twirled spaghetti around her fork and listened to them, Mina guessed she should have known they wouldn't think it was funny.

"You're awfully obvious about it," Belle interrupted, wiping tomato sauce from her chin with little dabs of her napkin. She wore a bathrobe to dinner because she was going out later, up to the mall in Salisbury with her current boyfriend. Belle changed boyfriends about as often, and as easily, as she changed hair styles. "I don't hear anybody complaining about *my* C's. It's pretty obvious about what you think of me."

Mina's parents let the subject get changed then, which told Mina that she might be in some real trouble. She caught Louis's eye on her, so she knew he agreed with her about that. She listened to Belle tell her parents about the movie she was seeing that night and who was going with them.

While Belle and Louis washed the dishes, and her parents had their evening cups of herb tea because coffee kept them awake at night, Mina had to stay at the table.

"What about this C?" Momma asked. Poppa sat and drank his tea and listened.

"He didn't have the nerve to flunk me," Mina announced, "which is what he really wanted to do. I'd have flunked me, if I'd been him."

"Why?"

"Because I have the nerve. If it was what I wanted to do, and if the only reason I didn't was because I was afraid of the repercussions."

"Has your work been that bad?" Momma asked. She was holding onto her temper.

"No. It's been good. Like perfect papers."

"Have you been disrupting the class?"

"No."

"He seems to think you have. I'd prefer the truth, Mina."

"I'm not lying," Mina said, getting a little angry herself. "You know that."

"I also know you're also not giving me any information," Momma snapped back.

Poppa drank at his tea.

Mina could see what her mother meant. That was fair enough.

"He's calling me disruptive because I ask him questions he doesn't want to answer."

"Like what?" Momma had to know exactly.

"Like—questions about blacks. It's supposed to be a history of Maryland, but he acts as if there weren't any blacks in the whole state. When I ask him, he kind of hesitates, and then he just goes right on with what he was already saying."

That defused Momma's anger, but she looked at Poppa as if she wanted him to say something in here.

"Are you the only one asking these questions?" Poppa asked.

Mina nodded.

"Are they all, all your questions, about black people?"

"Not all. He still doesn't answer. Like I asked him, why we didn't start studying with the Indians, because they were here first. And how the people in England could just give away things over here, like land, or trade rights. But mostly they are. About blacks." Mina wished she had a cup of tea or something to fiddle with her hands. Even her milk glass had been cleared away, so she just had a paper napkin. She couldn't rip up the paper napkin, because it was clean and could be used for another dinner. She laced her fingers together and unlaced them. She crossed her ankles and uncrossed them.

"What's he like, this teacher?" Poppa asked.

"White," Mina said. They didn't say anything. "He's the same one Zandor and Belle had; you know him. He knows who you are anyway."

"They didn't have any trouble with him."

"Yeah, well, maybe they didn't. I am, but it's nothing serious. Not serious for me anyway." Mina's spirits rose as she said this, because it was true.

Poppa reached over to cover the hand Momma had held out on the table. "Mina," he said, "we don't talk much about this—

it's not the kind of thing talking makes any difference to—but there are things that happen when you're a minority."

"But that's just it," Mina said. "More than half of the class is black. That's not a minority."

Neither of her parents said anything.

"Is it?"

"No," her father said. "But—in the whole country, we are. In history, we are."

"So what?" Mina said. "And what's so bad about being a minority anyway?"

Neither of them answered her.

"Besides, here we're not," Mina insisted.

"Which is one very good reason to be right here," her mother said.

"Is that true?" Mina wanted to know. "Poppa, is that true?" She heard how that sounded, calling him "Poppa" like she was a baby.

"There's a lot of truth to it," her father answered. "But, Mina, being a minority has only part to do with numbers. It has a lot to do with who has power, maybe more to do with that than anything else. Or money. And if you're black, you've got to understand that. You've got to accept the limits."

Mina didn't think she had to, and she knew she didn't want to. She wanted to ask them if they thought Mr. Shipp would say that, would agree with that.

"It's also possible that Mr. Bryce thinks you're trying to make him look stupid."

"As if he didn't know his subject," Momma explained.

"If he can't answer my questions then he doesn't, does he?" Mina asked, quite reasonably. They both kind of sighed. "He thinks I'm an uppity nigger," Mina said.

"Mina!" her mother said, quick and angry. Her father covered his eyes with his hand, which was a sign with him of being really troubled by something.

"I'm sorry, but what do you want me to do? Say 'Yes, sir' and pretend I look up to him, when I don't, just because he's the principal? Just because he's white?"

"I certainly do not," Momma said. Mina wasn't surprised.

"I only want you to understand what you're doing," her father said. He removed his hand and looked at her, straight in the eye. "I want you to understand what you're up against."

There was a silence, and the night lay dark outside.

"It has nothing to do with grades," her father said.

That melted Mina. She knew that. "I know, Poppa, I know. And I know it's hard on you, because your children are supposed to be better behaved and not get in trouble. I'm not disruptive. Honest. He's not much to be up against, come to think of it," she said, grinning, unable to stop herself.

Luckily, her parents seemed to find that pretty funny.

"That's not what Zandor and Belle thought," Momma said.

"I'm not Zandor and Belle," Mina pointed out.

"I know it. Don't I know it. You were bound to run into trouble, sooner or later. She was, Amos, we both know that. And, being Mina, sooner rather than later. I blame that camp, I do. I wish you'd never gone to that dance camp. I never liked it, not for a minute, but Irene said what an opportunity it was for you. . . . All right," she said to Mina's father, "I promised I wouldn't talk about it and I won't. I'll stop. But Mina—I *am* going to say this, Amos—have you ever thought that . . . there are men who don't like girls, women, to be too smart."

Mina never had.

"Read a little history, Mina. If you want to do some thinking about oppressed minorities, read a little history and think about women. Who didn't even have the power to vote until this century."

"But women aren't a minority," Mina protested.

"In terms of power they were. They still are. You said you knew what you were up against," Momma reminded her. "It's not just being black."

Mina was about sick of that word, black. It was a dark, heavy word. It hung down over their shoulders, like snow weighting down the long branches of pine. She was about ready to agree with Mr. Shipp that she liked the word "colored" because it covered everybody, from Mrs. Beaulieu with her mahogany-toned skin to her own father, whose skin was as dark as the bark on dogwoods, when the bark was wet with spring rain.

"And I'll tell you something else. Sometimes people will be prejudiced in your favor, just because you're black. Blacks, and whites too. And that's just as bad. It's never easy, Mina."

"I'll manage," Mina said.

CHAPTER 16

Mina managed, all that year. There wasn't a day went by when she didn't remember the man away up north. Sometimes she wanted to go to sleep, like a tree in hibernation, and come to life again in spring. Sometimes she was almost grateful to Mr. Bryce, because standing up to him made her almost forget. She didn't mind that Tamer Shipp would never love her, she just minded him being where she couldn't see him, or ever talk to him and know him better. She even wrote a letter to Alice that fall, not about anything important, but it felt—while she was writing—almost as if she was closer. The only answer she got was a Christmas card and the list of signed names didn't look like his handwriting.

It wasn't as if nothing was happening in her life. They had a fine Thanksgiving. Everybody came home for the holiday. Even Eleanor and John flew over for the long weekend, bringing little Mary and Lucas with them. John liked to work Christmas Day and New Year's, when he could make really good money. CS usually had some girl or some job, or both, to keep him away for Christmas. Thanksgiving was when the family really celebrated.

Mina and her mother worked for about two straight days, getting everything ready. Mina liked those long hours in the kitchen, working with her momma. They'd talk about different things, and it felt to Mina like Momma was about the best friend she'd ever had. That wasn't true, Mina knew, but it was true in a way.

There were things she never even hinted at, that she was thinking about, because her mother got het up when she thought her kids were being discriminated against, or left out of something, or acting in a way she wouldn't want them to. Momma got upset when somebody suggested she should spend more time on herself too, even if the someone was Mina. If Mina told her mother she ought to have a new dress, Momma would carry on about money and vanity and having made her choices about what was important. "I'll thank you not to try to reform a life I'm pretty proud of," she'd say. Even so, working and talking with her mother was one of the best times Mina had all that year. Momma liked it too, that was part of it.

While Mina worked the lard into flour to make pie dough, Momma doctored up jars of mincemeat. She didn't have time to make her own, but she always added her own ingredients to the store-bought, stirring it up hot on the stove, smelling it, adding some brandy, adding some raisins, adding this and adding that.

They all felt Miz Hunter's absence at the long table, with the food spread out and Belle's bowl of flowers moved to the sideboard because there wasn't room for it anymore. Poppa mentioned it when he was saying grace, after he'd thanked God for absent friends. "Gather into your bosom our friend Eustacia Hunter," Poppa said. "Amen."

"What's the church going to do with that house now, Dad?" Ellie asked. "Is somebody else going to move in?"

"Either that or we'll use it for church activities," Poppa said. He dished out potatoes while Momma carved the big turkey. CS had the vegetables. The plates started out empty and got filled up as they were passed along the table. "Youth fellowship, evening classes, Bible studies. We need more room. We're trying to decide if we need the room more than somebody might need the home."

John had Lucas in a high chair next to him, which was pretty distracting, but he asked, "How about one of these displaced families—Vietnamese or Cambodian? Central American?"

"They surely need homes," Poppa said. "But—well, their agencies aren't any too eager to take advantage of what a black church has to offer. In their way, they're right. Things are hard enough for foreigners in a strange land. We're also considering a kind of summer program, letting inner city families have the house for two weeks at a time."

"Isn't there someone like Miz Hunter who could live there?" Louis said. "She was like a grandmother or something, right next door."

"Most people don't want to go out to strangers when they get older," Momma told Louis.

Then they heard about John's promotion and listened to him try to puzzle out whether he wanted to take a desk job, which was the next step up. He wasn't sure how high a black man could go in the electric company, and because of that he wasn't sure that he wanted to stay on with them. CS was studying computers, because he figured there would be a good employment market anywhere you wanted to work. Zandor was all wrapped up with being a college man. He talked about his friends, he talked about parties and the athletics program; he didn't have much to say, as Momma remarked, about his classes. Over the pies, Zandor started in on Mina, telling her she ought to play some sport to keep herself in trim or no man—and especially Mr. Shipp, he said, winking at her, who had a wife that looked like Alice—would look twice at her. Zandor didn't listen to Mina saying she wasn't coordinated and would just as soon just take PE. "There's nothing but PE anyway that I can take," Mina said. This was getting oppressive and she wished he'd let it drop.

"What about one of the county summer tennis programs?

You could try one of those. Don't tell me you aren't coordinated, because you have to be to dance ballet. Coordination isn't the kind of thing you can lose."

Mina wondered. She didn't feel like going into it, about how she'd grown too big, outgrown her own frame. "I'll think about it," she told her brother, to shut him up.

"What'll it be then?" he insisted. "Track? Softball?" But she wasn't about to commit herself. Because he didn't know anything about her, "Develop a little competitive spirit," he advised, sitting back and lighting up a thin cigar. That was something else he'd learned at college: how to smoke a long thin cigar. He'd come home with a moustache that looked all right, and what he called a goatee, which was so wispy and stringy that it didn't take more than two hours to laugh him into the bathroom to shave it off.

All that vacation, the house was jam-packed with people. At night, there wasn't any room except the kitchen that didn't have somebody sleeping in it. Mina knew she was all interconnected with her family, like roots all interconnected underground, but she still felt different.

That feeling was made stronger by the job she got herself, babysitting every day after school. There were two kids, twins, first graders, two little blonde girls. Mina walked them home after school and kept them amused until their father got back from the store where he worked, or their mother came home from the real estate office where she worked. Mina didn't really want to work for whites, but blacks didn't hire babysitters. Black kids went to a friend's house, or a neighbor who was there to keep an eye on them, or an older sister or brother would have the job. So she wasn't surprised to find herself being interviewed by a white lady when she answered the ad. Mina made fifteen dollars a week and gave twelve of it to her mother. Because her mother took it, with thanks, Mina knew money was pretty tight.

She didn't much care for the people who employed her. They were the kind who would be an hour late without calling up, and they never paid her for extra time. They paid her on Fridays, the woman handing over the bills with a pursed-up mouth and pursed-up eyes, as if she was sorry they had to pay her anything. They'd have made great slave owners, Mina thought. They were like Mr. Bryce, in the effect they had on her. Mina was getting tired of her running battle with Mr. Bryce, bored by it, but she stuck with it. He thought she'd get worn down and start toeing his line; but Mina was more stubborn than that. It was only until June. She could keep it up until June.

Mina lived that year waiting for summer. She wondered if that was going to be the story of her life, just waiting out the year from September to June, so that her real life could begin in summer. There wasn't anybody who could really get through to her, because—because the only thing that really mattered to her was Tamer Shipp. So that, when one of the twins told Mina, "I don't like your color, its ugly," Mina didn't even mind. That surprised her: Even while she was getting angry enough to smack the kid, she didn't care what she'd said, not really. She didn't much care for white skin, if it came to that. It all looked to her like the undersides of fish at the market, like fish bellies. But Mina didn't say that. That would be fighting them at their own level.

She moved along all right among the whites in her school, even though she didn't care about them one way or the other. Maybe that was why they seemed to want to be friends with her, although she noticed they didn't invite her to their birthday parties or slumber parties. That didn't surprise her. She understood whites. But it wasn't so very different with her own friends, except in how she felt comfortable among them. She'd go along with whatever was going on, played spin-the-bottle in the coatroom during dances, went out roller skating and to movies with whoever asked, did a little kissing, a little flirting, and a lot of listening to peoples' problems, with their parents, with their boyfriends, with their girlfriends. Mina wondered if she'd known Tamer Shipp when he was in seventh grade, what he would have talked about.

The days and weeks rolled on by. Winter in Crisfield was a dismal season, wet and cold. What Mina liked best about winter was Sundays, with the warm church and choir singing and the big Sunday dinner after. Spring kind of dribbled in, one day a couple of green shoots, then a few forsythia blooms, maybe a daffodil in somebody's yard and a warm breeze up from the south for a day, and then you noticed that spring had already arrived and you'd missed it. Mina turned thirteen in the spring, and she had a hard time remembering she was that young. On the other hand, she couldn't believe she was already that old either. Inside herself, age had nothing to do with who she was. Let everybody else count up numbers as if they were real, as if they made a real difference.

Mina ended the year with all A's, even in Social Studies. That A meant, she knew, that she had worn Mr. Bryce down. She was class valedictorian at the graduation ceremonies, so she got to sit up on the platform, right next to Mr. Bryce. Mina enjoyed that.

But she was really waiting, and the time was coming closer: waiting for her father to pack up their car and drive away; waiting through two long days of cleaning, polishing up the Beerce house so that there wouldn't be a smallest corner, or a single windowpane, that wouldn't be sparkling clean. Mina did the work, singing aloud, and the other women sang with her. "O, what a beautiful city," she would start, on her knees with a scrub brush to get the linoleum clean. "There's twelve gates into the city, Hallelu-liah." That Halleluliah echoed around her heart, sounding like a whole orchestra was playing it.

* * *

On the day they were due to arrive, Mina waited on the front porch to greet the Shipps. Supper was ready, under cloths on the kitchen table. The icebox had basics in it, and the beds were made up. Mina sat in the expectant silence, entirely patient. She had told her employer that she wouldn't work that summer. The woman asked her to work full time, watching the little girls (and cleaning their house, and doing their laundry and "maybe a little cooking too, if you can cook—you do cook, don't you? We love fried chicken"). She'd find another way of making money. She didn't like the way the man teased her, calling her "Our Own Little Mammy." She had no immediate plans, but she had a couple of ideas. For now, all she wanted to do was say hello to Tamer Shipp and his family and know that he was right here in the Beerce house. She would ride home quickly; she'd promised her mother she wouldn't hang around long.

The corn was low in the field, just a fence of green. You could hear cars going along the road. Then one car turned into the dirt driveway. Mina stood up. Her heart thumped painfully.

The Shipps arrived quarreling, the way families do after a long drive. Samuel had punched Dream in the arm and Selma wouldn't move to sit between them, and Alice was almost in tears because she said Mr. Shipp wouldn't do anything to stop them fighting even though he knew how it wore at her nerves.

Mina looked at Mr. Shipp, standing beside the open door of his car, and she thought for a terrible minute she wouldn't be able to smile at him. He looked worn out and ground down. It wasn't just the droop of his shoulders, or the exhausted way his arms hung, or the way he wasn't saying anything. It was his eyes that got her. She remembered his eyes as looking out with a whole mix of feelings, but now he had stepped back from them, he was somewhere way behind them, as if he couldn't come out at all because it was too hard, and it would hurt too much. "Stop that whining, Alice, and do something useful," were the first words Mina heard him speak.

Everybody was surprised to hear that. The three children got silent. Alice got silent and then burst into tears and ran into the house. He didn't even look at Mina, as if he was ashamed to see her there.

Mina knew what he needed. "Mr. Shipp, why don't you go for a walk, up to the beach. We'll unload the car and get supper out onto the table. It's all cold, so you can eat it whenever."

The eyes looked at her from under his heavy eyebrows, but not even really seeing her, she thought. That wasn't important. "You look like the fresh air would do you good," she said.

He didn't answer, but he did shed his jacket, dropping it onto the hood of the car, and turned away.

Mina didn't wait to watch him move so slowly up and away, toward the creek and trees. She organized the two older children, telling Dream that if she'd just take her own suitcase up and unpack it, that would be all. Dream gave in.

There wasn't much Selma could carry, but Mina took some boxes out of the grocery bags so she could do something. They carried the bags in first, Samuel and Mina and Selma. Alice was sitting despondently on the sofa in the living room, with the skirt of her dress crunched up in her hands where she was using it for a handkerchief. Mina sent Selma out to get the tissues from the glove compartment for her momma, while they unpacked the staples the Shipps had brought down from New York.

"I'm glad to see you," Samuel said, putting spices into the cabinet.

"How was school?" Mina asked. She lined up a couple of wine bottles on the counter. "Did you like it?"

"There's an awful lot of sitting down," Samuel said. Mina started to laugh, and he laughed with her. "Wait'll you hear me read. Momma didn't want to come with us," he said.

Mina made murmuring noises, and they went back to unload suitcases and the boxes and bags of books and toys. She and Samuel unpacked the children's things into the bureaus and shelves. Dream, who seemed cheered up by the task of arranging her drawers, helped with the games and stuffed animals. When they went back downstairs, Alice was in the kitchen with a glass of wine, her eyelashes still damp but seeming to feel a little better. Selma was lifting the cloths and looking to see what was under them.

"Is that for dinner?" Alice asked. She had to know that it was, but Mina guessed she didn't want to say thank you, or something.

"Yes. I've got to be going now."

"You won't stay and visit? Where's your little friend, what's her name—"

"Kat."

"She's so pretty," Alice said.

"We'll come by soon. Promise," Mina said to Samuel and Selma. Dream stood beside her mothers chair, winding her fingers in her mother's hair. "Mr. Shipp went for a walk," she told Alice.

"He always does," Alice added.

Mina went outside. The evening was getting cool, the way June evenings did. In June, there were cool, dark nights after warm days. She looked up the pathway to the creek and saw Mr. Shipp returning. He was running.

Mina stared for a minute. He wasn't jogging, he was really running. It wasn't running away from something chasing him, or running to some destination. It was—just running. She lifted a hand and waved, but he didn't raise a hand to answer, so she guessed he hadn't seen her.

"Mr. Shipp looked terrible," she reported to her mother.

Momma was reading at the kitchen table, a big book about Mary, Queen of Scots. "Tamer always does, the first week or so—looks like a man after a war, or something."

"Raised from the dead, more like, and none too glad to be back," Mina said.

Mina's mother raised her face from the book and took off her reading glasses. The overhead light shone along the curls of her hair. She stared and stared at Mina, until finally Mina said, "What's so funny looking?"

"Oh. Oh, nothing. I wasn't really seeing you. Sorry, honey, my mind was elsewhere. We probably can't even imagine what Tamer's ministry requires of him, I was thinking that. Did you eat?"

"I'm not hungry."

For a wonder, Momma nodded and went back to her reading. Mina discovered she was hungry after all, and she cut some ham to make herself a big sandwich. She ate it out on the back porch, alone.

CHAPTER 17

The next morning, Alice and the children came by the house, bright and early. Louis took Dream and the little children out to the backyard to play, because Belle was sleeping in upstairs, while Alice sat down for a cup of coffee and a visit. "Tamer's already started out seeing people." She sighed. "I wanted to get these dishes back to you."

"We're glad to have you back," Mina's mother said.

"And Tamer said, last night, when he got back and saw how fast everything had been settled in—because he doesn't want me to feel tied down too much, because he says it's bad for a person to feel tied down—Mina, will you come work for me and help out? The children like you and you seem to have more patience than I do. We can't pay very much, just twelve dollars a week, but you can't get a regular job at your age anyway, can you? You're not sixteen yet, are you?"

"Far from it," Mina said. "Yes, thank you, I'd like that."

"Because Tamer said he wants me to take the High School Equivalency Test—do you know that one, Raymonda? The one that gets you a high school diploma. Because I never did get mine, so I'll have to study," Alice said. "And I'll have time to make more friends. So I'll be happier," she concluded happily. Mina just smiled at her, glad at the thought of working for the Shipps, amused by Alice's butterfly mind, the wings of which just touched things gently.

Mina liked the work. Early in the morning, when night coolness still filled the air, she would bike out to the Beerce farm. Mr. Shipp was usually gone by then, and everybody else was in the kitchen, finishing breakfast. Alice would let Mina know whatever plans she had for the day, if she had any. Together they'd get the house tidied, and then they'd do whatever. Alice went out in the afternoons. Somebody or other would come by in a car for her and she'd get in to go to the beach or to the mall or to a movie or just out for a drive. "I feel like a kid again," she said. "I didn't have much chance to be young," she told Mina. Dream always wanted to go along with her mother, and sometimes Alice took her. Rainy days they stayed inside. They played board games, or Mina read aloud, or they all baked and frosted a cake. Nice days they moved out of the small house, even if they only went as far as the porch. Alice wasn't doing much studying that Mina could see, but she'd come back from her outings all giggly and happy. She'd take off her high-heeled sandals and sit on the porch with a glass of wine, waiting for her husband to come home so she could tell him what she'd been doing. Sometimes Alice stayed out late for a movie, and Mina made sure Dream knew how to serve up the supper.

Mina didn't even see that much of Mr. Shipp, except she spent her days in his house with his family. She saw him in church, Sundays. Some evenings, if it was rainy, she'd stay and eat out there and he'd drive her home after supper. In late July, Alice went back up north for a week's vacation. Mina practically lived at the Beerce house then. That same week old Mr. Crofter died, and Mr. Shipp sat with him. Mina fed the kids and got them into bed and then sat out on the porch. Mr. Shipp would drive her into town when he got back. Dream was old enough to look after things for a few minutes. If he wasn't too late getting back, he'd ask Mina to wait while he had his dinner, which he'd bring outside to eat in the cooler air. Most of the time, when they talked, it was just about ordinary things, but the night Mr. Crofter died there was a change.

Mr. Shipp was sitting in the darkness of the porch. He was eating the tossed salad Mina had made. She could hear him crunching on the lettuce and celery and carrots. She was on the steps, feeling tired, feeling happy. In the dark air, fireflies flickered.

"I look at them," Mr. Shipp's voice came from behind her, "and I'm reminded—we're all like that, aren't we? Like fireflies in the black night of time."

Mina had her arms wrapped around her legs and her chin resting on her knees. In front of her the little yellow lights flicked on, flicked off. Maybe so, but why did he say night was black. The sky was black, the night was dark. Her mind drifted. She couldn't have been more contented.

"Mina, do you believe in God?"

His voice sounded all right, no longer strained the way it had when he first arrived. His eyes were back to normal. After a few weeks of summer, he was himself again. She'd watched that. But it was a strange question.

Mina had never thought about believing. "That's like asking me"—she tried to think of a true comparison—"if I believe in my own spinal cord. Or something." She turned around to look at the shadowy figure in the rocking chair. He'd taken his shoes and socks off, taken his jacket and tie off.

"I thought so," he answered. "Your father too, he has the same feeling. He wears his godliness like his own skin. Some men do. And women," he added, with laughter in his voice.

"Do you?" she asked him, meaning, do you believe. He knew what she meant, just as she knew that for some reason he needed to talk about this.

"I guess I must. Some people find Him easy, but not me. I don't seem to be able to leave Him alone."

"Does He want to be left alone?" Mina wondered. For once she felt her own spinal column, held straight as a habit from those years of ballet; for once she was aware of how it ran down her back and everything was built around its strength. Then she forgot it in the conversation.

"If I knew," Tamer Shipp's voice said. "For a long time, I was running away and He was chasing, and now I'm chasing and He's running away. I think, the way I go after Him, sometime He'll turn around and just belt me one, any minute now." He chuckled. "But I wonder about troubling Him the way I do. How can He be easy, the way the world is. How can I expect Him to be as simple as people are."

Mina didn't think there was anything for her to say.

"Do you think He has a purpose for you?" his voice asked her.

"I never thought about that," Mina said. "You feel like He might have one for you," she guessed, because it was only that feeling that would make him ask her that question.

"I wish I knew. I wish I knew that, and if I knew He did, I wish I knew what the purpose was," he said. Mina could feel how that question worried him. He didn't need her to say anything. He just wanted to frame the question into words, to get it out from inside her. "I guess I'd better take you home before Raymonda starts to get het up."

"She doesn't get het up when she knows where we are," Mina told him. But it was time for her to go.

After that, Mr. Shipp talked more with her, about all sorts of things, none of them really personal, but a lot of them more personal than personal. He talked about his children and what he hoped they'd be like. "I can almost see what they'll grow up like," he said. "Sometimes." They were walking down the driveway to the road. Mina was wheeling her bicycle, and Mr. Shipp was taking a walk, after sitting down all afternoon in a meeting.

"What about me?" Mina asked. She knew by this time that she could ask that kind of question.

"I don't know who you're going to be," he said, his eyes studying her, interested and sympathetic, with the readiness to laugh behind them. "You'll be yourself, that's all I know."

"T-rou-ble," Mina smiled.

"I expect so. Like Selma, she's another one coming along. It's funny, I thought it was my girls I'd be most anxious over, down in Harlem—"

"Down in Harlem, among the coloreds," Mina joked, remembering their first conversation and knowing he'd understand that she wasn't wising off.

"But it's Samuel. I wish he was stronger sometimes."

"He's plenty strong, mentally," Mina pointed out. The late afternoon heat was so thick that she moved in slow motion, her body filmed with sweat, sweat running down the sides of her cheeks and the backs of her calves, sweat oiling her arms. The macadam roadbed shimmered in the heat and showed what looked like pools of oil, but were only mirages.

"I don't know if that's enough," Mr. Shipp said.

"Enough for what?" Mina rested on her bike.

"Enough to . . . see him through to his own life?"

Mina didn't know the answer to that. She rode off, thinking. Samuel was her favorite, although Selma always handed her a kick. Dream—Dream was growing up into another Alice, so she'd find someone to look after her. Mina didn't turn around for a last look at Tamer Shipp.

Her family teased her about Mr. Shipp. She didn't mind, because they didn't know what they thought they knew, or what they knew wasn't even that close to the truth. "I've never met anybody like him," she told her mother. "Sometimes, I'm just so thankful we live now, and not before."

"He'd not have lasted long as anyone's slave, Tamer wouldn't," her mother agreed. "I'd have done all right, I think. I don't know about you, after your go-round with that Mr. Bryce. What do you and Tamer talk about?"

"Lots of things. His children. God. People."

"Somebody should be talking to him about his wife," Momma said. "She's drinking too much."

"Just wine."

"The trouble is, she's so crazy about him. She thinks she's not anywhere near good enough for him and she's afraid he'll see that. I feel sorry for Alice."

"I don't," Mina said. If she let the thoughts out, she was plain envious of Alice.

"He knows you've got a crush on him," Mina's mother said. They were in the kitchen, alone in the house with humid darkness wrapped around outside.

"He doesn't know you really do love him," Mina's mother said.

Mina didn't know what to say. She got up and poured herself a glass of orange juice. She took out the ice tray and slowly picked out a couple of ice cubes to drop into the glass. Half of her wanted to talk to Momma, talk from her heart. Half of her knew that there was nothing more to be said on the subject.

"Arrgblgh," was the sound Mina chose to utter, letting her mother think that whatever the words were, they were muffled by orange juice in her mouth.

Mrs. Smiths leaned back in her chair and just laughed, a sound that rolled like music around the room. "I could weep," she said, still smiling. "I feel for you, honey, and I'm so proud of you—you are such a trouble to yourself—but love gives what's best in us to us, I think. And I've been thinking, if you can give something to Alice of what's best in her. For Tamer. I don't know the situation, myself, but I do know you . . . so I thought I'd ask."

"They don't care about the same things," Mina said, sitting down, holding the glass of juice in both her hands.

"He'd be a hard man to be married to. He'd make you feel unworthy, if you were Alice. Not that he means to," her momma said. "I'm just asking, honey. I know you're only thirteen, I'm just wondering."

Mina tried to think about helping Alice, but she couldn't think of anything. She couldn't see herself telling Alice to be more thoughtful about things, and not care as much about good times as about God. She couldn't see herself trying to teach Alice the kinds of things Momma did for her preacher husband, to help him in his work, to help the church in its work.

August came again and with it a heat wave, broken by squally thunderstorms that rolled up the bay. When the storms came, Mina would go out onto the porch to watch them. She'd see the heavy clouds rushing across the sky and feel a sudden cold edge to the wind. The trees, leaning with the gusty winds, would turn up their leaves, showing the pale undersides. First the thunder would crack the sky apart, and then the rain would fall, beating its way into the soil. After the front passed, the rain would taper off, and then the sun would come out again. Steam rose in the yellow light, making the fields of corn like some tropical jungle country. The storms that passed during the heat wave never broke the edge of the day, they just made a temporary respite before things got worse. But the crops were growing well under this weather, the corn tall and tasseled, tomatoes swelling out ripe.

One Saturday afternoon, there was a movie up in Salisbury that Alice said she'd just die if she didn't see, so could Mina please come out extra? Mina had the three children at their little beach and Mr. Shipp came to join them. He had a towel around his shoulders and just his bathing suit on. His dark skin glistened with sweat. He dropped the towel beside Mina where she sat reading and belly-flopped into the creek. Water sprayed up around, and all three of his children threw themselves on top of him. He played in the shallow water with them, tossing them in, his deep laughter mingling with their shrieks of delight. Then he came out and spread his towel and sat beside her.

"That feels better," he said. He watched his children. "We're working you overtime. You can go home, if you like. You can stay, if you like. Whatever. It's a little cooler out here than in town. What're you reading?"

Mina showed him, *The Autobiography of Malcolm X.*

"What do you think of it?"

Mina thought. She wished she could think of something intelligent to say. But she couldn't. "It gets me so confused—I don't think, I just react. It's hard for me to believe it's true. It makes me glad I live here."

"I know what you mean. I prefer Baldwin, myself—James Baldwin," he said, to her expression. 'That man's got a soul. But I know about what this man's gone through." He put his hand on the book she had closed beside her.

"I don't," Mina said. "I'm glad I don't."

"This isn't a bad place to grow up. Cities are bad places for blacks to grow up in, or try to. I used to live here, years ago, did I ever tell you?"

"You said you went to school here."

"It was when we were first married and Dream was—just a baby, just a little baby. I finished my last two years of high school here. And collected a few bruises—those weren't easy years. But Alice had some family on her father's side, and she wanted to be near some family."

"So you already knew people when you came here," Mina said. That explained how he had so easily become a part of the community, of the church.

"I knew some people from school. Although, we're all so different now, grown up. It's easier now, around here, for blacks. For coloreds," he corrected himself, a private joke between them. She watched him as he watched the kids and the water flowing in the creek.

"I was quite an athlete in those days."

Mina looked at his broad shoulders. She could believe it.

"Tell you a story. You want to hear a story, Mina?"

His words sounded like he was teasing, but his voice didn't. Mina thought that, for once, he wasn't saying exactly what he meant and she listened.

"I always like stories," she said, waiting to hear whatever it was.

"I ran hurdles on the track team, and there was this white guy—Tillerman. Samuel Tillerman—he was on the track team too. I knew the kind he was, and I wasn't about to give him an inch. I hated him. Bullet, he called himself. He drove me—I never knew I could work so hard. The thing is, he taught me more about myself than anybody else, and in his own way, he won me the scholarship I needed, for college. And I never loved anybody the way I loved him."

It didn't make any sense, and it made perfect sense. But what was the story? "What happened to him?" Mina asked. "Where is he now?"

"Dead. Killed. In Vietnam," Tamer Shipp said. His adam's apple moved up and down. "When I heard that—I've never—it was like teeth in my heart."

Mina was shocked: She knew that exact feeling, and those exact words for it.

Mr. Shipp looked over at her. "I guess that's a little too fanciful for you to stomach." Mina shook her head, unable to find words to say anything. "Or because he was white, and prejudiced—because he was. Well, it shocked me too, Mina, to feel that way."

Mina nodded her head, because she knew the feeling, however different the cause was. She waited for him to tell what happened.

"Even now, it's years ago, whenever I think of it, think of him—those teeth bite in. That grief—it doesn't ease up. I don't know why, and I don't even know if I want it to. But whenever—"

"I'm sorry," Mina finally said. That wasn't anything to say, but there was nothing else she could say. She meant it, for what that was worth—those teeth had left her heart alone for a long time now. He called it a story, but he didn't tell it like a story. He told it like—like for once, this was something he couldn't set his mind to and make orderly sense out of. Mina had listened to his mind, Sundays in church, and she knew how strong and true it was. But this, this Bullet thing—she couldn't call it a story—this he couldn't even tell in an orderly way. This lay at his heart; she could hear that in his voice and in the ways he couldn't talk about it, and it hurt him. And there was nothing she could do or say to ease him. "I'm sorry," she said again.

"I am too, sometimes. Life would have been easier if I'd never met him," Mr. Shipp said. "You want to hear a piece of naked vanity? I always wished I'd been able to save him. Not save his soul." He turned to smile at Mina and she thought if ever she came to meet Jesus, she'd have already seen His eyes. "Only save his life. His soul was—just fine."

"It's Bullet you named Samuel after, isn't it?" Mina said.

"You have a phenomenal way of seeing into the corners of a story, Mina."

"I guess so," she said. She didn't tell him that she always

studied every word he spoke, each gesture, anything he did, or . . . until she could etch him into her memory without her even trying.

Mr. Shipp's eyes were on his children, splashing cool in the creek.

"Who was he? What was he like?" Mina thought if she had a picture of him in her mind she could understand more.

"I never knew anything about him, really. We weren't what anybody would call friends. His family had a farm around here, I think. They hated blacks, I guess. But he wasn't the kind of man you think of as having any family at all," Mr. Shipp said. "Hard. He was hard. I think God might be hard like that. Because there wasn't a false bone in his body. Then he got killed off, in that useless, senseless war before . . . You should have seen him run, Mina, he was—it wasn't that he was good, although he was good, really good. He was just so—right. To watch him move . . . it was so right. I admired that boy, and he got to respect me, I'm pretty sure of it. But—"

"You said he was someone you knew," Mina remembered.

"I knew him," Mr. Shipp said. "I never met anyone like him, and I wish he'd have lived, so I could have known him."

He turned his head back to look at Mina again. She wasn't crying, although she felt like it, like weeping—for this dead young man and for whatever grief Mr. Shipp was carrying around. But if she started in crying that would get in the way of her listening.

"Do you love God, Mina?" he asked her.

Mina didn't know what to say. He was asking her about why God let things happen like Bullet Tillerman being killed; he was reminding her that God wasn't easy, it was God who made blacks and whites; and he was telling her that this was a question he was asking himself. He was wondering all these things because of Bullet. Mina didn't know what she could say to ease Mr. Shipp so she told the truth. "I think I don't know much about love," she said. And she didn't, although she also did.

Tamer Shipp was looking at her and looking at her. The children laughed and splashed before them, and the air was muggy all around them, filled with bug noises; but in all the world, all Mina heard was what he said to her without saying a word.

He knew she loved him, and he wished she didn't because that was hard on her, but he was glad she did too. Mina was glad herself to read that gladness as part of his glance, but she pulled her eyes away. It was bad enough that Mr. Shipp had Bullet in his heart, to pain him, and she could see now—see what it would be to meet something that might be the best and have it just wiped out, erased, taken away so you couldn't ever know it. Ended and finished as if it had no value. With nothing left behind.

Mina wasn't about to add in any small way to what Tamer Shipp was troubled by. The world troubled a black man enough; it had troubled this man enough.

She heard Mr. Shipp chuckle, but she kept her eyes on Dream dancing around in the knee-high water of the creek in a bright red bikini, even though she didn't need the top yet.

"I'm like the ancient mariner," his laughing voice said, sounding normal again. "Except I never did tell anybody straight out before."

Mina didn't say that she didn't think she'd been told anything straight out, because she knew he was changing the subject. "Who's the ancient mariner?"

"In a poem. You'll read it."

"A black poem?"

"No, Coleridge."

"Do you ever wonder," Mina asked, while half of her mind was busy being amused that this subject was safe ground for conversation, "why there aren't many black poets?"

"I've thought about it," he said. "In this century, there are some," he reminded her. Then he said, "That dance camp really got through to you, didn't it."

Thinking about his Samuel Tillerman, Mina shook her head. "Nothing like they could have," she said.

"Miss T-rou-ble. I bet you got through to them more than they did you."

"I don't think so," Mina told him. She watched Selma move out to knock Dream over and end the dance. The little girl's concentrated glance never wavered from her sister as she plowed through the water. "Selma!" Mina called. "Don't you do that, you hear me?"

Selma stopped, looked at Mina, then turned back to the shore. Samuel splashed water at her and she joined in the new game.

Mina took the subject even farther away. "What about Alice and this equivalency test she told us about. When does she take it?"

"You take it whenever you think you're ready. Why?"

"Why do you want her to?"

"It'll be a good thing for her."

"To know that stuff?"

"No. I'd just like her to know she has a high school diploma. Alice could find work, something to do with retail clothing, if she had a diploma. She'd like the work, and she'd like herself a little better. That's my way of thinking about it. I like her fine, but she doesn't like herself so much. You know?"

Mina didn't know, but she could understand, she thought. Alice had no idea, she thought. Alice thought Tamer was ashamed of her, that he wanted her to improve herself. And Alice thought she'd fail.

Mina had seen some of those test booklets in the library, set on a whole shelf of test booklets for different jobs. She'd take a look at one, and see how hard it was. Alice loved her husband enough to try, if she thought she had a chance to pass. Mina thought she'd take a look at the questions and see if it would be fair to persuade Alice to study for it. At least there was something she could do something about for Mr. Shipp.

CHAPTER 18

The more Mina thought about it—and she thought about it a lot—the more she wondered about this Samuel Tillerman. It wasn't anything Mr. Shipp had exactly said that made her want to know more. It was his voice, the sound of his voice. Thinking about it, wondering about it, listening to his voice in her ear's memory, Mina tried to understand what she'd heard. His voice had been like—a bassoon. Usually his voice was like a cello, melodious and round. But this wasn't his usual voice, when he talked about Samuel Tillerman. There were new resonances, and his voice got heavier. It was as if he opened up his chest and spoke out of his secret heart.

Mina knew about secret hearts in people. But if she were to do what she had never done, talk to someone about Tamer Shipp, she didn't think her voice would change in that particular way. Mina thought probably he carried a grief that was both sharp and long in him. Like a bassoon where you could always hear that it could go higher or lower even though it didn't actually do that, he hadn't ever built up any edges for this grief. There was no missing a bassoon, even in a full orchestra, as it played its notes out.

Thinking of all that, Mina smiled to herself, and then laughed within herself: She guessed that dance camp was turning out to be good for something, if it was helping her to understand why what Mr. Shipp had told her troubled her so. She wished, for Mr.

Shipp, that what lay at his secret heart was as good as what lay at her own secret heart. She wished there were such things as healing hands and that she had them and that she could lay them on Mr. Shipp, on this grief. She wondered about Samuel Tillerman.

One September night, just before school started, she asked her parents. "Did you ever hear of anyone called Tillerman, any family around here?"

"I don't think," her mother said. "Why? Is this somebody you've met?"

"No," Mina said.

"There's one I know of," her father said. "She's a widow, and I don't think she has any children. She's a strange one." Her father was taking a week off again, a vacation with his family after the long summer.

"Strange?" Mina asked him.

"A hermit, or as near as makes no difference. She almost never comes out and the farm is going slowly to ruin. It was never much, but now it's rundown. Neglected. She doesn't have a car or anything. She keeps entirely to herself. Kind of wild-looking, she brings a boat into town maybe three times a year. You've probably never seen her, Raymonda."

"Is she the one who smashed the window at the phone company?" Minas mother asked. "Is she dangerous?"

"Is she crazy?" Belle wanted to know.

"I couldn't say," Poppa told them. "I'd hate to say, seeing as I don't know anything about her. I expect she's just terribly alone. Her people just—just let her be alone. Whatever made you ask, Mina?"

"I heard the name," Mina said, "and I wondered." She guessed someone who was a widow could have had a son. But she couldn't think of anything to be learned by trying to talk to some crazy old white hermit lady.

"I don't understand how her people can just leave her alone like that," Poppa said.

"When I get to be a crazy old lady," Momma said, "I expect you all to take good care of me."

"Then you better not get too crazy," Belle answered. "I don't want to have to explain to my children that their old granny is a nut case."

"I'll take care of you, Momma," Louis promised.

"Why should you get crazy?" Mina asked.

"For one thing, if I do, then I can do all the things I've wanted to, and nobody will make me feel guilty. I can sit around and eat chocolate bars and read until my eyes pop. I can—oh—say what I think the way I think it and nobody'll take me seriously enough to give your father grief about his nasty wife. Life might be a lot easier."

"Then who'll take care of me?" Poppa asked.

"I will," Momma told him. "For you I won't be crazy. Or maybe you won't know the difference."

"I'm glad to know that the perils of our old age together are so well planned." Poppa laughed.

"It's the perils of this coming year I'm having trouble with. If Zandor loses his scholarship—"

"That'll be his own fault. For playing around so much," Belle said.

"That's no consolation," Momma answered. "I don't know where we'd get the money to make up the difference."

"If Zandor does let his grades slip and loses the scholarship," Poppa announced, "he will have to make up the difference himself. But I doubt he will. He's a quick student, even if he's not dedicated."

"Besides, he can work, he got himself a job for the summer, so he must be serious about getting through college," Mina reminded her parents. Like CS, Zandor found summer work up near school, where pay was better.

"Admit it. Aren't you glad now you've got one child who doesn't want to go to college?" Belle asked.

"You know, I'm not sure I am," Poppa said.

"It's up to her, Amos," Momma repeated her old argument. "I can see why Belle would rather do a secretarial course and work in Washington, or some large city. Crisfield doesn't have that much to offer by way of marriageable young men."

"Mother!" Belle protested. "You act like all I think about is getting married."

"Why shouldn't you?" her mother asked. "You'll do a good job of it and you'll like it. As long as you've taken some training, you'll have skills should you need employment."

"You make me sound like . . . like Alice," Belle muttered. "With that equivalency test."

"Oh no," Momma said quickly. "Alice is ever so much prettier."

"You don't ever take me seriously," Belle said. But Mina was already laughing, and Mina's laughter carried the day.

Momma was genuinely worried about money. She didn't know where Louis's new school clothes were going to come from, and she kept looking worriedly at Mina, who at least seemed to have stopped shooting up and out. "Maybe you've done all your growing," Momma said.

"I don't mind not having new clothes," Mina told her. She didn't either. Her old clothes were just fine. Denim never went out of style. "Mine still fit." There was that hollow feeling these days, since the Shipps had packed up and driven north again. She'd get used to it, she knew, but it felt pretty hollow and bad, for now.

"You aren't nervous about starting the high school?" her mother asked.

"No," Mina said. "Besides, it's really only eighth grade and—I don't expect any trouble." She didn't know what she expected, except to get top grades. She only knew that she didn't plan to sit quiet. She planned to enjoy herself, somehow, as she waited through the school year until next summer arrived. She figured that her position in the class was a sure thing, even with new people coming in from the other elementary school. It wasn't, she hoped, that she was conceited or overconfident; she just knew herself. She recognized that most people didn't have her amount of personality. That's what they meant when they said t-rou-ble.

Mina was even looking forward to school. She'd talked some to Alice about the questions in the practice test booklet, and that had gotten her going. There was a lot she didn't know, and it was about time she started learning it. Mina was also looking forward to getting back in with her friends, finding out what they'd done over the summer, who was going with whom, who'd gotten up to what with whom. On the first morning, she sat down in a desk in homeroom with her new notebook in front of her and thought how funny it was that CS was a senior in college and she was just beginning high school. She was one of the first people in the room, before even the teacher. She watched people drift in.

Kat and Rachelle and Sabrina all sashayed in together, looking all brand new, shoes, skirts, and blouses. They sat with Mina, making a little cluster of conversation. "You sure do look fine," Mina said. She was wearing one of Zandor's outgrown cotton shirts and a denim jumper that had worn down to a soft, bleached-out blue. "What did you do to your hair?" she asked Kat, whose head looked like something from one of Alice's magazines, short in the front and brushed back sleek into a kind of tumble of long curls down the back.

"It's a permanent. Isn't it neat?" Kat turned her head so Mina could admire it.

"Not neat, terrific looking," Mina said. Kat just got prettier and prettier. It was a pleasure to look at Kat.

"I'm going to make my mother let me have one," Sabrina said. "Rachelle's half asleep after a heavy date, right 'Chelle?"

Rachelle just smiled, as if she had a big secret.

Mina felt so good, she felt like laughing. Instead, she started out talking, not bothering to keep her voice down. "I've got it figured out," she said, talking to her three best friends and anybody else who might care to be listening, ignoring the teacher at the front of the room, in her blue suit with an ironed blouse and a little pin on her lapel. "I'm going to sit up front, right about here, in every class. By the door."

"Why?" Sabrina asked.

"If you sit up front, they think you're really interested, so they assume you must be a good student, so they expect you to get good grades, so that's what they give you. And you can get out quickly when the bell rings, that's two. And, you can sort of angle around in your seat," Mina demonstrated, "and watch everything that's going on, without looking like you're not paying attention. In fact, they take that to mean that you're really interested. How do you think I get my A's?"

Everybody around was listening. She could hear that. "Hey, Mina," people from her old school greeted her. "Where you been?" She smiled and waved and greeted them back. "Hey, how was your summer?"

The homeroom teachers name was Miss Eversleigh. She was pale, washed-out looking, with her washed-out-looking suit and her plain pumps, and her washed-out-looking hair held away from her face with combs, and her washed-out fish-belly face. She held her thin body straight and wouldn't say a thing until everybody was absolutely silent. Mina had her figured in less than a minute: a female Mr. Bryce. She had a flat, fish-belly voice.

They were having a long homeroom, Miss Eversleigh told them. There were four forms to fill out—one card for the school office, one for the counselor, one for the PE department, and their class schedules, of which they needed to make four copies from the master she would give them, one for the office, one for the counselor, one for the PE department and one for themselves. The master schedule, she pointed out in her flat voice, was her own copy, one she had made herself.

Mina looked up at that. There were about—she counted—thirty-eight kids in this homeroom. That was an awful lot of extra work for a teacher. She was sorry for Miss Eversleigh if she didn't have anything more interesting to do with her time than fill out those thirty-eight schedules.

They were supposed to do the schedules first, step by step. Miss Eversleigh told them what to put on each line at the top and in each box for the periods of the school day. They were supposed to all work together.

Mina went on ahead and filled her schedule out, then made three more copies. The rest of the class was on sixth period Tuesday when she finished her last copy, so she went on ahead to fill out the two student information cards. Name and address, parents' occupation, previous school, religious affiliation. There was a place for sex, circle M or F. There was a place for race, circle W or B or Other (specify). Mischief rose up in Mina. She thought of filling in Other, specifically colored. Or maybe specifically *homo sapiens.* She wondered if they'd notice if she inserted Other (specify) under sex. When they asked her to say if she planned on going to college, she thought of asking them back how she was supposed to know at her age. There was a final blank, Track Level. Mina couldn't figure that out, so she shuffled her papers until she came to her schedule. Track Level A, she saw, and filled that in. She hoped it meant what she thought it meant. She figured this homeroom was operating at about Track Level Z.

Thinking that made her chuckle. Chuckling brought Miss Eversleigh, who was going up and down the aisles checking, to Mina's desk. "Now," Miss Eversleigh said, "once again fill in your lunch period." Her pasty white hands came down on Mina's papers.

Mina watched the teachers face as she looked the papers over. Mina expected a lecture, and she hoped it wouldn't be a long one. She knew she deserved a little trouble, because Miss Eversleigh had been pretty specific about not going ahead.

But the pale eyes just studied her for a minute. "You'll stay quiet," Miss Eversleigh said.

"Yes, ma'am," Mina answered, giving her word. She thought that was fair enough. She settled back to think, not looking around her at all.

In the limited time she had, Mina let her mind dwell on Mr. Shipp. Her memory settled on that day there were just them at the creek, and she played it back slowly to herself, from the minute she felt his towel drop beside her. She could almost see Bullet. He'd have bright blond hair and blue eyes, a strong build; her imagination couldn't make him run. Mostly she heard Tamer Shipp's bassoon voice. She heard that voice playing over her different feelings like wind playing through the leaves of a tree. For a minute, she wished, she really wished—

The bell rang, and they handed in their cards and filed out into the hall. Mina had signed up for tennis, she wasn't exactly sure why since she'd never played it and didn't have a racquet. But she'd heard of Arthur Ashe and Yvonne Goolagong. After this first day, she'd start each day off with tennis. Then she'd have classes, Math, Science, Social Studies, English and Home Ec. All the girls had to take Home Ec, no matter what your track level was. All the boys had to take Mechanical Drawing.

These were minors, half as important as the major courses, Miss Eversleigh had told them. Miss Eversleigh was the Home Ec teacher. Mina wondered how she'd do in Home Ec, because she already knew an awful lot about it, from her life.

As the first morning crept by, and she filled in sign-up sheets for textbooks and heard what they'd be doing all year, she noticed that people in this school stuck together pretty close. There were also more white people than black, because the other elementary school was kids from the other side of town. They were better dressed, a lot of the girls, and most wore makeup. Boys wore jeans, whoever they were. Most girls wore skirts, but some wore jeans.

People stuck with their friends in classes, Mina noted, settling down at a high table in Science, watching how the white kids all gathered together, even pulling an extra stool over if there was somebody extra. She guessed she was really in a minority now, although—she counted heads while the teacher called out roll—she didn't see how you could be that much of a minority if—the teacher called, "Wilhemina Smiths," and she answered, "Here"—you numbered a third of the total. "Tillerman," she heard the teacher call out.

Mina stared at him, registering the name too late to turn and see what voice from the back answered, "Here." She swung her head around, scanning the faces. The trouble was, they looked so alike, whites. They all had these bones on their faces that looked like they'd break with one good slug. Well, not all, but most. They all sat so joined together, except for the sullen looking kid in a T-shirt. Mina looked at the boys in the class, trying to match up one of the faces to the story Mr. Shipp had told. That was pretty stupid, since the young man was long dead. She thought she'd pay more attention to roll call from here on. This was a Track Level A course, so he might be in English. If not, she'd know tomorrow, during Science.

Mina watched people settle into desks for English, while the teacher humped and bobbled around behind his desk, with his bright red hair sticking up and his face pretending that the paper-shuffling was Important. There were some whites she recognized from earlier classes, and that sullen kid again, a girl. Mina had no trouble remembering her because she wore cut-offs—about the only person in the whole school in them—and she looked so poor, with her sneakers that should have been thrown out about seven years ago. The girl kept her eyes on her desk, sitting alone at the rear of the room. Mina felt sort of sorry for her. She didn't know anyone and she looked, from her face, as if she was probably in the wrong track level. She looked half asleep, or as if her mind was permanently elsewhere.

Mr. Chappelle called roll slowly. This was a trick some teachers had, if all they wanted to do on the first day was hand out textbooks and thus get one more day of vacation time for themselves. He went creeping through the alphabet, asking questions about nicknames, making slow notes on his roll book, killing time. Mina had trouble sitting still it was so boring.

"Wilhemina Smiths?" he asked, looking over at the blacks as if he already knew she'd be there.

"Here." She raised her hand.

"Are you Isabelle's sister?"

Mina nodded, wondering if he thought she was going to be like Belle. If so, he had a couple of things to learn.

"And Alexander's?"

"Yes." He must have been teaching for a while.

"I've been teaching for a while in this school," Mr. Chappelle said, and Mina had to stop herself from laughing out loud. He was saying that to show off to the rest of the class. "Moreover, Reverend Smiths is a distinguished member of our community," he said, with a smile for Mina.

Thanks a lot, she thought to herself, hearing the muttering among the kids she didn't know. She didn't want them to get the wrong ideas about her, to get off on the wrong foot with her, all these people. "Don't hold that against me," she said to Mr. Chappelle, smiling broadly at him so he wouldn't take her for fresh.

A few people chuckled. He hesitated, before going on in his roll call.

"Steven Stevens—I guess your parents like that name," he called out. Mina waited through this last S and a Terrence and wasn't surprised when he called, "Dicey Tillerman."

The kid in cut-offs raised her hand. Dicey? Mina thought. Bullet? What kind of names did these people have. If they were even related, she reminded herself.

"I don't know anything about you," Mr. Chappelle said.

Everybody turned around, staring. Mina waited to hear the answer.

Dicey Tillerman thought at first she wasn't going to have to answer. Then, she saw that he was going to make her answer, and her eyes snapped angry. She was scrawny, but no mouse, Mina decided.

"I'm new to town," she said.

"Would you like to tell us about yourself?" Mr. Chappelle asked, looking at the clock to see how much more time he had to kill.

The girl's chin went up. "No," Dicey Tillerman said.

Mina grinned. She thought she might like to know more about this Dicey Tillerman, whether she turned out to be one of Tamer Shipp's Tillermans or not.

CHAPTER 19

When Mina showed up at PE the next morning in gym shorts and sneakers, she discovered that of the ten girls taking tennis, she was the only black. Four of the others were obviously best friends, and the remaining five all wanted to get into that group. Mina didn't know any of them. They all came from the other feeder school. None of them was at all interested in her.

The coach was a tall, rangy woman, who bounced on the toes of her sneakers as she demonstrated, and her short hair bounced on top of her head, and her words bounced around as she handed out racquets to those girls who didn't have them (the four had brought their own) and showed them how to grip for the forehand. Her name was Mrs. Edges and she was so tan she looked as if she must have spent all day all summer out playing tennis somewhere. Her eyes kept going to Mina where she stood at the end of the line of girls. Mina could see why: When they came to divide themselves up over the three tennis courts to practice hitting, everybody went somewhere else than where Mina stood. Mrs. Edges finally called out, "There's room for one more girl over here," and waited through a long two or three minutes, before saying, "Bonnie, come over here."

Bonnie was one of the outsiders, the furthest outside. When she was told to hit with Mina, she did it. Nobody said anything.

Nobody needed to. Mina felt like she had been transported

back to dance camp, that second summer. The first summer too; only she had been too dumb to notice it. She wondered if she should try to switch into a regular PE class, which was what her friends were taking. Swinging her racquet, she got one ball over the net, where it plopped just beyond Bonnie's reach. Bonnie forgot to move, so she swung and missed. She giggled and looked at the other two courts to see if anyone wanted to join in the joke.

"Hey!" Mina called. "Over here, I'm over here. See if you can hit it to me."

On her third try, Bonnie succeeded in getting the ball over the net. Mina watched it, moving toward where it was going to land at mid-court and got her racquet back in time to stroke at the ball. The return went to Bonnie's backhand and she stood still, watching it go by.

Mina almost groaned aloud. This was going to be a real drag, a waste of her time. She didn't know what she could do about it.

Mina also didn't seem to be able to figure out how to meet Dicey Tillerman. After a week of school, she hadn't even said hello to the kid, which was strange even if Dicey was a white. People at least pretended they didn't notice black and white. Dicey always wore the same clothes, except they got cleaned in between wearings. She always sat at the back of the class, without seeming to pay any attention, but she always knew whatever answer the teacher called on her for. Mina tried to catch her eye, but Dicey didn't look at anybody. She moved around on long skinny legs, with her toes showing through holes in her sneakers, as if she was alone in the world. Mina watched her, going down a hallway or moving across a classroom to her desk. Mostly, her face was expressionless, but sometimes it seemed to wake up, or come alive, if something interesting was going on. What interested Dicey, and this interested Mina, was never anything the kids got up to; it was something that somebody said, a teacher or a kid. This had happened only in Science class, so far. Dicey obviously hated Home Ec, but did the diagramming in English without any trouble. Mina learned some about Dicey by keeping an eye out for a chance to start a conversation. But she never got that chance. Dicey kept herself clear of everyone.

Mina asked around a couple of times, but wasn't surprised to hear that nobody knew anything about Dicey. She didn't seem to fall in with any group—she was a minority of her own, Mina figured, watching the dark eyes across the class as they observed what Mr. Chappelle was doing and then turned to the sky and treetops outside the window.

Mina figured she had all year, she had time. Meanwhile, she had her own life to lead. She didn't drop tennis, because she liked it. She liked pulling the racquet back and then swinging it forward, using her whole arm for the stroke, using her strength and her weight to stroke it properly. Mrs. Edges often volleyed with her, letting the rest of the corps de ballet (as Mina called them in her mind) arrange themselves on the other courts.

Kat's advice, given as they walked home from church together the second Sunday after school started, was to switch to PE. "It isn't bad, we're doing gymnastics now. You're good at that, you always were."

"I stopped being good at it."

"Is that what happened? At least, you never work up much sweat in PE," Kat continued. She was walking with small steps, because she wore low heels now to church. Mina watched Kat. It always rested her eyes to watch Kat.

"Katanga Beaulieu," Mina said, "you're—you could be a model, I bet."

They weren't in any hurry. It was a muggy day at the end of a muggy week, and Momma was serving a cold chicken salad for lunch.

"You always know, before I tell you anything," Kat answered.

"If I were old-fashioned, I'd think you used voodoo. Because that's what I want to do, and I think I could. Models make an awful lot of money. My dad says he'll send me to modeling school, when I get old enough. But he thinks I ought to wait until I'm older, out of high school. He says, if I promise to finish school then he promises to send me to the best modeling school I can get into."

"That's great," Mina said.

"But it's all so long away. Anyway, there's a beach party tonight. Do you want to come?"

"I don't know."

"It might be one of the last. You ought to. If you do, you have to bring something to drink or something to eat. You could make brownies. I bet Bailey Westers would like it if you came."

"Maybe I will. Not for Bailey Westers, though." Mina enjoyed the parties. She always enjoyed getting together with people, the youth fellowship group or just a bunch of people gathered around a fire on a beach. They'd bring radios and dance, and some couples would slip away for a little private necking, but you could say no easily, in a group with no particular dates, to someone who asked you to go walking on down the beach. Mostly Mina said no, because . . . anyone who wasn't Tamer Shipp was just someone who, when she closed her eyes, she might be able to pretend for a minute was Tamer Shipp. Which wasn't the same.

What Mina didn't like about these parties was the conversations the next day, about how far a girl ought to go with a boy, if she loved him, if she only liked him a lot, and the kinds of questions they asked each other. "Have you French kissed much?" Mina always interrupted those conversations with jokes—"No tongues!" she would cry, her hands up in horror—but she couldn't interrupt them for long. Sometimes she went to the parties, sometimes she went out on dates, and sometimes she stayed home.

"Boys like you," Kat said to her that day, walking slowly home from church. "I think because they know you're not going to be serious."

"I think it's my maternal streak," Mina said. "They tell me all their troubles."

"I want a big wedding, with a dozen bridesmaids and a band at the reception," Kat said. "Do you?"

"I never thought about it. We can't afford it anyway. How's your aunt?"

Kat's aunt Grace, her mother's sister, had moved in with them temporarily, to get over her divorce. "She's bored. She says there's no night life and she's going to wither on the vine. Just what Dad said she'd say after three weeks with us. I think she's going to move to L.A."

"Like Miss LaValle. I wonder what there is about the West Coast."

"It's more integrated, I think. Like Paris, or Europe; they don't even care about mixed marriages, can you imagine?"

"What do you think happened to Miss LaValle? Do you ever wonder?"

"Nobody ever heard from her, after a couple of letters. She was always so sad. I'd never let a man live with me without marrying me. Would you?"

Mina thought about that. "It would depend on the man," she said. She really meant, it would depend on how much she loved him, but she didn't tell Kat that. Kat wouldn't know what she meant, not yet. "Like how rich he was."

"You don't mean that." Kat laughed.

Mina asked her father, one night out of the blue, because even she didn't know where the idea came from, if he'd mind if she stopped calling him "Poppa."

"What did you have in mind?" he asked. "'Father' sounds distinguished. I like father."

The boys called him "Pop," but that didn't sound right to Mina either. "Dad," she said.

"You already used to call me that, once," he reminded her. "You don't need my permission."

"It's just that Poppa sounds so childish."

"And Dad sounds more white, is that why?" her mother asked.

"No," Mina said. "I wouldn't make that mistake again."

"Oh?" her mother asked, looking at her father.

"I know what that kind of significant look means," Mina told them both, letting them know she didn't much care for it. Parents had a way of dragging up dead history against you.

Momma almost took offense, then she started laughing. "Oh, I do like the way you're growing up, Mina. You're growing up to be quite something."

Mina wondered if quite something was the adult version of t-rou-ble. She thought she'd rather be t-rou-ble, because it seemed more honest to her. But she didn't tell her parents that.

Louis turned ten that week and had a birthday party and gave Mina more information about Dicey Tillerman. He had made out his list of ten guests, one for each year of his life, and presented it to Momma, who would have to give the party, and to Mina, who would bake a rocket-shaped cake for him. "Willy and Josh," they read down the list, recognizing familiar names. "But who's Maybeth?"

"She's a girl," Louis explained. They didn't say anything. "She's in third grade." Mina and her mother exchanged a look. "They just moved to town."

"What church does she go to?" Momma asked.

"I don't know."

"Where does she live?"

"I don't know."

"It doesn't sound like you've talked to her at all. How come you want to ask her to your party?" Mina asked.

"She's pretty," Louis told them. He made himself look back at them as if it was nothing, but he had a goofy smile on his face.

"What will Dream say?" Mina teased. But Louis did like pretty girls. She didn't blame him. She liked to look at handsome boys herself.

"Dream just teases me anyway. Maybeth is nice."

"Will she mind being the only girl?"

"I don't know." Louis's eyes filled with tears. "Please let me."

"I guess, if you really want to—" Momma waited. She knew already, as Mina did, that Louis would stick by what he said. He was quiet, but he had a way of knowing what he wanted. He nodded his head. "What's her last name, we'll look her up in the phone book."

"Tillerman," Louis said.

"But—" Mina objected. She tried to communicate with her mother, but her mother must not have made any connection. "But, Louis," Mina asked carefully, "isn't she white?"

"I don't mind."

"Oh, but, Louis," Momma joined in. "You've got to consider the little girl's feelings, honey. She'll be the only girl, the only third grader, and the only white person. Use your imagination, Louis. Can you be sure she'll have a good time? Can you promise her she'll be glad she came?"

Louis shook his head sadly. His mouth quivered.

"Think of someone else you'd like to invite to make the tenth," Momma said.

"There's nobody else. I'll just have nine."

"Are you terribly unhappy about this?" Momma asked. Sometimes you had to ask Louis.

"No, I can understand."

"Then why don't you, if you want to, you could take her a

piece of your birthday cake. So she'll know you want to be friends," Momma suggested.

Louis liked that idea and went away happy, while Momma happily made lists of what food and prizes they'd need, what games they'd play.

Everybody was happy except Mina, who was itching with impatience to get Louis to herself and question him. But when she did do that later in the evening, after Louis had finished up his day's homework at the kitchen table where she did her math, he didn't know much of anything.

"There are three of them," he told her. "She's got two brothers."

"Can't you find out?" Mina asked.

Louis shrugged. Mina knew what she'd have done, she'd have gone right up to Maybeth and said, "Who are you; do you have someone called Bullet in your family who's dead?" But Louis was gentler and more considerate than she'd been. "Can you try?" she asked him.

"Sure," he said.

It was the middle of the next week before he had anything to tell her. Mina had almost forgotten that she was waiting to hear, she was getting so griped by the corps de ballet. It seemed to Mina that they were getting a little ruder every day. Nobody stopped them, so they were making a kind of group joke out of her. The outer five especially were saying things and looking things. Mrs. Edges seemed to notice nothing. Kat and Sabrina said she ought to drop tennis, and Rachelle said she ought to report them to the counselor. "If you let them get away with this," Rachelle advised, "they'll just try something else." But Mina had always fought her own battles.

Moreover, Dicey Tillerman barely ever even crossed eyes with Mina in any of the three classes they had together. Probably prejudiced, Mina decided, and who cared? It was the poor whites who were the most prejudiced, that was what people said. And immigrants. Because people needed to be sure there was somebody lower than they. Well, Mina didn't consider herself lower than anybody. Frankly.

But high school *was* different. Things were somehow more complicated in high school. The kids from the other elementary school weren't—weren't kids like the ones she'd always been to school with. And they were changing things for the whole class, Mina thought.

So when Louis closed up his spelling workbook and told her, "I found out," Mina didn't know what he was talking about. They were alone. Momma was at work, Belle was at a friend's, and her father was across the way at a church meeting.

"Found out what?" Mina was whipping through a couple of pages of math problems.

"About the Tillermans."

"Them."

"What's the matter? You sound angry."

"I do?" Mina listened to her voice. "I do. I didn't mean it at you. It's just—I'm finding life pretty difficult these days. I'm sorry." He listened to her, serious, his eyes like their father's. "Tell me."

"They live with their grandmother, the one who's crazy. The oldest boy is in fifth grade, James. He's in the special accelerated section so I guess he's smart. The little brother is in second grade, and he's quiet too, like Maybeth. He kind of stands around at recess. Sammy."

"Sammy?"

"I said. Didn't you listen?"

Samuel Tillerman, Mina heard the name with a bubble of laughter and her eyes filling up with tears. She heard Tamer Shipp's bassoon voice saying it. She felt like getting up and calling him up on the phone to say, "I found him for you." She could imagine what Mr. Shipp would say.

"I didn't know you cared that much," Louis asked her. "Maybeth stayed back a year, where they lived before, so she should really be in my class. She's the nice one. She's got friends, lots of friends. I talked to James a little at lunch one day because he looked lonely. I don't know if he was boasting, but he said they walked all the way here from Annapolis. Could they?"

"Across the bay?"

"I don't think he was lying, but he might have been boasting."

"Where are their parents?" Mina asked. She knew she couldn't call up Mr. Shipp. But she didn't know how she'd wait all the time before next June to tell him. First, though, she had to make sure.

"James wouldn't say anything about them. That's all I know. Except, they've got an older sister."

"I know about her. She's in my class," Mina said. "Her name's Dicey, and she's not—not too friendly."

"Maybeth is friendly," Louis said. "She—" He didn't know how to say what he was thinking.

Mina knew, but she wasn't going to let him know she knew his private thoughts. Instead, she told him, "Do you know what Mr. Shipp once said about Alice? He said he thought God had done fine work when He made Alice."

Louis liked that. "It doesn't matter if she's not black," he said. "She's still pretty, isn't she?"

"I wish I could figure that out," Mina told him.

CHAPTER 20

It clearly mattered to the corps de ballet that Mina was black, and it was making Mrs. Edges nervous. Less and less of their PE time was used playing tennis, because drill exercises were the only way Mrs. Edges could keep the class in control.

It wasn't a terrific way for Mina to start out the day. When she thought about it—which was no more often than she had to, because thinking about it made her feel helpless and dangerously angry—she thought the easiest way would be to start in picking on Bonnie. When you want to claw your way up the pecking order, you start with the person on the bottom. But Mina didn't want to claw her way up—if it was up. She wanted to play tennis. What she really wanted was to go for the girl named Harriet, who set the styles for that group and set the tone. Leader of the pack, Mina called her, to herself. They were like a pack of dogs, and they treated one another like dogs—casually cruel if they thought Harriet would find them clever, cruelly careless about what they said to one another, and then they tried with emotional apologies to act as if they didn't mean what they'd said. But it was such a contest, what they called their friendship—who had the most records, who had the most lipsticks, whose father had the best job, which boys liked whom.

Mina ignored them, mostly. If they started hedging her in too close, all she had to do was look at Harriet and look at her. Harriet wasn't about to tackle Mina straightforwardly. Mrs. Edges gave up the hope that everybody would get used to things and get along, and she would take Mina onto a court herself. They volleyed, or played a few games. Mina had a good, strong serve. The serve was the easiest part of the game for Mina.

Harriet didn't like this. She came hippity-hopping over one early October morning to say, "Mrs. Edges? My father says I'm not getting the quality of instruction he expected. He wants to come in and talk to you about what I'm learning." The rest of the corps de ballet stood behind her, nodding their heads to show that their daddies felt the same way, smirking to see a student win a power play over a teacher, any teacher.

Mina couldn't have stopped herself if she wanted to. She took one look at the scene and started to laugh.

Harriet whirled around. "What's so funny?"

Mina couldn't help it. "You are," she laughed. "You and the rest of your corps de ballet here."

Harriet's henchman, Sandy, the only one with whom Mina had any classes, looked at Mina, looked at Mrs. Edges, whose temper was starting to show; and looked at Harriet. She grinned at Mina. "Nice try, Harriet," she said, "but she's got you."

Mina stopped laughing. She told herself that she couldn't just slam somebody on the head with her tennis racquet. It wasn't even her own racquet, it belonged to the school, and what if it broke.

"Wanna play a game?" Sandy asked her.

Mina wanted to say no and walk away. She didn't want to have anything to do with them. She didn't want Sandy thinking that Mina would be grateful for this little friendly gesture. She'd seen what their friendship was worth. But she also wondered how she'd do, and it was a beautiful morning out there on the tennis courts, the air cool and tasting good, the sun warm, the leaves dark green on the tall trees. It was too beautiful a morning to let go to waste.

"Sure," she said. "Two out of three? Shall I serve first?" she asked, smiling with all her teeth, Uncle Tomming the girl.

Sandy was dark-haired and round-muscled, with the body of a natural athlete. She was sure of herself, because she was the best of the corps. "Fine by me," she agreed, her generosity put on as bright as her lipstick.

Mina aced her, all four serves, one after the other. She overpowered the girl. That took care of the first game. When Sandy served, they had to volley, and Mina concentrated on always getting the ball back over the net. They crept up to deuce, then the add point went back and forth, with nobody able to take the final point that would end the game. Mina stopped thinking about beating Sandy and started to think about winning the game. When she did that, she had to admit to herself that it had been fun to play against Sandy. Mrs. Edges was so much better than Mina, their games weren't really games; but Sandy made a genuine opponent.

"That's some serve you've got," Sandy said. Mina nodded, but didn't say anything more. "Is that what you call us, corps de ballet?"

"Why not?" Mina asked. She had worked up a sweat winning the second game.

"With you as Odile," Sandy cracked.

That got Mina's attention. She looked down into the white girl's tanned face and noted the crooked nose and short front teeth and the unmistakeable gleam of intelligence in the brown eyes. "Odile-Odette," Mina answered.

Sandy laughed, a short quick laugh, and went off to the gym for a shower.

The next day, Sandy started off the class saying that she and

Mina would take on anyone else in doubles. Mina said, no, but she and Bonnie would if anyone cared to play them. Bonnie wasn't sure she wanted to, but Mina made her, without saying a word, just by assuming they would and summoning her onto the court. But the next day, Mrs. Edges took Mina aside at the end of class and said she was switching Mina's sports assignment.

"It doesn't bother me," Mina said.

"It's not that," Mrs. Edges said, embarrassed. "It's because you're too good."

Mina's jaw wanted to fall open, but she held it closed.

"You've got excellent coordination and real strength. You move well, with natural grace. You're unusually disciplined. I want you to be in an intermediate class, not a beginner's. You'll be behind at first."

"That's okay," Mina said.

"But I think you'll catch up in no time. Miss Bower—she's the varsity coach—agrees with me. We want to build a tennis team. I think you're a good bet for it. We want you to take tennis for your spring sport too, if you'd like to." Mrs. Edges waited, and then added, "So would you like to do that?"

Mina nodded her head while her mind was still trying to figure out words like natural grace and coordination. She wondered why Miss Maddinton had told her she'd grown up clumsy. She wondered why she'd believed that long-ago teacher. She wondered if Miss Maddinton just hadn't remembered that people grew and kept on growing; she hadn't looked with a long eye. Maybe, Mina thought, because a long eye wouldn't show her what she wanted to see.

"Thank you," Mina remembered to say.

Since things were going along so well, Mina decided that she'd pair herself up with Dicey Tillerman when the science teacher announced that he wanted them working in pairs for a rock classifying unit. It wouldn't do Dicey any harm socially. Mina's position in the class was becoming more what she'd expected. Everybody knew Mina Smiths, or knew who she was, or was going to. Moreover, she'd seen Dicey talking to a boy after school, while the boy played his guitar, so she thought Dicey must be coming out of her initial shyness. Then, which was most tempting, she'd seen Dicey's face wake up a couple of times in English class in response to something Mina had said. For all of those reasons, but mostly because of Tamer Shipp's Bullet, mostly for Tamer Shipp, Mina went over to sit beside Dicey Tillerman at the lab table in the back of the room.

Dicey looked up, not exactly pleased. Mina piled her books onto the table. "I'm Wilhemina Smiths, Smiths with an S at both ends. My friends call me Mina. You're Dicey Tillerman," she added quickly, because she wouldn't put it past this girl to not introduce herself.

Dicey looked at her. Probably, like Mina, she was hearing the buzzes of conversation around them. Mina ignored her friends and met Dicey's eyes. They were hazel eyes, and suspicious.

"We're the smartest ones in here," Mina kept her voice low to say that, even though she thought it was true.

Dicey didn't say any of the things Mina expected her to say. The usual responses would be, "Oh I don't think so," with false modesty, or, "I know," with pride, or, "Thank you," for the compliment.

"How do you know that?" Dicey demanded.

Mina got busy arranging her books and kept her eyes on her hands to hide the laughter bubbling up in her. "I know about me," she said, "and I've been keeping an eye on you." That was certainly the truth, if Dicey only knew. "Don't worry." Mina looked back at the hazel eyes, which were entirely alert now in the narrow face. "I won't eat you."

Dicey was surprised to hear that, and then she just grinned at Mina, mischief and confidence all over that face now. The eyes flashed some different colors Mina couldn't catch. "I'm not worried," the girl said, and Mina could have cheered aloud, if class hadn't started in right then. *Whoo-ee*, she said, inside her head.

They worked well together. Dicey knew how to work with someone, although she always knew what she thought, loud and clear. When they disagreed on what kind of a rock it was they were classifying, or what was the best proof, they argued back and forth about it. Sometimes it turned out Dicey was right, sometimes that Mina was right, and sometimes their arguments got them to a new answer, which they both recognized as better than either of their own suggestions. Dicey didn't ask Mina any personal questions. Mina very carefully didn't ask Dicey any personal questions either, but she figured they had begun to be friends. Mina could never boss Dicey around, and she liked that.

When Mr. Chappelle assigned an essay in English class, Mina had such a good idea right away that she could barely stop herself from trying to talk to Dicey right then in the middle of class. She waited by the door for Dicey to come out. She told Dicey she had an idea she wanted to talk to her about.

"Sure," Dicey said, not even slowing down.

Mina suggested after school, and Dicey said she couldn't. Mina suggested that the girl come by her house, but Dicey said she couldn't. There was a sinking feeling at Mina's heart—and a little anger at the way this girl just—dismissed her. She wondered if she'd been all wrong about Dicey and what she was like. Independent, just for starters. She didn't think so, because she was pretty smart about people, but she was watching the sharp face and she knew she didn't even have all of the girl's attention. Mina decided to turn it into a joke. "You sure are a hard person to be friends with, Dicey Tillerman," she said.

She waited for some answer, but there was no answer given. Mina guessed that was a pretty clear answer.

But if Dicey thought Mina didn't know the smell of prejudice when she ran her nose over it . . . if Dicey thought Mina was short on friends . . . it wasn't Dicey Mina was interested in anyway, it was Bullet, if anybody wanted the truth of it.

Kat said it one day, walking down the hall behind Dicey's cold shoulder. "What do you want honky friends for anyway."

"The way you talk, Katanga Beaulieu." Mina prissed up her lips and minced on down the corridor.

Mina wrote her English essay the night before it was due. She had the house to herself that night. Louis was at Boy Scouts, Momma was at the hospital, and Belle had gone with their father to the meeting about plans for the Halloween party for teenagers. Halloween hadn't used to be like that, Mina remembered. Halloween hadn't used to need a party to keep the older kids at the church and out of trouble, or grown-ups going out with the little kids to keep them safe. On Halloween her father went out walking along the streets of the neighborhood, "doing his Mayor Lindsay act," Momma had said.

"Who's he?" Mina asked.

"He was Mayor of New York during the riots after Dr. King was shot," her dad said. "He went out walking on the streets those nights, trying to keep trouble down. It was a brave thing, and it certainly helped."

"Those were terrible days," her mother added. "You were just a baby, but . . . it was so terrible that Dr. King was shot, and the riots were so terrible, blacks tearing apart their own neighborhoods. I could sympathize, but I couldn't sympathize, if you know what I mean. I was glad we were down here, you can believe that. Things were tense down here, but not terrible."

Mina sat at the kitchen table, with the dark empty house

around her. The assignment was to write about a real person having a real conflict. She had decided right away to write about herself, and she wrote it pretending she was writing about someone else, so no one would know until the end who it was. She picked out examples of conflicts anybody could have, because when it came to the point, she didn't want to write the real truth. She really wanted to write about dance camp, to say how bad it was the way those white people acted. More than that, she wanted to write about Tamer Shipp and wrap her memories around with words. But she didn't want to write out her real feelings for anybody else to know.

The essay sounded as if she wasn't hiding anything, but she was hiding everything. Mina liked that. She knew, if they had to read them aloud, everybody would like it too, because they'd know it was Mina making her own form of mischief. It was a good essay. It made her laugh as she wrote.

Everything was rolling along right for Mina that fall, except Dicey Tillerman. The intermediate tennis class was fun, classes were pretty easy, and wherever she went people liked her. She was even getting to know some of the upperclassmen. One of the ones she wanted to meet was that guitar-playing boy Dicey talked to, because she'd heard him playing out by the bike rack a couple of times and she liked the sound of his music. Besides, she said to Kat, who also wanted to meet him, he was pretty good looking, even if he was white. "Good looking?" Kat said, staring back at him, hoping he'd notice her. "He's beautiful."

Mina was having a fine time in her life. Dicey Tillerman was no worse than a little splinter of discontent, the kind of little splinter that you can't quite get out, although you are aware of its sharp and irritating presence. Mina would have liked to show Dicey, but that wasn't anything to do with Dicey or anything Dicey actually did. Dicey didn't pay any attention to Mina. To try to get her would be like letting the splinter work its way in closer to your bloodstream, deeper into your flesh.

Mina got all A's on her report card, and she asked her parents if they'd get her a tennis racquet for her Christmas present. "I don't know if it's too expensive," she said. "The school has some, so it's okay if it's too expensive. But I'd like it."

"Why?" her mother wondered.

"I'm good at it," Mina said. "I'm not uncoordinated."

"I know you're not uncoordinated," her mother said, "but—"

Mina's mood got out of her control at that "but." She didn't know why, except that she'd felt sad all day, maybe because she'd dreamed about Tamer Shipp, dreamed that she was looking for him and couldn't find him. Maybe some of it was the strain of convincing herself that she was more interested in the many friends she did have than in the one she didn't, or pretending to herself that she didn't care if Dicey was the kind of person who rejected someone because she was black. Maybe she was just tired of waiting around for her English essay to come back, tired of Mr. Chappelle's weak excuses. Whatever the reason, she heard her voice get high and say, "You don't understand, you just think everything has to do with being black, or female, you just don't know anything about me and you act like you do. I'll save up and buy the racquet for myself since you feel that way." She burst out of the room and up the stairs to her own room. Up there, she slammed the drawers for a while until she felt a little better.

The day Mr. Chappelle finally returned their essays, he said he wanted to read a couple aloud. Mina's was the first one he chose. She wasn't surprised. She listened to it, to how it sounded, and listened to the response it got. It was the response she expected. She kept her eyes down, enjoying herself. Then she started listening to what she'd written, and she stopped enjoying it, because she hadn't told the really important things. She'd talked about laughing and crying and seeming confident, but being insecure. She'd made it sound like she was being perfectly frank and open. But she hadn't had the courage to tell the real truth.

Mina wasn't any too pleased with herself, even though at the same time she was really pleased with herself. She wondered if black people just never did talk about what was true, the way she hadn't. And if that was the case, how could they expect whites to understand? Maybe they really wanted to stay back angry, maybe she did—so she wouldn't have to face up to things. Really face up to them. Mina sat there, enjoying how smart she was and wondering, but hiding the wondering. It was nobody else's business, was it?

When they got to the last line of the essay, where she identified herself as both writer and subject, everybody thought it was terrific. Mr. Chappelle got her to stand up. He was pleased with her, because reading her essay made him look good to the class. Dicey was impressed and didn't try to hide it. Mina was pleased and didn't try to hide it from herself. But even as she sat down again, smiling broadly, she knew what she hadn't had the courage to do.

Mina settled back to listen to the other essay. This was about someone called Mrs. Liza, and about one sentence into it, Mina realized that somebody was talking right to her heart, right from whoever's heart it was that wrote it. The essay wasn't about feelings, but it touched Mina's feelings about this poor lady who lived with her kids and no husband, who walked "like a song sung without accompaniment." Mina could see that, even while her memory supplied a better word, *a cappella.* This person told the real truth. Whoever wrote it had the courage for that. When it ended, with Mrs. Liza somewhere absolutely alone, worse than where she'd started out, Mina thought it was about anybody who'd ever been beaten down, by one other person or a bunch of other people or society. She didn't know who Mrs.

Liza was, but she'd met her before, a hundred times she'd bet. Miz Hunter's great-grandaddy was Mrs. Liza, and so was Miz Hunter too, and Mina sometimes, and Mr. Shipps' bassoon voice because there was something helpless in it, something lost, something good just thrown away.

Mina felt as if she could have cried for how true the essay was. Instead, she broke the silence by making a joke. "That surely *is* a horse of another color. I guess it beat me around the track before I even got out of the starting gate." She looked around, to see who had written it, because she meant what she said. She didn't mind being beaten out by something that good. She'd only mind not getting a chance to say how much she liked being beaten out by something that good.

Even, she realized, watching how hard Dicey was fighting to keep her face expressionless, if it was Dicey Tillerman. She wondered, for a minute, who the lady was, maybe the grandmother who was supposed to be crazy anyway. Mina let the class talk on around her, her heart still reverberating from what she'd heard. She wished, she really wished—she thought, her eye on Dicey's profile with its straight nose and large mouth—she thought, angrily, that Dicey should know that Mina was a friend worth having. Except Dicey didn't seem to think that.

After some questions back and forth, Mr. Chappelle told Dicey to stand up, because she had written the essay. Mina made herself smile across the room—because it was good, whatever else Mina was thinking—but Dicey just stood there, her eyes fixed on Mr. Chappelle's face, as if she knew something nobody else did.

"Do you have something to say?" Mr. Chappelle asked Dicey. Mina heard it in his voice: He thought she hadn't written the essay herself.

Dicey didn't move a muscle and Mr. Chappelle talked on. He was edging up on the accusation. Everybody else caught on, and the whole air of the classroom got that excited silence, like people gathering together around the scene of an accident, people watching somebody else's trouble and pain.

Mina looked at Dicey, who wasn't giving Mr. Chappelle an inch, not a word. She was so disappointed. She really wished Dicey *had* written the thing herself. Mr. Chappelle paced his sentences out slow, talking about plagiarism. He knew Dicey was helpless. He knew anything she said or did wouldn't do any good. So he kept on slow, making it as hard on her as possible. Everybody was enjoying it too. Nobody liked Dicey, nobody cared about her because she didn't pay any attention to anybody, so they were almost glad she was the one chosen to be humiliated like this.

Served her right too, Mina started to think to herself; and then she realized that if Dicey had cheated on the essay, then Mina was entirely wrong about everything she'd thought about the girl. Mina didn't think she could be so entirely wrong about something, not entirely like this, and she started to think that the kind of person who would cheat wouldn't just stand there like that, not giving an inch.

"What I primarily resent is the deceitfulness of it," Mr. Chappelle said, dragging each word out, "the cheap trickery, the lies."

Nobody in that room could begin to think that Dicey cared enough about them to go to so much trouble. Mina was on her feet before she thought any further. Whatever Dicey Tillerman might think of her personally, she thought more of herself than to stay quiet. Mina figured if she had to choose, she would choose to be among the people who were willing to stand up for the truth. One of the minority who stood up against. . . whatever was trying to press people down by lies. She was already stuck in a couple of other minorities, she thought to herself, she might as well join this one. "That's not true," she heard herself say.

She met Dicey's eyes across the classroom. Mina's mind stayed cool as she talked, but she didn't feel cool in any of the rest of her. She was angry at everybody, at the teacher for doing this to a kid, at the rest of them for allowing it, and at herself for not having the courage to write out the truth. The bell rang before Mina was through, but she told everybody, including Mr. Chappelle, to stay there.

As Mina said that, she felt herself spreading out her whole personality, like limbs from some big tree, over everybody in the room. They stayed put, and she had known they would. The only one in that room she couldn't keep in place by the force of her personality alone was Dicey, and Dicey's eyes looked like the eyes of somebody walking home after a war, someone whose side had lost and was going to have to rebuild a whole life.

Mina didn't let her sympathy get in her way, and she didn't try to stop herself from enjoying herself. It took about five questions to show everybody that Dicey would never have cheated. Mina asked those questions. Dicey answered them. Then Mina nodded her head and left the classroom without a backward glance.

People caught up with her in the hall, to tell her how terrific she was and to laugh about the teacher's embarrassment. Mina heard them, but didn't count them for much, because these people had been just as ready to let Dicey stand alone there and be lied about. She didn't expect Dicey to do anything so commonplace as say thank you, so she guessed she wasn't disappointed to be ignored in Home Ec. Besides, Mina admitted to herself, she hadn't done it for Dicey Tillerman, or for Tamer Shipp either. She'd done it for herself, Mina Smiths. She hadn't done it for pity, but for her own self-respect.

CHAPTER 21

When the phone rang, late that evening, Mina was drilling Belle on a list of vocabulary words for Math. This was Business Math, and there was a lot of accounting in the course, Belle said, which made it harder. You had to know the vocabulary to understand the way the problems were stated. "Invoice," Mina asked. Belle started to spell the word, and Mina watched her sister's face as she concentrated. Belle was proud of being practical; her standards for herself in this course were as high as her standards for personal appearance. The phone rang, and her father called out from the living room that he'd get it. Mina watched Belle and decided that she'd probably make a really good secretary.

"Do you know what time it is?" their father's voice asked.

Belle smiled at Mina, sharing the joke. It was probably one of the boys who often called Belle up. Their father was pretty strict about phone calls, and he wasn't too wild about Belle being so popular. All of their friends had been grilled by him for calling up at what he considered the wrong time.

They heard him say, "I'll get Mina," which surprised them both. He came into the kitchen with an odd expression on his face to tell her a Dicey Tillerman was on the phone. "Don't talk long," he told her, following her back to the living room.

"I won't, Dad," she told him, and she didn't. Dicey had just called to say thank you. Mina made conversation, from the front of her head, but most of her mind was thinking how weird it was: What kind of a person wouldn't realize for hours that she wanted to say thank you? It didn't sound like someone was forcing Dicey to call, so how come—having put it off for so long—Dicey didn't wait until school.

Mina's father was watching her, and she knew he was going to have something to say. She knew he remembered the name.

"What was that about?"

"Oh," Mina said, still standing by the phone table. "It was just . . . the teacher accused her of cheating today, and I . . . kind of defended her."

"Mina?" Belle called from the kitchen.

"She'll be a few minutes," their father answered. "Sit down," he told Mina. She sat across from him on the sofa. "Why did you defend her? Is she a particular friend of yours?"

Mina watched the way her father reserved judgment. He wasn't ever hasty. He waited until he had the information that he thought he needed. His eyes looked at her, waiting to understand.

"I guess I like her. I'm not sure how she feels about me. But—I knew she wouldn't cheat."

"Do you know her that well?"

Mina shook her head. "She's new this year. It wasn't just rooting for the underdog, Dad, I know that's what you're thinking."

"I'm not saying there's anything wrong with looking out for the underdog."

"It's that she just wouldn't. Some people are like that. Like—Zandor might cheat, but Louis probably wouldn't, and Selma Shipp, you couldn't make her, ever. You know what I mean?"

He did.

"So I was certain, and Mr. Chappelle *was* pretty awful about how he did it, accused her." Mina laughed: "It was fun, the way I knew what questions to ask her. It was a pretty dramatic scene."

"That's why you were lit up like a roman candle at supper."

"Yeah, I guess I feel pretty good about it."

"So you're satisfied you did the right thing," her father asked.

Mina was. She thought it was the rightest thing she'd done in a long time. She wished her father could see it that way, although she was glad he didn't know the wrong things that made this so right, worth being proud of. Mr. Shipp would understand, she thought.

"Right for whom?" he asked her.

She didn't understand what was bothering him. "Right in general, because she really hadn't cheated. Mr. Chappelle didn't say anything—but he wouldn't—but he knew."

"Was it right for this girl?"

"Of course. You weren't there, you don't understand. How could it not be right?"

"Sometimes people get into the habit of letting others fight their battles for them."

"Dicey's not like that. The opposite, if anything. It wasn't like that."

Her father believed her. Because she knew that, Mina wanted to explain. "It was right for me too, because I don't want to be the kind of person who sits by, sits safe, while somebody else is being done wrong to."

"And in God's eyes?" her father asked. He sat so quiet when he talked, and he so seldom brought God in like this, Mina knew he thought it was important.

"I can't really know that, can I?" she asked him. He was asking her, by asking her that, all kinds of questions. Her father didn't push religion at them, not that way. But he tried to know what they were thinking, without pushing it. Mina thought privately that if it was right for what was good in her, it was probably right for God. But that sounded too conceited to say. "Dad, everybody was just letting him go after her, and she—I don't know what she was thinking, she didn't say anything. I don't even know why everybody else let it happen. It was almost as if nobody could think it out, that somebody who doesn't care about what people think of her doesn't care enough to cheat. Or if it's because people are scared to do what's right, because then they'll come under fire. But nobody was objecting at all, not even to the way he was trying to shame her, and—I couldn't just sit there, could I?"

"I guess not. Although you do know you could have, that it's possible. Sometimes it's the best thing, Mina."

"Maybe," she said. "Not this time though."

"Well, your mother will be proud of you," he said.

"What about you?" she teased.

"I think I am too," he admitted. He didn't want to encourage her to be t-rou-ble, she could see that. She could also see why. She went over and kissed his cheek, rough now at the end of the day.

"Thanks," she said. She wasn't the kind of person to be slow in giving thanks.

"Her name is Tillerman." He stopped her on her way back to the kitchen. "What do you know about her family?"

"Next to nothing," Mina said. He was worried about that too. He was a worrier, her father. Neither of them was going to say that word, white.

For one day, Mina and Dicey were the stars of the school. They walked down the hall like they were a triumphal procession. Mina knew it was a fake; it would only last a day and then the excitement would blow over; but she didn't mind. Dicey knew it too, but she minded.

Mina walked Dicey downtown to her job, and on the way Dicey told her that they lived with their grandmother. She knew what people said about her grandmother, Mina saw, but it didn't bother her. So maybe she knew better, Mina thought.

Dicey worked at Tydings's grocery store, down near the docks. The only person besides Mrs. Tydings in the store was a little boy, a little blond boy about eight years old. Dicey introduced him to Mina. "This is my brother, Sammy."

Sammy's face was marked up, as though he'd been fighting. Mina barely noticed that and paid little attention to their conversation, because the suddenness of the whole thing had her entirely off balance. For about the first time in her whole life she wanted to ask God to stop time rolling, because she couldn't keep up. She needed a few minutes to step aside and notice everything that was happening, to be sure she didn't miss anything. Usually Mina could keep up with the pace of things and stay ahead, but Dicey—Dicey was about the most sudden person Mina had ever met. There were no half measures with Dicey. Either, Mina guessed, you were nobody at all, or you were a friend.

She was glad to be considered a friend, but she thought Dicey made things pretty hard on herself being that way. And pretty hard on her friends too, probably.

But it was Sammy Mina wanted to talk to right then, because he must be Samuel Tillerman. Since all he wanted to talk about was marbles, she asked him to teach her how to play. They went outside and tried the wood porch of the store, but the marbles rolled too quickly. Mina didn't care, but Sammy did. "It's no good," he said.

Mina sat back. "You look like you were in a fight. You look like you did all right."

"I did." He sat back on his haunches and looked at her, measuring her.

She was measuring him too, and recognizing that made her laugh.

"What's so funny." He stood up. He was ready to tackle her too, if he thought he needed to.

"That's for me to know and you to find out," she told him. She got up herself and handed over the marbles she still held in her hand.

"Maybe I will," he said. Mina was willing to bet money he didn't even notice how much bigger and older she was.

"Maybe you will," she agreed. She was teasing him, and he knew it, and he didn't mind. She knew this little kid, she recognized him—he was t-rou-ble.

Mina didn't meet Dicey's grandmother until Thanksgiving weekend. By that time, she had laid out for Dicey exactly who she, Mina, was, in case Dicey wanted to change her mind about being friends. "I'm smart," Mina had said, "and I'm black. I'm a black female. And look at me." Mina just laughed to herself, remembering it. None of it had been too important to Dicey. Dicey didn't say much about herself and certainly didn't talk about herself the same way. Mina wondered if Dicey knew about herself in that way or whether she just *was* herself. Mina didn't care, and it wasn't a matter of either way being better. She was simply curious about Dicey, and excited too, because every day brought her closer to Bullet. She was going to find him, in some way, and be able to give him to Tamer Shipp, in some way. As if she could wrap all her love in a single box. Feeling love, Mina thought, was easy; it was finding the ways to give it that was hard.

When Dicey invited her to their farm for the Saturday after Thanksgiving, Mina rode her bike out, expecting just about anything. The only thing she hoped for was to find out if this grandmother was any relation to Bullet, but that was a question that she didn't need to have answered right away. She had time.

Mina rode her bike around to the back, where other bikes were parked. The front of the house, set way back from the road, looked blank, behind a big tree that began to spread out its limbs close to the ground. She'd never seen a tree that grew in that spreading fashion; it would look like a coolie hat with leaves on it. Trees were supposed to rise up straight along their trunks, Mina thought, and then spread out limbs. Even the Tillermans' trees didn't act the way they were supposed to.

Mina went up the sagging back steps and knocked on the door to the kitchen.

A woman opened it. She didn't say anything. Her hair was a tangle of gray curls and she had to look up at Mina with suspicious eyes, dark hazel like Dicey's. She wore no makeup, not even lipstick, and if her hair had ever been brushed it hadn't made much impression on the curls. She wore a loose cotton blouse over a long skirt, and her feet were bare. She looked at Mina as if she didn't know whether she planned to greet her or not. Mina wondered if she had done something wrong.

Mina moved her face into a polite expression and opened her mouth to ask if Dicey was home.

"You're Wilhemina Smiths," the woman told her.

For once in her life, Mina felt tongue-tied, outgunned.

"Your father's the minister."

Mina was still standing there, outside the door.

"Well, come in," the woman said impatiently. "Although I don't know what your father will think. Does it matter what he thinks?" She stood aside to let Mina enter a big kitchen.

"Of course," Mina told her. She wondered if she shouldn't have come here, if Mrs. Tillerman minded having a black in the house as a guest. Dicey didn't, but you couldn't tell about a person's family just by the person. "He's my father," she said to Mrs. Tillerman.

Then the woman smiled at her, a quick smile, and held out her hand, which had flour on it. "I'm making cookies. I'm Abigail Tillerman. Dicey's grandmother." Her grip was firm. So maybe you *could* tell about people's families, sometimes at least. "They're out front. You can hear them."

Mina could. There were people singing, and a guitar. They were singing "Amazing Grace." For a minute, she just listened. "When we've been here ten thousand years," the voices sang. A soprano, unusual in that it was both clear the way it was supposed to be and also round in a way sopranos almost never were, dominated the trio. The other two voices sang harmony, behind the soprano. "Bright shining, like the sun." The guitar played a quiet background, making part of the song.

It was a good sound, coming into the warm kitchen with its long, scrubbed wooden table, and the smells of chocolate and sugar and baking. . . .

Mina smiled and said, "How do you do, Mrs. Tillerman." The woman was watching her, still wary, so she said more. "Can I go ahead in? I'm an alto."

She earned another smile and followed her hostess down a hallway.

Jeff Greene was there with his guitar, and Dicey and two younger boys, one of them with Dicey's dark hair and the hazel eyes Mina was starting to expect. A girl sat cross-legged in front of the guitar. She looked up when Mrs. Tillerman introduced Mina. Maybeth: Solemn and a little frightened, or maybe shy, she stared up at Mina out of huge eyes, light brown and mixed with colors. Mina looked over her head at Jeff, whose gray eyes, quiet as a sky with low cloud cover, seemed to be trying to communicate something she couldn't understand, but something about this little girl. Maybeth was entirely delicate, Mina thought, delicate not fragile, with the slender bones all over her body, chin, wrists, shoulders. She thought how she could tell Louis she'd met Maybeth and that she agreed with him. She included the little girl in her general smile, not singling her out, trying not to just stare at her. This was some of God's finest work, she thought.

"She came to the back door," Mrs. Tillerman announced. Then the woman's face turned back to Mina. "Not what you think," she said.

Mina could have laughed aloud. "I know," she said. Mrs. Tillerman's mind just jumped around, and Mina guessed she could understand how she got her reputation.

When they settled down to sing something else, they asked Mina what she wanted. Her mind had been running on friendship, so she named, "Oh Lord you know, I have no friend like you." For a wonder, Jeff knew it. Mina didn't sing out; she kept her voice at his tone, so the voices would blend. Mrs. Tillerman sat down to listen for a while, and Sammy charged over to sit on the arm of her chair. Mina knew what he was thinking, sitting there like that, and she wished she could tell him he didn't have to worry about her. She thought Mrs. Tillerman was a lot like Dicey, and Dicey was a loner, but she wasn't crazy. She looked across at the little boy and grinned at him. After a minute of staring, he grinned back at her.

One of the things that struck her hardest about the Tillermans' house was how like her own it was. The rooms were bigger and more worn down, there were more rooms and a lot more land around outside, but it was a house that took naturally to being filled with people.

The other thing that struck her was Maybeth. Her eyes wanted to stay on the girl, but Mina could tell that would make her uncomfortable, and it wasn't as if it was only her blonde prettiness that made Mina want to stare. Mina couldn't figure out what it was, and she could see that Jeff knew better than she ever would how to act around Maybeth. Maybeth made her think of a dogwood tree in blossom. She watched Maybeth sing, all wrapped around within the music. She tried to name to herself the color of the girl's cheeks. It was like nothing she had ever seen, except milk maybe. It was rich white, tinted with some creamy color underneath. It was a beautiful color.

Looking at the little girl, listening, her mind wandering, Mina just barely stopped herself from jumping up and yelling, *Whoo-ee*. Oh, Tamer Shipp, she thought, you're right. Colored does cover just about everything. She knew him better than to wonder if he had known what he meant when he said that.

CHAPTER 22

In the middle of that week after Thanksgiving, when the house had finally settled down and been cleaned up after the mess it got into by being crowded with family, Mina got home just in time for dinner. She'd been at the library with Kat and Sabrina, working on a science paper, a fact sheet that was supposed to teach them how to use scientific sources. Belle was cross at her for not being there to help with the dinner preparation. "If you think I'm going to do the washing up too, you're wrong," she told Mina as they sat down.

"I don't. I'm not," Mina said. "I told Momma where I was going."

Everybody seemed pretty snappish at the table, except Louis. But Louis never got snappish. Mina asked him what was wrong. He shook his head; he wouldn't say or couldn't say. Momma dished up the pork chops and rice. Mina's father, she knew, was tired from trying to fix up Miz Hunter's house for a church activity building. Things kept costing more than he'd planned on and taking longer, and people didn't always do what they said they'd do to help. Belle had probably had a fight with her present boyfriend, or was between boyfriends; Mina couldn't keep up. Momma was worried about something, and Mina thought she knew what. Zandor's letters were getting shorter and telling less, which meant there was something he was carefully not telling.

Mina bent her head while her father said grace, adding a silent thanks that her own life was going awfully well. For once, they ate in near silence. Mina tried to start a couple of conversations, talking about the science assignment, but there were almost no responses.

Finally, her father laid down his fork and knife on the empty plate. "Mina, we had a visitor today. Your mother and I."

"Oh?" Mina asked.

"A Mrs. Abigail Tillerman."

"Oh," she said. Uh-oh, she thought. Her father was going to tell her something he thought she didn't want to hear.

"I opened the door, and she was standing there, and she said she'd come to put a face to the bogeyman," he told Mina.

Mina couldn't help it. She laughed. She could just see Mrs. Tillerman doing that. She couldn't wait to tell Dicey.

"It's not funny," her father said.

"Mina turns everything into a joke," Belle said. "She's a regular clown."

"Belle," Momma corrected, "that's not a kind thought."

"Well, how would you feel if everybody was always talking about your sister?"

"I'd try not to feel jealous," Momma snapped back.

"You think I'm *jealous*?" Belle didn't like that. "I'm embarrassed, not jealous."

"Why bother?" Mina said. "It's my problem, not yours. If it's a problem."

"If you girls would save your squabbling for some other place, I'd be profoundly grateful," Mina's father interrupted. "I want to ask Mina why Mrs. Tillerman felt it necessary to come calling."

"To meet you, Dad," Mina said. "Because—she probably knows what people say about her and. . . ." She couldn't think of how to finish.

"It's not a family I'm sure I want you associating with," her father told her.

"You don't even know them." Mina didn't like what her father was saying, didn't like him saying it, and didn't like this feeling of being angry at him.

"I know enough," he said.

What did he know? That they were white. That Mrs. Tillerman didn't act like everybody else. "You don't know anything," Mina told him.

"I know that, because of them, you're speaking to me as you never have before," he pointed out.

"See what I mean?" Belle said.

Mina didn't know what to say. Louis sat unhappily beside her. She looked to her mother for help.

"Amos, are you being fair?" her mother asked.

"Why do I always have to be fair?" Mina's father asked his wife. "Do I have to be fair? Because a man is a minister doesn't mean he's got to be perfect, does it? Mina, that woman . . . none of your other friends' parents have ever felt the need to come calling like that. She didn't even sit down. We stood in the hallway. She's not—normal."

"Well, I didn't mind her," Mina's mother said. "As I said to your father, she must be all right, she didn't ask me if I'd come clean her house. I think she came because she didn't want us worrying, Amos."

"Well she's *started* me worrying," he said.

"She just thinks differently and talks differently," Mina said. "I like her. I thought she was pretty funny."

"See? She turns everything into a joke," Belle pointed out.

"And I plan to be friends with Dicey," Mina announced.

Her father's eyes looked like she'd just told him she was pregnant, or wanted to convert to Judaism, or maybe cannibalism.

"Amos," her mother said. "Did you ever think how—Americans want everything to be alike? Not different. Like homogenizing milk or . . . the way everybody's teeth are supposed to be perfectly straight. The white society—all those people on television talk alike, even blacks, you've noticed that, you've commented on it. The white society wants to erase all the differences. In Europe, Mrs. Tillerman would be called eccentric. That's not bad, eccentric. It's bad to call things, or people, crazy because they're eccentric. Amos, Jesus was eccentric. He said what the majority didn't want to hear, he acted the way they said you shouldn't act. Amos?" she asked.

Mina's father got up from the table and walked out of the room.

"He's worried, he's worried about you, Mina," Momma said.

Mina guessed she knew that.

"She came to my school," Louis said. "She was playing marbles with the little kids. It was weird."

"My guess is she had her reasons," Momma said.

"You know, she's taken all four of them in," Mina told her mother, asking her. "There are four kids, and their father ran off and their mother is—I think she's in some hospital. It sounds like some kind of nervous breakdown, a really bad one. But Mrs. Tillerman is going to adopt them. If it was one of Dad's congregation that did that, he'd call her a saint."

"Have a little faith in your father, Mina."

Since the subject didn't get raised again, Mina guessed she was right to have faith in her father to understand. The next Sunday, he gave a sermon about The Peaceable Kingdom, where the lion lay down with the lamb. He talked about the differences in creatures, in their natures and their needs, in what you could expect of them. He said, at the end, that some people thought it was impossible for the lion to lie down with the lamb. "I don't believe that," her father said. "But I do know something. For that impossible dream to become real, to make God's kingdom here on earth, or to bring ourselves a little closer to it, the lion had better not be hungry."

"Who *is* the lion, Dad?" Mina asked him over Sunday dinner.

She didn't know at first why he looked at her so lovingly. "You were really listening," he said.

"I always listen. This is about my favorite, I guess. But I wasn't sure who you thought was the lion, and I wondered."

"Maybe, anybody hungry is the lion," her father said.

"So the slaves were the lion, and the whites were the lamb?" Mina asked.

"In a way, yes. I've been taking your mother's advice and trying to think with a more historical perspective."

"Well, well," Momma said. "And it's only taken me, what, twenty-seven years?"

"I don't see how anybody can live with another person for twenty-seven years," Belle said.

"People change, and keep on changing," Momma answered her.

Dicey changed, got silent and withdrawn and—but Mina figured, after the days Dicey had missed from school, probably her mother had died. There wasn't anything you could say to someone about that, so Mina just kept close, but not too close. Jeff asked her, finally, what was wrong with Dicey, and she told him her guess. He said, "I can see that," and it sounded like he could. "Their uncle died too," he said.

"Bullet," Mina said, without thinking, wondering how she knew that was who it was so certainly. She didn't need to find that out after all.

"In Vietnam," Jeff said, his voice quiet, but angry for some reason. They went out to the Tillermans' that winter, Jeff more than Mina. Dicey never came to Mina's house, but Mina thought that had more to do with Dicey wanting to be near her own family than with anything else. Mina thought Mrs. Tillerman didn't mind having her out there, because if she had she'd have said so, not minding the embarrassment of saying something like that. Maybeth played the piano, Bach, while Dicey and Mina sat to listen. It had been a long time, Mina thought, as the piano notes wound into her ears. Too long a time.

"It's the counterpoint I really like," she said to Dicey.

"Counterpoint?"

Mina explained what she remembered. Maybeth wasn't listening, just playing. Finally, Mina said to Dicey, who sat quietly in front of the fire, with the flames at her back, "There's such a big difference between knowing about something and actually doing it."

"My mother was like that," Dicey said. She didn't say any more, but Mina could hear a lot in what she didn't say.

"I thought I was going to be a ballet dancer when I was little," Mina said then.

"What happened?"

"I outgrew it—literally," Mina said, making it a joke. "They told me I'd grown wrong, too big. I used to be tall and skinny and coordinated."

"You told me you played tennis," Dicey objected.

"They were wrong about me, as it turns out. 'But it took me awhile to figure that out. It was a special camp, up in Connecticut, for gifted dancers," Mina said. She made herself add, "They were all white."

Dicey looked up at her then, as if she was hearing things Mina wasn't saying. The piano played on.

"I used to listen to a lot of this kind of music too. Because of the camp. I stopped that too. Which was stupid of me," Mina said.

Dicey agreed. Mina just smiled at her. She could talk to Dicey about almost everything. The one thing she never mentioned was Tamer Shipp and Bullet. She was saving that, just as she was saving the Tillermans for Tamer Shipp when he came back that summer. Because she had that gift saved for him, Mina could get through all the days, waiting.

The thing she almost didn't say to Dicey she got around to one early spring day, when a March wind was blowing up from the water, and she had walked with Dicey to work. "Maybe I shouldn't ask you this," Mina started.

"I dunno, Mina; if even you are hesitating, it seems to me that you probably shouldn't," Dicey advised.

"You've never met my family."

Dicey nodded, not making any excuses.

"But I wonder—because, you know, you've been like a mother to your brothers and sister. The way you take care of them. But there's more to being a mother than that. You're your own mother, in a way. That's what makes you so grown up."

"Am I?"

"Yeah. Or, I think. You know that." Mina was impatient. "But I've been wondering—if you ever need a mother-figure, or a mother-substitute, for something you can't talk with your grandmother about—I can recommend mine."

"I couldn't do that," Dicey said.

"Because she's black."

"Don't be stupid," Dicey said. "Because she's a stranger."

"That's why I want you to meet her. My dad too, but he's a harder nut to crack."

"Okay, maybe," Dicey said. "See you tomorrow, okay?"

Mina knew how to interpret Dicey's abrupt exit. It was nothing personal, it was just the way she moved through the world. She was finding that being friends with Dicey was an education in itself. She looked at people more carefully now, whites especially. Dicey had olive undertones in her skin, but Miss Eversleigh's face was like onionskin typing paper, and Mr. Chappelle's had a dead white tone, chalky. Mrs. Tillerman, who worked outside except during winter, faded to coffee ice cream color. Zits, Mina noticed with some ungenerous pleasure, looked a lot worse on whites than on blacks.

Mina was playing tennis again, as her spring sport, and she thought probably she'd play it all through high school. She'd try out for the tennis team next year. The exercise of playing felt really good to her body, the way it used her whole body, like dance used to. There were only a few blacks who played tennis, but since the ratio of blacks to whites on the tennis squad was greater than the number of tennis players compared to everybody else in the school, the blacks just kind of mixed into that tennis-playing minority. It was a colored team, Mina said to herself, storing the thought up to tell Mr. Shipp. She had gotten a racquet for Christmas and she used part of her babysitting income to buy cans of tennis balls. It wasn't easy to find someone to play with on weekends, when she had time, until Sammy asked her to teach him how, holding a racquet that Jeff said had been given to him years ago but looked suspiciously new to Mina.

Sammy was young, and smaller, so Mina had to play gently, but he enjoyed batting the ball back and forth. He never got tired, never got bored. It got so they could have some good volleys. Dicey spent most of her free time on a sailboat in their barn, which she wanted to get into the water for the summer. Mina wasn't interested in sailing. She was interested in tennis. Teaching Sammy made her own game better in some weird way.

One Saturday, she suggested they stop off at her house for something cool to drink, before he rode home. He said yes with no hesitation. Little kids didn't notice color so much, Mina knew; the older you got the more you noticed.

Mina's mother was reading at the kitchen table when they entered. Mina had forgotten that her mother would be home. "This is Sammy Tillerman," Mina said. "Sammy? This is my momma."

He stood in the doorway, staring. "Hello, Sammy," Momma said.

The little boy didn't answer. He just stared. Mina went ahead and poured two glasses of lemonade, wondering what was going on. Maybe little kids thought grown-up blacks were different from black children, so you couldn't relax with them. Maybe kids forgot that black children had black parents. Mrs. Smiths looked at Mina, who raised her shoulders to say she didn't know what was going on, and then they both looked at Sammy.

He was standing there with his arms drawn up in front of him. His fists were all balled up, as if he wanted to push his fingernails into his palms and hurt himself. His mouth was stretching out wide, so that it hurt Mina to look at him, trying to pretend that was a smile. He didn't want to cry, and he wasn't going to—whites didn't, not with the same ease blacks did, and they didn't laugh as easily either, or yell out glad or angry. But this was worse than crying.

Before Mina even had time to finish thinking all this and to wonder what was wrong with him, her mother was up from her chair with the pages of the book flipping over. Momma put her arms around Sammy. "It's all right," Momma said. "I understand."

That was more than Mina did, for a minute. Then she realized that she'd forgotten—but Sammy hadn't, and how could he—that his own mother had died. Mina was angry at herself: She should have known better than to forget. Sammy just leaned up against her mother's body, resting there with his head on her shoulder and his face buried into her neck, not crying, not saying anything, just more tired than a kid should have to be. Momma crooned and cuddled him. Mina stood by the table.

"I'm sorry," Sammy mumbled, but he didn't move away from Mrs. Smiths's arms.

"Don't be," she said, wiping her own eyes dry. "There's nothing wrong with sorrow. It's as much a part of God's world as anything else." She let him go, but kept her dark hand on his yellow head. "Are you a little better now?"

He nodded his head.

"You can come back, anytime, for the same treatment," Momma said, standing up. "I'm a nurse, you know."

Sammy thought that was funny, and he looked up at Momma for a while, while she looked down at him. "Good-o," he finally said.

Mina thought to herself, watching, her momma was the kind of woman she wanted to be, wherever else she got to in her life.

CHAPTER 23

It was a warm spring, that year. By early May the magnolias were in full flower. Their heavy waxy leaves spread out like dark green hands, hands without fingers—or maybe fingers without hands, thick flat green fingers. The blossoms within also opened out, thick waxy white cups. There was an old song Jeff had sung for her: "Southern trees bear strange fruit." The song was talking about blacks hanging from the trees, strung up by the KKK, and Mina couldn't think about that while she went to sleep at night, unless she wanted not to go to sleep. But these magnolia blossoms were pretty strange looking too, she thought, they were strange in their own right. And Crisfield wasn't really southern, because Maryland wasn't. Maryland had been pretty well split in half about what side to fight on in the Civil War.

May set Mina's mind dreaming, like another one of Jeff's old songs. "I know where I'm going, and I know who's going with me." It was an Irish song, a sad line of melody running through several verses, and when Maybeth sang it *a cappella* it made Mina smile. "I know who I love," she would sing, "but the dear knows who I'll marry." It was like May, that song, poignant and lovely.

One warm night in mid-May, Zandor came home unexpectedly, just walking into the kitchen Friday night. He had shaved his moustache and he wore an ironed cotton shirt, with slacks and polished shoes. Mina took one look at him and asked, "Do you want us kids to clear out of the house?"

"You might as well stick around, you'll hear all about it anyway," he said. "But thanks."

He'd been suspended from school for the rest of this semester and through the summer. He could go back in the fall, if he wanted to, but he wouldn't have any scholarship. He'd been caught smoking marijuana in his dormitory room.

Mina had never seen her father so angry. He seemed to swell up with anger and explode it all around the kitchen. Zandor sat up straight and listened to what his father had to say. Every now and then Momma would cut in with some sharp, angry remark, as if she couldn't hold back, but mostly she let her husband speak. He didn't say that much, and he didn't talk for that long, but Mina was impressed with the way Zandor could sit there and hear him. "Now what are you going to do with yourself," her father thundered. "Now where are you going to go?"

Zandor waited, to be sure that was really a question. Then he answered it: "One of my professors, Sociology, said I can live with his family. He's working on setting up a survival camp, like Outward Bound, for black kids. He'll hire me to be his assistant; he's gotten enough funding and enough people to run one session this summer."

"I'm amazed he'll trust you," Mina's father said.

"Luckily, I had him for Soc One last year. He seems to like me. I talked it over with Charles Stuart. CS said I should tell you it sounds all right to him. CS said pretty much what you said to me too," Zandor told his parents. "It was stupid. It was a stupid thing for me to do."

Zandor had about grown up over this, Mina thought.

"I should be able to go back in the fall. It won't cost me anything to live there, because I'm going to do housekeeping for them, in exchange for room and board; his wife works too. I've got a job at one of the McDonald's and I think I'll be able to pick up another part-time job on weekends, especially if I can learn how to run a cash register. If I'm careful, I can save enough. This has fairly well shot my chances for student loans, as well as everything else."

"I would think," Mina's father said.

"I told the dean I wanted to tell you myself, but he's going to call on Monday morning, to be sure you know."

"I'll be here."

"CS said I should tell you about this too," Zandor said. He looked from his mother to his father. "There were maybe half a dozen of us on my corridor who were smoking. I know that doesn't make any difference, not really. But I'm the only one they suspended."

"Why?" Momma wondered.

"And I was pretty angry, because—well, probably because it was the only thing I could blame on somebody else." He smiled at Mina, getting more relaxed now that the worst was behind him. "I mean, it's not as if I could blame it on racial prejudice or anything. They're as black as I am, all of them. I guess that's one advantage of a black college. Anyway, CS pointed out to me the others are all local kids, and one of them's father has a good dry cleaning business, two of them are lawyers, one of them's a union official. Since ministers don't have very much clout, the school could make its point on me. They'd figure that the ministerial minority wouldn't raise too big a stink—you'd have more invested in being on the side of law and order, and all that. It doesn't mean I didn't do it, but—it makes a difference to me. In how I feel about myself. So I can't see there's any need for you to . . . do any apologizing to him, Pop."

Mina's father nodded his head slowly a couple of times, then excused himself from the table. They heard him leave the house. He was probably, Mina thought, going to church.

"Well," Momma said. "So much for your news. How is your brother?"

"I think he's serious about this girl, and I don't blame him. She's cool, and she's nice too. You'll like her, Momma. I think he's going to be calling you up soon to say he wants to get married. How'd you like to be a bridesmaid, Belle?"

"A big wedding?" Belle asked.

"He can't afford marriage. Does he even have a job lined up?" Momma worried.

In May, Mina's father also learned that he wouldn't have to go away that summer, or ever again. He had done it for so many years, the board wrote to him, and it was exhausting work. They felt he had done enough. Mina had a hard time feeling good about that, because she didn't know what Mr. Shipp would do when he came to Crisfield.

Then she learned, when Mr. Shipp telephoned her father, that he wasn't coming to Crisfield at all. He called at night from New York, when rates were cheaper. Mina listened to half the phone conversation. As she listened, wishing she wasn't hearing what she was hearing, she learned that he had taken a new job, not with the church at all. It would be good for the children. The pay would be better. It would have duties.

Mina sat back on the sofa, eavesdropping, feeling heavier and heavier. She felt like she'd swallowed a big black stone and it was sinking in the pit of her stomach.

"Mina? They want to talk to you." Her father handed her the phone.

The stone disappeared like magic. If they wanted her to go with them for the summer? Or even if he just wanted to say a special good-bye to her?

"Mina?" Alice's butterfly voice said. "I passed. Can you believe it?"

"Passed?"

"The equivalency test. I have a high school diploma with my name on it and all. Tamer took me out for dinner to celebrate, and dancing after. Aren't you proud of me?"

"It's wonderful, Alice," Mina said. She made her voice sound glad, because she was glad. It was just this stone, settled in her stomach. "How are the kids?"

"They're properly impressed with me. Tamer's having it framed. Dream gave me a picture—a drawing of me teaching school, isn't that silly? Selma doesn't understand, really. But even my mother-in-law has to admit it's something I've done right. It's lucky I decided to get it, because with this new job of Tamer's I'd be really stupid if I didn't have it. Well, this is running up a big bill, I just wanted to tell you."

"Thanks, and—I'm really pleased for you. Congratulations."

She hung up, then turned around and waited for her father to tell her the bad news, the worst of it. He was already back reading the Bible, looking for the text he'd want to speak on.

"Dad," she demanded. "What's going on?"

"Nothing. It's pretty good news. Tamer's taken a job at a college, somewhere in the Midwest. I've never heard of the place. He's going to be the assistant chaplain. He can maintain his church affiliation, that's no problem. I think he's pleased to get his family out of New York. I would be."

Mina turned away. She didn't know if she could stand this. She knew she could stand knowing that Tamer Shipp was married and too old anyway ever to love her back. She knew she could stand only seeing him in the summers and even then not really seeing very much of him. She didn't think she could stand never seeing him again.

"He wanted to know if he could come down for a few days after school gets out. He's going to stay in Miz Hunter's house with just Samuel. Alice has to stay in New York because they'll move out to—it's in Ohio, Mina, did I tell you that?"

So she would see him, just once again.

At least nobody knew how she felt, really, inside herself. Mina thought she was glad of that, but once or twice she thought it would feel so good just to talk to somebody. Dicey maybe might understand, even though the way Dicey talked to Jeff (who was head over heels about her, if ever Mina had seen anybody head over heels with anyone) showed Mina that Dicey hadn't ever thought about this kind of loving. She was tempted to talk to Dicey, who thought about things so differently, who thought about things.

In the end, only her mother said anything, and all Momma said was, "It's hard for you, isn't it. There aren't too many people in this world who have the capacity to love deeply. It's a mixed blessing to be one of them." Mina nodded. She thought Jeff too was one of them, and she knew what her mother meant.

But if she was going to have to say good-bye to Tamer Shipp forever, Mina thought, then there was something she was going to give him too. The trouble was, she didn't know how to go about doing the one thing she wanted to have done, before she said good-bye to him. Forever.

* * *

Two days before he was due to arrive, Mina rode her bike out to the Tillermans'. It was the first Wednesday after school got out, and she knew that Dicey would be at home that afternoon. Dicey worked mornings during the summer, while James and Sammy went crabbing with Jeff. Mina rode her bike around to the back of the house. Maybeth and her grandmother were in the vegetable garden, weeding and loosening up the soil after the night's heavy rain. Dicey was in the barn, painting her sailboat. Mina walked into the shadowy barn. "Hey," she said.

Dicey had paint spattered all over her T-shirt and shorts, all over her arms and legs, all over her hair. "Hi. What's up?" she asked. Mina knew nothing would budge Dicey from finishing the job she was working on—although why Dicey cared so much about learning how to sail, she couldn't understand. She leaned against one of the stall doors and said, "I've got a favor to ask."

"Not this afternoon," Dicey said.

"What if it was," Mina demanded, half teasing. "What if it was a matter of life and death, and this afternoon?"

"It isn't, though, is it?" Dicey asked, turning around to look at Mina, worried that it might be and she would have to make a choice.

"No. It's for next Sunday morning. I want you to come to our church."

Most people would have asked why, but not Dicey. "I've never been to church," she said.

"That's all right."

"You know, you never do ask anybody for anything," Dicey said.

Mina hadn't realized that, but she guessed it was true. "Neither do you," she pointed out, in case Dicey missed that similarity.

"What time is church?"

"Ten-thirty."

"Okay," Dicey said.

"Good," Mina said. "And who else can come?"

"Who else?"

"I thought—maybe Sammy?"

Dicey lay the brush across the top of the paint can, then wiped her hands on the seat of her shorts. "I can't go—"

"You have to," Mina interrupted. She really didn't want to have to explain herself. "Or if you can't—" She wanted Dicey there for her own sake, but Sammy for being Samuel Tillerman. Sammy was the one who mattered.

"Not without asking Gram," Dicey said, before Mina finished her sentence. "I keep forgetting—she says we decide things together, and she'd be angry if I went ahead, and she'd be right. I'm sorry, Mina, I'll ask her right now."

Mrs. Tillerman didn't say anything when Dicey asked if she and Sammy could go to Mina's church. Mrs. Tillerman stayed crouched by a row of tomato plants, working the soil with a claw-fingered hand tool. Maybeth worked on quietly, and Mina studied the way her cheeks got dusted with a golden tan color. Every time she saw Maybeth, for some reason, Mina felt good about the whole world. It made no sense, which didn't bother her.

"Is it all right if we all come?" Mrs. Tillerman asked.

"Of course. I'd like that. I would have asked but I didn't want to impose."

"I'll just bet you didn't," Mrs. Tillerman said, knowing better.

Mina grinned.

"It's no imposition," Mrs. Tillerman said.

"I know," Mina answered back.

* * *

She was in the choir when they entered the church. They had all of them come: Mrs. Tillerman with her chin up high and an old-fashioned blue straw hat on her head, Dicey with Maybeth, both wearing denim jumpers, then James and Sammy. James looked around him, curious and alert. Mina smiled at them once they'd gotten themselves seated, about halfway up the aisle. Hearing the talk, Momma turned around once, briefly, then looked at Mina with an eyebrow raised, and then concentrated on worship.

When the service started, nobody talked anymore and only a few people kept staring at the Tillermans. They started off with a traditional hymn, "The son of man goes off to war, a golden crown to win." Mr. Shipp and Mina's father were at the front of the church, facing the choir. Mina sang out her harmony line. She could hear Maybeth singing among the congregation and saw that the people around could hear it too. They liked what they heard, and they wanted to turn around, but they didn't. Mina watched. The bubbles in her stomach just bounced around and there was devilment all over her face that she couldn't keep hidden. This was, she thought, sitting down again, much better than standing around feeling dismal about the last time Mr. Shipp would speak a sermon in their church.

The church was filled with people who wanted to say goodbye and good luck to Mr. Shipp. Samuel sat next to Louis, looking serious, watching his father come up to read the text. Mina sat up, ready to listen, thinking that she couldn't hear a thing because her own thoughts were all tangled up and, deep under the dark surface of her, mixed together. She could barely wait for the moment when she introduced Sammy to Tamer Shipp. She wanted to slow down every second that was ticking past.

Mr. Shipp stood at the lectern and opened the book. He read from Isaiah, the Old Testament prophet, but he had a way of skipping back and forth in his mind between the Old and New Testaments, so Mina couldn't predict what his sermon would be about. He read the text like a poem: "The people that walked in darkness have seen a great light." When he finished, he closed the Bible and looked up.

He couldn't help but notice the Tillermans then. Mina saw his eyes briefly on them, and his eyebrows went up. Nobody was staring. It would be bad manners to stare at people just because they were the only whites in the room. But everybody was so carefully not noticing, you could see how much they noticed.

He didn't talk for long, and he was talking about the Prince of Peace from Isaiah, but his idea was that the people at Jesus' time didn't want a prince of peace at all. "They wanted a prince for war, a hero who would scourge out the oppressors, a man invincible in battle with mighty armies to come behind him where he rode over the earth, burning the earth clean for God. But God sent them a man of peace, a man of sorrows, a man of righteousness, instead. I think, if we think about it, we can understand why the people wanted a man of war—their anger, the injustices of oppression, the sufferings they had lived with. We can understand the desire for a burning out of the oppressor. But"—Mr. Shipp changed the notecards from which he was speaking—"I think we have also lived close enough to a war to glimpse God's purposes. How many of us still carry grief for our sons, our brothers, sweethearts and husbands, grief for friends forever lost," he said in his bassoon voice. The congregation murmured agreement, and a few people called out, answering him with names. Mrs. Tillerman sat there with her face unreadable, but Dicey was looking at her grandmother. "So God sent us a man of peace, knowing that what we wanted was not what we needed," Mr. Shipp said.

After the service, Mina made the Tillermans wait, standing out under a tall pin oak, with its narrow leaves and its bark that twisted up along the trunk and branches. "He used to come down and minister for the summers," she explained. "He's got a new job, so this is his last sermon. His name is Tamer Shipp," she said. "His new job's at a college in Ohio. So everybody's saying good-bye. I want you to meet him," she finished, not looking at anybody in particular.

"It was an interesting sermon," Mrs. Tillerman said. She didn't say any more.

"I liked the singing. I'd like singing in your choir," Maybeth told Mina.

Mina thought she was asking. "You can't, even though I'd sure like to sing in a choir with you."

"I know, I'm the wrong color," Maybeth explained.

Mina couldn't help it, she got a fit of the giggles. People were walking by, carefully not staring at the strangers as they went by, returning to their houses and their dinners. Mina's parents had come to be introduced and to ask the Tillermans back for lemonade. "I haven't seen you for an age," Momma said to Sammy.

"I love lemonade," Sammy told her. Mrs. Tillerman, as wary as Mina's father, watched all this, and every now and then her eye would come back to Mina, but she didn't ask any questions.

Finally, Tamer Shipp was free and Mina waved him over. Samuel trailed behind his father.

Mina took a deep breath. "Mr. Shipp," she said. "I want you to meet some friends of mine."

"I did notice you all, in there," he said, laughter in his voice.

Mrs. Tillerman flashed one of her sudden smiles at that, a smile that flickered on and off across her face.

Then Mina didn't know what to say or how to say it. She felt so much, all at once, all she felt was big and clumsy. "Mrs. Abigail Tillerman," she said, starting with the oldest.

"Mrs. Tillerman?" Mr. Shipp sounded surprised, but also not at all surprised as he checked carefully what he'd heard.

Mrs. Tillerman's chin went up and she met his glance, to meet whatever might make him ask that question, that way.

Mina hurried on. "And her grandchildren. Dicey"—they shook hands—"James, Maybeth and this is Sammy," Mina concluded.

For a minute Mr. Shipp didn't say anything and then he did something that Mina—even though she hadn't known what she expected—would never have expected. He turned to Mina and wrapped his arms around her in a hug. He was so big that he lifted her off the ground. He turned her around in a circle, with her feet off the ground, and then he set her down and kissed her on the cheek and kept his arm around her shoulders. Mina's heart was beating so hard she thought she'd explode. "Oh, Mina Smiths," he said, his voice low and rich, like a bassoon, as he said her name.

The Tillermans were just staring. Dicey knew something was up even if she didn't know what it was. Mina was terribly afraid her own face was giving away more truth than she wanted it to. She made a face at Dicey, feeling like a goop.

But Mr. Shipp had moved away to take Mrs. Tillerman's hand, not to shake it but to put it in both of his. He looked down into her face. He was trying to think of what to say. Mrs. Tillerman was waiting, but Mina could see she didn't know what to make of it.

"I admired your son," he finally said.

"Bullet?" she said, asking a question.

He nodded.

"That wouldn't have been easy to do," she said.

"Oh no, he didn't make it easy. But it was the most natural thing; you couldn't do anything else. I couldn't. I—I was on the track team with him—his last year, before he dropped out. He was—" Mr. Shipp couldn't finish that sentence, as if he'd come to the outer limits of his voice's range. "It's so good to meet you."

Mrs. Tillerman didn't say anything, just stood there with her small hand in his two big ones, looking at him. While tears went down over her cheeks.

Mina wondered if she'd done something wrong, or unkind. Sammy moved over to stand in front of his grandmother and to glare up at Mr. Shipp.

"Gram?" Dicey asked, worried.

Mrs. Tillerman put one hand on Sammy's shoulder, without taking her hand away from Mr. Shipp. She nodded her head. She paid no attention to her own tears.

"I was so sorry," Mr. Shipp said. "And angry too. I've wanted to say that to someone who'd understand."

"Yes," Mrs. Tillerman said. She took her hand back then and wiped her eyes. Her eyes were smiling. "I thought of him, when you spoke—"

"I thought of him, writing it—"

"I'm pleased to meet you, young man. These aren't his children."

"I didn't think so," Mr. Shipp said.

This wasn't going at all the way Mina had expected. He was giving his attention to Mrs. Tillerman, not Sammy. They were looking at each other, the older white woman and the grown black man, as if they were the only adults there . . . Mina laughed then. Because they were, and because she had wrapped up this gift for Mr. Shipp, but he had taken something she hadn't even known she was putting in. Mina looked at Tamer Shipp, at the familiar planes and curves of his face: He was glad, the gift had gladdened him. That was what Mina had wanted, so she didn't mind at all that what he had taken was not exactly what she had given.

When they all moved around to her back porch, Dicey kept Mina back, while Mr. Shipp walked ahead with the others, telling Maybeth he heard her singing.

"What was all that about," Dicey asked.

Mina, who was down to her last days with Tamer Shipp, said, "Tell you later."

Dicey didn't press her. "Okay. But you're right about him, Mr. Shipp. He's really something."

"I never said a word," Mina protested.

"That's what I mean," Dicey said.

As they drank lemonade, Mr. Shipp explained that he'd known Mrs. Tillerman's son years ago, and Mrs. Tillerman explained that Bullet had been killed in Vietnam, and Mina's mother shifted the conversation away from that to Mr. Shipp's new job. They sat at the long table on the back porch. It wasn't relaxed, but it was friendly enough.

"I've never been an assistant before," Mr. Shipp said. "I'm not sure how I'll do being somebody's assistant. And the college has as—and I quote—'its stated objective'—Why do they talk like that, Amos; haven't they ever read their Bible to learn good prose style? The objective is to improve relations between the different races. So they hired me—as a show and tell? You've got to look out for these liberal whites." He chuckled. "They think everybody's the same. They don't know the first thing about being hungry."

"It'll be a nice life for Alice and the children," Mina's mother said. "The schools should be good—you'll like school, Samuel. It'll be a small town. Lots of fresh air, trees and all that."

"They might let me teach a course," Mr. Shipp said. "Now *that* I'd be grateful for, a chance to try teaching."

"People must always be looking up to you," Mrs. Tillerman said, getting up to leave. She had sat pretty much silent, but listening. "That must be hard on you."

"She's right," Mina's father agreed, standing up to walk them around front. "You're absolutely right, Mrs. Tillerman."

"Call me Ab," she said.

"I've never thought about it from that angle," Mina's father said.

Dicey waved briefly to Mina, leaving last because she wanted to say she was glad to meet Mina's mother. When they'd gone, Mr. Shipp turned to stare at Mina across the table, and she couldn't guess what he was thinking.

But Momma wasn't satisfied, and she wanted to hear more. "It's a long story," Mr. Shipp warned her as Mina's father came back onto the porch to pour himself another glass of lemonade.

"With a happy ending," Momma said.

"No," Mina said and Mr. Shipp said, "No," at the same time.

"A happy ending isn't possible, Raymonda, but it's an ending that makes peace with a long grief, and that's something. You remember the sixties, don't you?" He moved down to sit beside Mina's mother.

Mina's father sat down next to her. He picked up her hand and held it. "That little girl."

"That's Maybeth," Louis said.

"We like Maybeth," Mina interrupted, so that her father wouldn't get too nosy about Louis.

"What a voice she has. Could you hear her where you were sitting?"

"I've heard her before too."

"You know, it's a real pity . . . I know she couldn't join the choir, but—"

"I agree, Dad," Mina said. "So you've decided they're all right, after all."

"It's not an easy life for anybody, is it?" he answered her.

"I dunno," Mina joked. "I think I've got it pretty good. If you asked me."

CHAPTER 24

Almost two years after she had last seen Tamer Shipp, Mina sat with Dicey in the crowded auditorium, watching Jeff's graduation. Ordinarily, underclassmen weren't invited, so they were two of just a few sophomores there, among families and faculty and anyone who played on the varsity teams with the graduating seniors. Kat was there, somewhere too, with her boyfriend's family. Kat always had a boyfriend, a steady boyfriend, but she didn't change her mind about wanting to be a model. Now, however, she said she wanted at least a year of college, to be sure about her choice. She had modeled some clothes for a big mail-order catalogue, hard work, Kat said, but it was a beginning. Kat didn't want to know Dicey and Dicey had no time for Kat, but Mina was friends with them both. When Mina was with them both, they all three got along fine.

Rachelle, who also had a boyfriend, also a senior, wasn't there, although she should have been; Rachelle was big with the seventh month of pregnancy and had dropped out of school and what she was going to do Mina didn't know, because that boy wasn't about to get married. Rachelle was living with Sabrina's parents for the time being, because her parents hit the ceiling and hadn't come down yet. What she'd do, she didn't know. Sabrina's parents said there were worse things, much worse trouble to get into, and they wanted Rachelle to be sure she did what she thought was right. Rachelle's parents said they were grateful, mostly, Mina thought, because her father had stepped in. He was minister to both families.

Somewhere in the audience also were Jeff's father and their monk friend, Brother Thomas. Dicey and Mina sat together separate from them. At graduation, the kids liked to stick together. They wanted their parents and relatives there, but they wanted them to go home right away, afterward.

The seniors sat on bleachers up on the stage, behind the podium. Mina had finally found Jeff, in the middle, between Phil and Andy. They tried to get the seniors to line up in alphabetical order, but the kids always chose to sit with their friends, regardless of the alphabet. Mina remembered that from Belle's graduation, and Zandor's. This was the fourth graduation she had been to, and she could tell Dicey with confidence, "It's long and boring."

Dicey bit her lip. She'd only come because Jeff wanted her to. She'd only gotten dressed up because Mina and Mrs. Tillerman had told her she had to and found a pattern that they thought would suit her and picked out a fabric Dicey admitted wasn't too bad. "Why that boy puts up with your antics," Mrs. Tillerman had grumbled at Dicey.

Mina, who had been in on the long relationship, thought she understood why. What she didn't understand was how Dicey managed to maintain the distance from Jeff that she did. Mina had changed from being a friend and sometimes advice-giver to Jeff into having a real crush on him for a while: There was something about his long, narrow body and his long, dark eyelashes that pleased her eyes, and something about his quiet courage to love Dicey that touched her heart. She'd known, while she had the crush, before it changed back into friendship, that Jeff never looked at anybody but Dicey. That was all right because she'd also known that having a crush on Jeff meant she was growing free from Tamer Shipp. Not entirely; not as a person; not as probably one of the best men she would ever meet. But when Mina had found her eyes lingering on the bony shoulders under Jeff's oxford shirt and found herself thinking that he looked like some Greek statue of what a young man should look like, part of the rush of feelings she felt was a sense of freedom, of being ready to grow upward even farther from the strong tangled roots of her life.

The principal started things off. Mina glanced over at Dicey, who was thinking about something else. What, Mina couldn't guess; some scheme, some plan maybe, although with Dicey it was just as likely that she daydreamed about Algebra. The dress Mrs. Tillerman had made was plain white, with a high collar and no sleeves, with a blousy top over a gathered skirt. Mina and Maybeth had forced Dicey to put on a touch of Mina's lipstick, which she was in the process of chewing off as she thought. Sometimes Dicey just made Mina smile, the way she was.

After the principal came the valedictorian. This year, it was a weedy-looking boy with sandy hair so long he tucked it behind his ears, who talked about commitment. Belle's year it had been a girl whose voice had barely whispered out, as she talked about what women were not able to do in the world. Mina figured she'd probably be valedictorian her year, and she was considering what she'd talk about: God, maybe, which would get some people squirming in their seats; maybe a quick history of race relations, which would sit people up, especially if she refused to take it too seriously, which might be fun to try and write. She figured she had plenty of time to think about it. She knew if she got Dicey to vet the possibilities, Dicey would smell out anything second rate.

The graduation speaker was somebody from one of the local community colleges who talked about what education could do for a person. Mina listened, in case he had anything interesting to say, but he didn't. After the speeches, one after the other, all alike in their black robes and mortarboard hats, the seniors moved across the stage, took their diplomas and shook hands and returned to the bleachers. When everybody was in place again, the ceremony was over. People flowed onto the stage and down from the stage; they flowed out into the aisles and back among the seats. People flowed all over the place.

"Let's go wait by the car. He won't be long," Dicey said to Mina. It took Mina a little while to get there, because there were some people to say hello to, but with Dicey tugging her along impatiently it didn't take very long. They stood by the Greenes' station wagon, which Jeff had for the evening. Brother Thomas would take Jeff's father home.

The lamps overhead that lighted the parking lot attracted most of the bugs, and it was pretty quiet outside. "Did you give it to him yet?" Mina asked Dicey. Dicey had made Jeff a strap for his guitar, out of the mainsail of her boat. She'd saved the big pieces of canvas when the sail blew out. She had put the strap together at work. Dicey had a job with a small-time sail-maker in town, so she knew how to handle canvas. Once she had the strap made to her satisfaction, she'd found fittings for each end of it, the boat fittings of polished brass, small enough to attach to the guitar.

"No, I haven't yet. What if he doesn't like it?"

"Dicey Tillerman, you could give him an old shoelace and he'd treasure it because it's yours," Mina told her.

"Yeah." Dicey grinned. "He's something, isn't he?"

"You look good too. Are you sure you won't go to the party?"

"Sure. He doesn't want to either. He just always asks, you know how he is. But I'm going to miss him when he's at school."

"Don't tell me that, tell him," Mina advised.

"He knows," Dicey said.

"Besides, he's only going up to Baltimore. He doesn't want to get too far from you."

"I know," Dicey said.

They waited without saying anything for a minute. A few people started to come out into the warm night. "Nobody knows," Mina started to sing, because the song had come into her head, "the trouble I've seen." Dicey joined in, both of them singing softly. "Glory, halleluiah," they sang. That was odd, Mina thought, because it was a trouble song, but with the glory halleluiah at the end, it was almost as if you should praise God for the trouble you'd seen. The song was a mournful, mourning song, but it was also a praising, thanking song. Mina had never understood that before; and now she wondered what else there was in that song, and in everything, that she didn't yet understand. She would have talked to Dicey about it, but Dicey was watching Jeff approach, working his way through the parked cars, with another boy behind him. "Who's that?" Dicey asked Mina, but Mina didn't know.

This other boy had slung his jacket over his shoulders because of the heat. He was bigger than Jeff, not so much taller as broader through the shoulders, built thicker, built muscular. His trousers rode low on his hips. Mina, for some reason, always liked the way that looked on a boy, especially when he wore a vest, as this boy did. The "Gambler Look," she named it to herself, liking it. Jeff introduced him, Dexter Halloway. "His family might be moving down here," Jeff said.

"Down from where?" Mina asked.

"Baltimore."

"Crisfield's not down from Baltimore," Mina declared. "I've been there, I've got family there, Crisfield's not down."

The boy laughed. He had a good, rich laugh.

"We ought to get going," Dicey told Jeff. "Maybeth made you a cake. Sammy decorated it."

"I'm glad you came," he told her. "I like your dress."

"They intended you to," Dicey said.

Dexter asked, "Mina, where do you live?"

"In town, just a few blocks from here. Why?"

"I could walk you home. I'm supposed to chat up the locals, Jeff, and it's safe to walk around here at night, isn't it?"

"Except for the mosquitoes," Mina said. "But the mosquitoes are pretty vicious."

"My dad's having a drink in the hotel bar with your father and Brother Thomas, and there's no way I'll get lost. So I'll see you around."

"Is that okay with you, Mina?" Jeff asked.

Mina didn't want to be a third party tagging along. "Sure," she said.

"But you have to look out for Mina," Jeff warned Dexter. "She's t-rou-ble."

After the station wagon had driven off, Mina waited for Dexter to start walking. "Do I want to move to Crisfield?" he asked her. He had about six inches on her, maybe five. He didn't move.

"How would I know?" Mina asked, waiting. "It depends on what you're looking for."

"Sanctuary, I think. At least, that's what my parents are looking for, although they don't say so. A change of scene, for sure."

"Oh," Mina said, curious, but not wanting to pry.

Then they had nothing to say and were just standing there.

"Shall we go then?" Mina asked.

He agreed, but didn't move.

After another couple of minutes, he asked her, "I don't know where you live."

Mina threw back her head and laughed, causing people passing nearby to look curiously at her. "I'm sorry. I was working so hard to be feminine, you know, letting you take the lead. It's this way." She was still chuckling when they left the parking lot and moved toward town.

"You don't look fifteen," Dexter said to her.

"I never looked fifteen," Mina answered. "I looked ten for a while, then I started looking twenty-eight. How old are you?"

"Seventeen. I'll be a senior next year."

"You're going to move before your senior year?"

They made their way along one of the main streets, then turned off to where there were no streetlights, just lights from the windows of the houses. She couldn't see his face, if she had looked.

"One of my sisters—she's gotten in with a bunch of kids—My mother thinks the best thing is to relocate. She got picked up for shoplifting, that's what precipitated the crisis," his voice told her. "But we none of us suspected that . . . that she was up to anything. It's hard on a family when that kind of thing happens. Especially—it's my mother's second marriage, and she had these three kids and Dad took us all on. I'm the oldest."

Their steps matched, and Mina was wearing heels, so he must be abbreviating his, she thought, listening to their footsteps down the quiet street. They passed houses on one side and cars on the other as they walked down the sidewalk. She heard TVs and sometimes voices. She thought about what he'd told her. It bothered him, about his sister.

"If you're the oldest, that probably means you're the responsible one, and the big achiever in your family. That's the way the oldest child usually is. I'm second youngest in mine," she said.

"So you're irresponsible? An underachiever? Immature?" he asked, his voice telling her he didn't believe that.

"Not everybody goes according to the usual rules," she agreed.

They walked on in the humid darkness, past a couple of big old houses, built at the turn of the century for huge families and their servants, but now crumbling into disrepair. One of them had a round tower running up its side, showing dark against the sky, the tower shadowy black and the places where there were windows shiny black. "Wait," Dexter said. "Wait a minute."

They went back to stand on the sidewalk in front of the dark house. A couple of magnolia trees grew in the front yard, and the porch was a dark strip behind its railings.

"Is this empty?" Dexter's voice asked. He was almost whispering.

"It looks it. I wouldn't know. Why?" She wondered if he was the kind of person who wanted to break into an empty house. She wondered how well Jeff knew him.

"Because it's the kind of project my mother could really get her teeth into. She could spend years on it. If we bought it." Mina couldn't see his face, but his voice sounded excited. "See"—he moved to the steps and looked up at the house—"she never worked at a job, she never had to and she doesn't want to. She's got some money of her own, which is lucky because my father—my real father—isn't the kind of guy you can rely on. He's—"

"The perfect youngest child?" Mina suggested, giving him a way out.

"Yeah. Dad's not like that. Mom did fine the second time. But—do you think it would be okay if I just went up onto the porch? You have to touch something, to get a feel for if it's all right. Or I do anyway."

"Go ahead," Mina said, embarrassed at what she'd been thinking about him.

He went up and stood there, a dark figure. He lifted his shadowed face as if he could see up and into the house; he stood there, quiet, as if he was listening. Then he jumped down, over all four steps, and came back to join her, still looking back to the empty house. "It'll do, if it's only on the market, if we can only afford it. My dad's a professor and I don't know how the prices are down here—up here," he corrected himself. "It feels right. What's the neighborhood like? We could be in it by midsummer, and Mom would have five years work ahead of her so she'd be off Clarissa's back. Because she gets on people's backs, worrying, and that's the thing that'll drive Clarissa right away, into drugs or who knows what else, and they both know it, but knowing it doesn't help much. Does it? What's the neighborhood like? You didn't answer. Is it a bad neighborhood?"

Mina didn't know what to answer because—because she didn't know what he'd think was a bad neighborhood. The neighborhood was starting to be mixed; a couple of white families had moved in, taking advantage of lower prices in this part of town. He came from Baltimore, a city, and his father was a professor, so probably he wasn't frightened of whites the way someone from a more insulated environment would be. But she didn't know if city neighborhoods had the same economic mix most Crisfield streets did: Some of the families on this street were respectable middle class; some of the families had troubles, some of the troubles were bad ones, and some of the bad ones were troubles of their own making. Mina wondered how to frame this question; to ask Dexter the precise kind and degree of his various prejudices. Just the thought started her giggling.

"What's funny?"

"You are. I am. How old is Clarissa?" She hoped to distract him.

"Thirteen, which is . . . a bad age. I think. Is there something wrong with the neighborhood?"

"Come on back to my house, we've got lemonade, if you're not in a hurry?"

"I'm in no hurry to get back to the hotel," his voice said.

He was another one of those exact ones, Mina thought. She walked along the three more blocks to their house and up into the small living room. "I've got to be sure my brother's all right. Both my parents are out," she explained, trying not to just stare at him.

He nodded, his smile showing her he understood about little brothers and sisters. Mina kept herself from running up the stairs, walking up normally even though she was in a hurry to get herself hidden for a minute, to get her feelings covered up and kept private. Laughing at herself, she watched Louis sleep for a while, before she took off her shoes and danced on back down the stairs to join Dexter.

They sat on the screened porch, with the candles lit. "It's an okay neighborhood," she said. "Although, there *are* a couple of white families who've moved in."

"I'm not prejudiced." He smiled. He had a broad straight nose and a strong jawline. He kept smiling at her and she kept smiling back. "The school I go to in Baltimore, the University School, it's mostly whites."

Mina nodded her head. She knew how that was. His skin was the color of dark chocolate, semi-sweet.

"My dad teaches with Professor Greene, but he's in the Physics Department. Professor Greene's how we heard about Crisfield. Dad says he won't mind the commute if it's a good place for us kids. But I'm not really a friend of Jeff's."

"Oh?" Mina wondered what that meant, why he said that.

"I don't know him. I'd like to be, I like what I do know about him, but—I always move carefully with whites, because I always have the feeling I'm not sure I can trust them. Have you known Dicey long?"

"Long enough. So I guess you *are* prejudiced."

"I try not to be. I guess I'm just your standard, wishy-washy liberal type. Your father's a minister, Jeff said."

Why had he skipped to that? Mina wondered, as she nodded her head.

"I'm an atheist," Dexter told her. "Do you mind?"

"It's up to God to mind about that," Mina said. "It's none of my business."

He found this funny too. "I play lacrosse. What about you?"

"Tennis. I was on junior varsity this year." It was like they were exchanging data about one another.

"And I like classical music. I even play some."

"The clarinet," Mina guessed, because of the sound of his voice, the sounds of his voice.

"No, the flute. Why did you say clarinet? Do I look like a clarinetist or something? Do you like that kind of looks? Do you play?" He certainly asked a lot of questions and didn't give her any time to answer most of them.

Mina didn't mind. She could keep up with him. "I sing," she said. "In the choir."

"That's all right then. I'm probably going to medical school, which takes a long time."

"Why are you telling me all this?" Mina finally demanded.

"Because I want you to know me. Because I intend to see you again," Dexter said. "If it's all right with you. If we do move down here, which you can believe me I'll be arguing for with my not inconsiderable skill in debate."

"Modest, aren't you," Mina teased. Oh yes, she thought, it was all right with her. All right and then some.

"No," he answered, not treating it as a joke. His eyes looked serious and amused and interested and hopeful all at once. "I try to keep a clear reading on myself."

"I know what you mean," Mina said. She did like him, even if he wasn't what anybody'd call a relaxing or easy person. He had an unmanageable amount of energy, that was her guess.

"So, tell me about yourself; where are you going?"

"You mean to college?"

"Of course. Cornell has a good undergraduate premed course, and a good liberal arts school too. Or Duke."

"I see," Mina said. "We're going to the same school."

"You wait," he teased her. "You'll make a good doctor's wife."

"Yeah, but will you make a good lawyer's husband?" she asked him. This was just a game, some strange form of flirtation.

"Are you going to go to law school?"

"I might. I've been thinking about it. I might do about anything," Mina said, which was true. She knew he was feeling about her just as she was feeling about him, like they'd been born good friends, even if they'd just now met up with one another.

Dexter didn't stay long, and he didn't try to kiss her or anything, although he did put a hand on her shoulder, just briefly touching her. Mina almost wished he would kiss her, because she thought she wanted to kiss him with her eyes open, seeing who he was. But it was as if they had a long time before them and no need to hurry through it. Mina stood on her front porch and watched him walk back toward town. About half a block away, he started just running. She knew why he did that, she thought.

The lights were on in Miz Hunter's old house, where they were having a meeting about finances. The rest of the street was dark, and the branches of the trees were rustling in the wind. Mina stood on the front porch until she couldn't stand still any longer.

Mina leaped down off the porch into the dark yard. There she danced around in circles, as if she was on a stage, jetés and pirouettes. She didn't mind if anybody saw her, not that she wanted anybody to. She just wanted to dance, just for a few minutes, because sometimes there was nothing but dancing to really say what you felt. Even if someone had told you years ago that you couldn't dance, and you'd been silly enough to believe them, even if they were right.